THE
MEDICI
SECRET

Michael White has been a professional musician, a science lecturer, newspaper columnist, science editor for *GQ* magazine and a series consultant for the Discovery Channel's *The Science of the Impossible*.

First published in 1991, he is now the author of 26 books, including the bestselling *Equinox* which was his first novel. He was awarded the Bookman Prize in the US for best popular science book of 1998 for his biography of Isaac Newton, *The Last Sorcerer*, and is an Honorary Research Fellow at Curtin University. He lives in Sydney, Australia with his wife and four children. For more information visit Michael White's website at www.michaelwhite.com.au

Also available by Michael White

Equinox

THE
MEDICI
SECRET

MICHAEL WHITE

arrow books

First published in Great Britain by Arrow 2008

13 15 17 19 20 18 16 14

Random House, 20 Vauxhall Bridge Road,
London SW1V 2SA

www.randomhouse.co.uk

Addresses for companies within The Random House Group Limited
can be found at:
www.randomhouse.co.uk/offices.htm

The Random House Group Limited Reg. No. 954009

A CIP catalogue record for this book
is available from the British Library

ISBN 9780099571155

The Random House Group Limited supports The Forest Stewardship Council
(FSC®), the leading international forest certification organisation. Our books
carrying the FSC label are printed on FSC® certified paper. FSC is the only
forest certification scheme endorsed by the leading environmental organisations,
including Greenpeace. Our paper procurement policy can be found at
www.randomhouse.co.uk/environment

Typeset by SX Composing DTP, Rayleigh, Essex
Printed and bound by CPI Group (UK) Ltd, Croydon, CR0 4YY

For Carole

Chapter 1

Florence, 4 November 1966

When the warden of the Medici Chapel, Mario Sporani's eyes snapped open at 5.45 a.m. and he heard the shutters of the bedroom window smash against the wall of the building, he thought the world was coming to an end. Instantly awake, words from Revelations shot through his brain: 'And the serpent cast out of his mouth water as a flood after the woman, that he might cause her to be carried away of the flood.'

For a moment he thought he was trapped in a vivid nightmare, but then the wooden shutters flew back so hard they shattered the glass of the bedroom window, sending glistening shards across the room. The rain was slamming against the building with such force he thought the old stone would crumble and the entire structure might collapse. This was most certainly no dream.

In an instant, he was out of bed and pulling his

1

wife Sophia through the doorway and along the corridor leading to their baby's room. He could hear their son screaming above the pandemonium of the storm. Sophia snatched him from his cot and tried to soothe him.

'Sophia, you take Leo and stay in the back room, shutter the windows and lock them. I'll bring you a quilt and a torch. Then I must go to the chapel.'

'But Mario, you can't go out in this.'

'I must,' he replied. 'God only knows what damage has been caused already. The burial chamber could flood; and the bodies . . .'

He headed for the door. A few moments later, he was back with a bottle for the baby, a torch, some bread and the quilt from their bed. Mario kissed his wife and child. Turning, he ran out and locked the door before speeding along the hall, down the narrow wooden staircase, so dark he could hardly see the steps in front of him, and into the corridor leading to the front door.

The door almost knocked him over as he opened the latch and the wind bellowed into the hallway. He left the door pinned to the wall unable to move it back, and, his head down, took two slow steps on to the stoop. It was black outside. Storm clouds had blotted out the moon and it was obvious there was no electricity.

2

As Mario peered around the edge of the entrance to his building, the sky was lit up by an enormous lightning bolt. The entire street was awash. Muddy water rushed by, knee deep. It stank of sewage. He saw a bicycle wheel whirl along Via Ginori towards Piazza San Lorenzo. Taking a deep breath, he forced his way into the water.

The cold made him gasp. He couldn't be certain of his footing and the pavement under his boots felt slimy. There was nothing to hold on to except the damp brickwork and stone of the buildings. The sky lightened a fraction and the moon's rays broke through, casting a faint hollow light, just enough for him to make out the contours of Via Ginori and the walls of the Basilica di San Lorenzo ahead.

Mario tried to move faster but it was hopeless. He crept against the current an inch at a time. He had to pin himself against the wall, as a branch then a tyre, an empty box and a dustbin were swept past him by the wind before colliding with a building or landing haphazardly in the rushing mud.

By the time he reached the corner where Via Ginori met Via dei Pucci he was exhausted and covered in mud. His cheeks were stinging from the freezing cold and he could no longer feel his toes. The usually busy main street was deserted. The same brown sludge ran along the thoroughfare splashing up against the ancient stonework on either side. From far off, Mario heard a crash and the grinding of metal, followed by a scream. As he stared dumbstruck at the devastation, another lightning bolt ripped across the sky and the rain turned to hailstones that ricocheted off the roofs, and hit his face.

He pushed on across the main street finding a little shelter from the hail under the shadow of the basilica. Here the current was more powerful and it took all his strength to resist it. But then, as he approached the doors to the chapel, another branch whirled towards his head. He ducked, but too late. The wood smashed into his face and he fell backwards into the torrent.

The mud rushed over him spinning him around under the surface. Something hard jabbed him in the ribs, then he was scrambling to his feet, trying to find some purchase in the ooze. He almost made it, but his footing gave way and he found himself in the water again with a mouthful of mud. He spat it out in disgust and flailed around, suddenly terrified. With his right hand, he clutched at a metal ring in the wall of the basilica. He held on for dear life and pulled himself up, spluttering and gasping for air, a foul taste in his throat.

He was almost at the entrance to the chapel and could just about pull himself along, grasping the

4

wall. Manoeuvring himself carefully around a buttress of stone, he caught his first glimpse of the chapel doors. They had been ripped off their hinges and water was cascading inside.

With renewed determination, Mario ploughed through the torrent towards the entrance and down the half-dozen stone steps that led to the main floor of the crypt. Here the water was lapping around his calves; it was getting deeper and detritus was being carried in with the brown-grey water tumbling over the doorway and rushing down the steps. Just inside the doorway was a wall unit containing a torch and an axe. Smashing the glass, he grabbed the torch.

He almost slipped on the stone but made it to the floor of the main room. The sound of crashing water echoed from the low, arched ceiling. Around the perimeter stood monuments to over fifty of the long-dead Medici family buried in simple stone caskets under the floor. These memorials were mounted above floor level, but the water was rising and it would soon be lapping at the statues and ornate sarcophagi. But even this wasn't Mario Sporani's primary concern. Far more worrying was the possibility the water could find a way beneath the floor into the actual burial chambers. He must do everything he could to stop that happening.

Mario splashed towards the altar, a raised area at

the back of the crypt. There stood two huge stone angels perched on either side of a marble platform. Behind that was the entrance to the Medici family vault.

Mario moved as fast as he could through the freezing water towards the altar. The trapdoor into the burial chambers was surprisingly light and yielded easily. Inside, he could see a ladder. Probing into the gloom with his torch he could just make out rungs dropping away into the void. Water tumbled in ahead of him and he could hear it slap on to the stone floor below. Moving as fast as he could, he lowered himself into the hole and pulled the door down over his head. The seal was not perfect and water continued to flow down the ladder and into the chamber.

Moments later, Mario was on the floor of the chamber casting the torch beam about the ancient walls and the rows of stone alcoves along each side. The air was rank with mould, old earth and decay, but he was familiar with these and they no longer bothered him. Then he heard an ominous crack. Spinning round, he saw a block of stone move away from the wall and crash on to the floor. Water gushed in.

Mario was almost thrown off his feet. Energised by primal fear, he clambered up on to a shelf of stone immediately behind him. He could see, a short distance away, the opening into one of the burial alcoves and the edge of a shroud, frayed and grey. Then came another crash as a second stone fell, splashing water high up the walls of the chamber. His torch slipped from his grip into the water. He watched it sink and then abruptly snap off. The room was completely black. A voice was yelling in his head: He was an idiot to come down here. What possible good could he do? And now, the voice insisted, he was going to die here. He would join the dead all around him.

But the panic passed and a steely determination took its place. He could see nothing, but he knew the way out. Levering himself off the ledge, he slid into the icy water. It came up to his thighs and it was already lapping at the ledges where the ancient corpses lay. Ignoring the numbness in his legs and a growing giddiness, he pushed on back to where he knew the ladder stood. In the darkness, he fumbled for the security of the metal rungs, but they were still beyond his reach. With his hands outstretched, he forced his way on blindly against the rushing water still pouring in through the gaping hole in the wall.

Just as he was beginning to despair, his fingertips touched metal. He grasped the edge of the ladder and pulled himself up on to the first rung.

As he lifted his foot to find the next rung he felt the

ladder jolt and start to tear away from the wall. Mario threw himself forward and his weight forced the ladder back against the stonework. Above him he could see a chink of light coming from the edge of the trapdoor where it had not quite settled back into place. Filthy water cascaded down over his head and down his back. He could feel his heart pounding in his chest, as he eased his way up another rung. The ladder shuddered again. Six more rungs and he would be within reach of the opening.

And then he caught sight of something bobbing in the water no more than two feet away. It was a dark tube about twelve inches long.

Mario swivelled round as carefully as he could. Stretching out, his fingertips brushed the object and he just managed to hook hold of it. Thrusting the object into the waistband of his trousers, he scrambled with all his strength up the ladder just as the support bolts slid from their recesses in the wall. With an almost superhuman effort, he grabbed for the edge of the trapdoor. His fingers found the metal rim of the aperture. Water crashed down on to his face, and he could barely draw breath. Driven on by sheer terror, he managed to heave himself up. With his feet scrambling against the rough stone wall, he pushed open the trapdoor and threw himself gasping on to the floor of the altar.

Chapter 2

Florence, present day

Edie Granger locked her red Fiat in the private car park beside the Medici Chapel and strode across the cobblestones towards the front doors. She was five foot nine in stockings, and, thanks to a daily hour-long workout, she was extremely fit. Unusually for an English academic, Edie placed sartorial elegance high on her list of priorities, something that endeared her to her Italian friends, who only half-jokingly claimed she was a dead-ringer for the actress, Liv Tyler.

She studiously ignored the placard-carrying hooded figures in worn brown robes parading in front of the doors to the chapel, just as she had done every day for the past few months. The protestors were members of a strange group calling itself Workers For God. Led by a fanatical Dominican, a Father Baggio, they were opposed to any scientific research conducted in the Medici Chapel. To Edie they had long since become part of the landscape.

She waved her pass at the admissions booth just inside the doors, took the stairs two at a time, and strode into the part of the crypt where crowds of visitors milled around each day reading the inscriptions on the tombs of the Medici.

At the far end of the chapel an area had been cordoned off to the public, and a cream canvas tent concealed the entrance to a narrow staircase that descended into the burial chamber where deep alcoves on either side contained the sarcophagi. Entering the research area, Edie sidestepped a pair of dissection tables and passed through a doorway into the first of a pair of labs that led off to the left.

The burial chamber beneath the crypt of the Medici Chapel was a low-ceilinged room about ten by six metres. It was cramped and warm but the air was kept fresh with a powerful portable air-conditioning system. Around the walls of the lab stood X-ray machines, spectrometers and DNA analysers. Across the main chamber was the office of Carlin Mackenzie, where sealed cases of bones lay incongruously alongside a couple of souped-up Macs.

Edie had just settled down at her bench and was running through some read-outs from an infra-red spectrometer when Mackenzie walked in with two men in suits. She had met them before: the shorter of the pair was Umberto Nero, the Vice Chancellor of the University of Pisa; the other, younger man was a well-known local politician, Francesco della Pinoro, currently the hot favourite in the mayoral election.

'Ah, Edie,' Mackenzie said. The professor was a short, chubby man in his late sixties. He wore John Lennon glasses, had a shock of fine, white hair, and a soft, handsome face that had made him popular with TV documentary makers. 'Gentlemen, this is my niece, Dr Edie Granger.'

Della Pinoro extended a hand and Nero nodded. He and Edie had met on many occasions and they had never much cared for each other.

'Edie, I wonder if you could spare a few moments for our guests? Their car is due here in a minute; could you give them a brief tour?'

'Of course.' Edie managed to inject a little enthusiasm into her voice.

'Excellent. Gentlemen, thank you for your valuable comments and I will be in touch very soon.' Mackenzie shook their hands and turned on his heel.

'This way.' Edie escorted della Pinoro and Nero back into the central chamber to a long metal table. As they walked across the stone floor, she described how the bodies in the alcoves had been embalmed and preserved in this vault. Pacing around the table, she looked across at the visitors. Between them lay a 470-year-old corpse.

Brushing away a lock of curly black hair that had fallen across her face, she fixed the men with her burnt-wood eyes, folded her arms and stretched herself up to her full height, towering over both of them.

'This is Ippolito de' Medici, the illegitimate son of Giuliano de' Medici, the Duke of Nemours,' she explained. 'For almost half a millennium, mystery has surrounded his death. Some people have speculated that this young man – he was only twenty-four when he died – was murdered by his cousin Alessandro, who was then bumped off by another friendly relative, Lorenzino de' Medici. There was no proof though, until now. We've just finished working on these remains and have found clear evidence that Ippolito was poisoned.'

Nero looked up from the mummy on the table. Edie noticed he was a little pale. She quickly led the men into a smaller room off the main chamber. Here the smell of earth and old cloth was fainter. A man was seated at a workbench, peering into an eyepiece of a large microscope.

'This is the very heart of the operation,' Edie said.

'This room and the lab next door once contained up to a dozen coffins, but most of these were badly damaged in the flood of 1966. The bodies, those of minor members of the Medici clan, were reburied in another part of the chapel. This is now the principal lab where we analyse materials taken from the mummies in the crypt.'

'How can you be sure the man out there was murdered?' Della Pinoro asked. For the past few minutes, he had been taking particular interest in the V-shaped opening at the top of Edie's lab coat. 'Surely any evidence would have disappeared centuries ago?'

'A good question,' Edie said, feeling relieved she could demonstrate her knowledge. 'The main purpose of our work here is to ascertain the cause of death of prominent members of the Medici. These corpses may seem like lifeless husks,' she added and gestured towards the chamber they had just left, 'but they tell us an incredible amount that has remained hidden until now.'

'Such as?'

'Often we have to reconstruct a scenario just from skeletal remains. Usually this is all that's left after five hundred years. But even crumbling bones can tell us an enormous amount. Common diseases of the time, such as syphilis and smallpox, leave telltale signs in the fine structure of the victim's bones which we can study using immunohistochemical and ultrastructural analysis.'

Della Pinoro looked confused. 'In the case of Ippolito,' Edie went on. 'We've been able to make a detailed analysis of his skeleton which has revealed unusual levels of chemicals called salicylates.'

'And this proves . . .?'

'Well, Alessandro got away with the murder because, on his deathbed, Ippolito displayed all the normal symptoms of malaria: fever, rigors, excruciating headaches and severe abdominal pain. But poisoning with oil of wintergreen produces almost identical effects, and oil of wintergreen contains methyl salicylate.'

Della Pinoro was about to say something when a movement behind the men caught Edie's eye. 'Ah, they're bringing out the latest cause of disagreement.'

'Cause of disagreement?' Nero asked, as she headed towards the door.

'Apparently, this is Cosimo de' Medici, Cosimo the Elder,' Edie replied, leading the two men to another dissection table that stood head to tail with the platform containing Ippolito's remains. Mackenzie was there with his stepson, Jack Cartwright, the team's DNA expert.

'Apparently?' Mackenzie looked quizzically at Edie.

'We have conflicting opinions about the identity of this body,' Edie explained. 'My uncle is certain it's Cosimo, I'm yet to be convinced.'

Jack Cartwright, the tall, broad-shouldered man at Mackenzie's side stepped forward and introduced himself to the visitors. He had just returned from a morning at the University of Florence.

'And where do you stand in this matter, Dr Cartwright?' the vice chancellor asked, averting his eyes from the corpse.

Cartwright was about to reply when a young woman arrived, looking rather flustered. 'Sorry to interrupt,' she said. 'The car has arrived for our guests.'

The vice chancellor could not conceal his relief, and before della Pinoro could say anything, he had stepped up to Mackenzie. 'I'm very grateful you could make time,' he said. '. . . And thank you, Dr Granger, for showing us around.'

A few moments later, Edie returned having seen the visitors to their limo. Mackenzie and Cartwright were examining the body on the table. Mackenzie, with a loupe to his eye, was easing open a flap of a remarkably well-preserved silk tunic with a pair of tweezers. For two weeks they had been studying material taken from this body, running tests on tissue samples and bone structures using a portable X-ray machine. But only this morning they had agreed the body should be removed from its niche and inspected more closely. The body shared the alcove with another. Mackenzie believed it to be the remains of Contessina de' Medici, wife of Cosimo I, who had died in 1473.

'I do wish you wouldn't put out our dirty laundry for other people to see,' Mackenzie said, without looking up.

'I don't see any harm in admitting academics have disagreements,' Edie replied, plucking another pair of tweezers from a tray.

'Well, I do. I don't trust those people. They're always on the lookout for anything to cut our funding.'

'I think they were more interested in getting out of here as quickly as possible.'

'Quite possibly, but I consider Pinoro to be a viper.'

'Is that why you lumbered me with them?' Edie retorted.

Mackenzie glared at her. Edie looked away and quickly changed the subject.

'Exquisite texture to this silk jacket.'

'Indeed it is. Take a look at this,' Mackenzie

offered Cartwright his loupe. The corpse was dressed in a cream silk shirt and a velvet jacket which would once have been the most vivid and beautiful purple. The buttons of the jacket were solid gold. 'Adds weight to my theory, does it not?' Mackenzie muttered.

Edie shrugged. 'You would expect Cosimo to have been buried in the finest, but that could equally well apply to any prominent member of the family.'

'Perhaps. Found anything from the DNA samples, Jack?'

'We're still working on that,' Cartwright handed the eyepiece back to Mackenzie. 'It's proving to be more difficult than expected.'

Mackenzie sighed, carefully pulling back the crumbling jacket and exposing the crisp brown skin of the mummy beneath. It looked like a body made from papier mâché. 'Well, that's why we've dragged the poor fellow out,' he said.

Cosimo de' Medici, or Cosimo the Elder as he was sometimes known, had been one of the most important members of the Medicis, a man who had done more than anyone to elevate the family into its illustrious place in history. Born in Florence in 1389, he had been *de facto* ruler of the city for a generation. He ignited the Italian Renaissance and made the equivalent of billions for the family. Upon his death in 1464, he was honoured with the official title *Pater Patriae*: 'Father of His Country'.

Mackenzie ran a scalpel along the body's desiccated torso. The blade slid through the skin effortlessly and he drew it down then across the body to produce a Y-cut. The embalmers had worked with remarkable skill. The ancient corpse was very different to that of Ippolito, whose body, although buried more recently, had been reduced to little more than a crumbling skeleton. But under the crisp skin lay a dry cavity. The organs had shrivelled to a fraction of their original size and were as dry as the man's skin.

Mackenzie removed pieces of each organ and placed them in individually labelled test tubes which he then stoppered up. Edie placed these carefully in a rack on one side of the table. Probing deeper, he scraped away a tiny sample of the breastbone and a rib, placing the flakes into their own sample bottles.

Leaning forward, Mackenzie examined the void inside the body's chest. 'Odd,' he said after a moment. 'There appears to be an alien object resting against the spine. I can't see it very clearly. Take a look Edie.'

She swung a mounted magnifying glass over the cadaver and peered down at the area around the shrivelled heart. 'I can see something, a black

18

surface, it's embedded in the anterior epidermal layers I think. It certainly doesn't look like a natural artefact.'

'Help me turn the body over on to its side,' Mackenzie instructed them.

Edie and Jack Cartwright gently turned the corpse, raising one side two feet above the table. It weighed almost nothing.

'Just a little more,' Mackenzie said, squeezing his head and shoulders under the ancient mummy. With surgical precision, he ran his scalpel along the line of the spine making sure he inserted the blade in just a fraction of an inch so as not to damage the vertebrae. Straightening up, he raised a pair of metal tweezers up to the light. They held a thin and featureless black rectangle.

Carlin Mackenzie was alone in the burial chamber of the Medici Chapel. The digital clock on his desk showed that it was approaching 9 p.m., but he felt neither tired nor in any mood to shut down the computers and walk the short distance to his apartment on Via Cavour.

It had been an extraordinary day, perhaps the most extraordinary of his life, certainly the most remarkable of his forty-year career as a palaeopathologist. The nature of the artefact they had discovered inside the body of Cosimo de' Medici remained a total mystery; but the simple fact of its existence presented a conundrum. Save for the natural disturbance of the flood of 1966, these bodies had not been touched since they were buried. Yet here was this strange rectangular object concealed in the dried epidermal tissue of a man who had died over 500 years earlier.

The object was resting in a Petri dish next to Mackenzie's computer. He, Edie and Jack Cartwright had studied it as thoroughly as they dared without taking unnecessary risks. It was entirely black, a piece of granite-like stone measuring exactly 3.9 by 1.9 centimetres, and was just a few milli-metres thick. A single X-ray had shown it to be solid, apparently featureless and of uniform density. They had refrained from any form of chemical test until they could be sure these would not harm the stone. Using a powerful microscope, its crystalline struc-ture was revealed to be a blend of feldspar, quartz and potassium, an exceptionally pure granite called Amanorthosite.

Mackenzie began to write some comments in a notebook. He listed what they already knew: the object's chemical structure, mass, density, dimen-sions. Then, putting down his pen, he picked up the stone rectangle and held it up to the light between latexed finger and thumb. With a jolt, he realised something about it had changed. Across what had been a featureless surface, faint green lines had begun to appear. They were changing and merging even as he stared. He reached for his loupe and looked closer. This was truly remarkable. A faint green outline was forming close to one end of the rectangle. Below this, he could just begin to see some letters, and two-thirds of the way down, a set of lines appeared.

'This is amazing,' he heard himself say. For a few seconds he wasn't quite sure what to do. Then, he grabbed the phone and quickly dialled a number. An answer machine came on. He dialled another number from memory. A second machine clicked on, and without hesitating, he began to describe what he could see on the face of the stone tablet.

Two minutes later, he was about to make some final remarks when he heard a bleep and knew he had used up the memory on the answer system. He replaced the phone and stared at the wall. What he had seen thrilled but also scared him. He had never been a superstitious man. He had been trained as a scientist, but he couldn't deny his deepest fears. This was merely the latest in a string of weird events and coincidences that he had spoken of to no one. By leaving this message, had he done enough? Or had he done too much? Had he placed others in terrible danger?

He heard a faint noise from the chamber beyond. He looked towards the plastic screen dividing the office from the burial chamber. Silence.

He placed the tablet back in the Petri dish and removed the loupe. It was at that precise moment he felt a sudden, intense pain in his neck. He sensed rather than saw someone leaning in towards him. His hands flew to his neck and felt the cold steel of a garrotte. His assailant twisted on the wire with incredible force.

The scientist's eyes bulged. Gasping for breath, he tried to pull away and at the same time to force his fingers beneath the garrotte. But it was utterly futile. A terrible pain roared through his head and he began to lose focus. His attacker was pulling him further and further back, slicing into his neck. For a fleeting moment, Mackenzie believed he could twist free, but the man behind him was far too strong. Mackenzie's sphincter opened and he voided himself; a foul smell rose from his seat. There was a tiny almost imperceptible crack as Mackenzie's trachea was sliced open and darkness closed about him.

Chapter 3

Venice, present day

Jeff Martin eased the cashmere of his sweater away from his neck and ran a hand over the light stubble on his chin. It had been too late to shave before leaving his apartment earlier that evening and, when he had caught a glimpse of himself in the hall mirror on the way out, he had thought he looked tired, his skin a bit blotchy, his longish, light brown hair a little lank and lifeless. Jeff's intense blue eyes still possessed something of their old sparkle, he had reassured himself, but it could not be denied, he had definitely looked better.

Gazing now around Harry's Bar, he reflected, not for the first time, on what had gone through the mind of Ernest Hemingway as he had taken in the same scene more than half a century earlier. 'You find everything on Earth at Harry's . . . except perhaps happiness.' The place never changed; neither, he thought, had those sentiments. The half-timbered walls were still the same shade of cream they had been when it was first opened in 1931. The waiters, handsome and elegant, wore the same uniform of black trousers, white bow ties and crisply starched white jackets. The menu was very similar, the layout of the bar unaltered, and the arrangement of tables and chairs in this modest room was identical to the design dreamed up by the founder, Giuseppe Cipriani, who had called it Harry's after a friend, Harry Pickering, put up the two hundred pounds needed to open the place. And Harry's still exuded the same aura of genteel melancholia it had possessed so long ago.

'Another?'

The question snapped Jeff out of his reverie. He looked at his friend, Visconte Roberto Armatovani and nodded. 'Why not?' They hadn't seen each other for some time. Roberto, a world-renowned musicologist, had been on a lecture tour of America. They had met earlier in the evening and enjoyed a hideously expensive dinner upstairs in the restaurant. Now they both felt a little overfull, but relaxed. The waiter was at the table and two more Bellinis were ordered almost immediately.

'So,' Roberto said. 'How's Rose taking to Venice?'

'Oh, very well. She's at a difficult age but she's become quite attached to dear old Maria. Which is a relief.'

Rose, the only child from his ill-fated marriage, was the best thing he had produced in his life. Jeff wished he could see more of her, but her mother, Imogen, the woman he had been married to for thirteen years and divorced from for two, seemed determined to cause him pain and trouble. This was Rose's first visit to his adopted home and he had been able to see her only a handful of times since the dissolution of his marriage. Rose lived with her mother at Hogsdown, a vast, frigid stately home in Gloucestershire that Imogen had inherited from her deceased parents. With a momentary stab of sadness, Jeff realised his fourteen-year-old daughter was almost a young woman and soon he'd be losing his baby girl for ever.

He took a sip of his Bellini. Placing it back on the table, he glanced at Roberto who was as relaxed as always, a man completely at home in his environment. He was in his perennial uniform of black jeans, black polo neck and black leather jacket. His salt and pepper hair was cut short and his thin face, almost black eyes and high cheekbones made him look far younger than his forty-four years.

The two men had met five years ago. Roberto was

an authority on early music and in particular the compositions of Palestrina, the sixteenth-century maestro who had been a favourite of Pope Julius III. But there was much more to Roberto. He was also an extraordinary polymath; a superb violinist; the author of a clutch of popular books on a variety of arcane subjects, and, what had most drawn Jeff to him, he was an expert in the history of Venice. Jeff had been on two archaeological digs with him and helped with some of the research for his latest book, an account of the early settlement of Venice in the fourth century.

For Roberto, all his endeavours were elaborate hobbies because he was heir to one of the largest and most ancient fortunes in Italy. The Armatovani family could trace their ancestry back to the thirteenth century and it included half a dozen doges, cardinals and numerous warlords and local aristo-crats. Roberto was the youngest of four brothers and the only one to remain in Venice after his parents died. He lived in one of the few palazzos that had not been converted into sumptuous apartments or hotels.

'You going to tell me about your trip then, Roberto? I've been waiting for you to mention it all evening.'

'Oh God. To be honest, I'm so glad to be home I don't much care to think about it.' His English was pure Oxbridge. 'But it was . . . well . . . how shall I put it? An experience. I don't think they knew quite what to make of me. They believe that it's obligatory for European professors to wear tweed jackets and smoke pipes.'

They both laughed. 'What about the tour though? You knocked 'em dead no doubt.'

'Of course,' Roberto replied. 'They have some excellent young musicians. But what of you, Jeff? You're looking a bit run-down.'

'Oh, rubbish.'

'Is there something wrong?'

'Roberto, I'm fine. In fact, I'm more contented than I've been for a long time.'

'Contented? What a thoroughly disgusting word. It means nothing, nothing at all. Precisely halfway between agony and ecstasy. Very bourgeois of you, my friend.'

Jeff shrugged and drained his glass. 'All right, "fulfilled" then. I'm feeling fulfilled. Will that do?'

'Better.'

'You know more than anyone how depressed I was when I first moved here, but I'm over it now.'

'And you're not missing your old life?'

'Imogen?'

'No, not that bitch. Your illustrious career, being the young prodigy, historian extraordinaire.'

27

'No.'

'Why don't I believe you?'

'Well OK, yes. I sometimes find myself wondering what I would be doing now if things had turned out differently. I do try and keep up with things, even if I am *persona non grata* at Cambridge. And there's the stuff I do with you.'

Jeff beckoned the waiter and ordered another round. He was not being entirely honest with his friend. He loved Venice and had started to find real joy in working with Roberto. The problem was this research was only one of many concerns for Roberto who seemed to have a magical ability to juggle ten different projects at once. His recent trip to America had interrupted the flow of their studies, and Jeff knew that now Roberto was back he would immediately be throwing himself into at least half a dozen new plans. Besides which, he had to admit he was beginning to miss the satisfaction he had gained from being a respected member of the academic establishment, a fellow of Trinity College, Cambridge.

His ascension to world authority on the history of the early Middle Ages had been the stuff of legend, and at university he had been considered a genuine prodigy. Even before his finals he had written a ground-breaking paper on anti-Semitism in tenth century France published in the leading academic publication *Journal of European History*. He had then picked up a First from King's College, London before his twentieth birthday.

Moving to Cambridge, he had become a protégé of Norman Honeywell-Scott, a famed academic with important connections. Jeff felt no shame in admitting that he had ridden on Honeywell-Scott's coattails, but within three years of joining the historian in Cambridge, they had fallen out, never to speak to each other again. Honeywell-Scott had moved to the Sorbonne where he had become an even more luminous star in the academic firmament. The same summer, Jeff had met and fallen in love with Imogen Parkhurst, only child of the Tory cabinet minister Sir Maxwell Parkhurst, whose ancestors had made their fortune financing the Napoleonic Wars.

Imogen's father had never liked him (her mother had died nine years earlier), and Jeff knew that for all his brilliance and academic success, Imogen was way out of his league. He had been born in a two-bedroom flat above a shop in Wickford, Essex, and his father had run an electrical business. Intellectual clout could only partially make up for poor breeding. Imogen had vigorously denied that her feelings for him stemmed from a belated act of rebellion against her parents, but it was nonsense of course. Then out of the blue, Jeff learned that Imogen was having an affair with a family friend, Caspian Knightley, a distant cousin of the late Diana Spencer.

From that moment onwards, his and Imogen's lives began to diverge. Two months after they had separated, Sir Maxwell died in a helicopter crash and Imogen inherited the family millions. Jeff threw himself into work and put huge faith in a TV series about Charlemagne he had been chosen to write and present. The pilot for the show bombed and almost overnight he lost his chance. The failure, the first of his career, hit him hard. He had turned to drink and then, influenced by his media friends, he had dabbled briefly with cocaine. Before long, his academic life started to unravel. A few months later, with his divorce finalised, he had taken the advice of the Master of Trinity and left for an extended 'holiday' in Italy.

In some ways, he had been lucky. During his marriage to Imogen he had met some useful people who had become genuine friends. One of these was Mark Thornton who was one of the most skilful divorce lawyers in Britain. Thornton had never much liked the Parkhursts and had little time for Imogen. He had worked hard to secure Jeff an exceptionally good settlement which meant that the electrical contractor's son from Wickford was set up for life with a flat in Mayfair, a luxurious four-bedroom apartment on St Mark's Square in Venice and a few million in the bank. But Jeff knew he would have happily sacrificed the lot if he could have rewritten history and had more time to spend with Rose.

'Is there some babe at the bar?' Roberto asked suddenly.

'What?'

'You seem inordinately interested in something or someone over there.'

'Sorry, I was just thinking about Rose,' he lied.

'She's certainly blossomed. I could hardly believe it when I came to pick you up this evening. And she gets on with the irreducible Maria? That really is something.'

Jeff laughed. 'You never did warm to my house-keeper, did you Roberto?'

'No,' he replied. 'The woman can't stand the sight of me.'

'Nonsense.' Jeff looked at his watch. It had turned eleven. 'Look, sorry to be a bore, but I ought to be getting back. It's my shout.'

Outside Harry's, it was freezing, and their breath hung mistily in the air. It was the eve of Carnivale; a crisp February evening, Jeff's favourite season in Venice. Turning up their collars, they walked along Calle Vallaresso, past the designer stores on each side, towards San Moise. They parted at the junction with a promise to meet up for Sunday lunch at the Gritti Palace. Jeff plunged his hands into his overcoat and headed east towards San Marco.

It was quiet. Most tourists were tucked up in bed and the African street traders were putting away their fake Louis Vuitton bags and five-dollar Rolexes. He crossed the square close to its western edge and walked quickly through a short passageway. His apartment was on the top floor on the north side of the square. Turning right, he walked along a narrow lane behind the building, the silence broken only by the gentle lapping of the canal to his left. Reaching the door to the hallway, he felt in his pocket for the key. Just as he inserted it into the lock, he heard a quiet cough. He span round. Standing in the shadows was a man in a long black coat and hat. For the briefest moment, the light from a window in Jeff's building caught something shiny in the man's hand making it glint in the darkness.

'I'm sorry. I didn't mean to startle you,' the man said, stepping out of the shadows. No more than five feet tall, his face was lined and worn. He was wearing a scruffy overcoat and a trilby hat, under which his long white hair trailed to his shoulders. Taking a step towards Jeff, he leaned heavily on a wooden cane with a highly polished metal top. 'My name is Mario Sporani,' the old man added. 'You don't know me, but I have some information I think you'll find interesting. Could I possibly impose on your hospitality? It is a little chilly.'

'What kind of information?' Jeff asked, eyeing the man suspiciously.

'A matter of history.'

'History?'

'My apologies. I have travelled this evening from my home in Florence. I was once the warden of the Medici Chapel. There's a matter of great importance I need to discuss with you,' and he handed Jeff a frayed black and white photograph. It showed a much younger Mario Sporani holding a black cylinder about twelve inches long. At one end of the tube Jeff could just make out a crest, an arrangement of five balls and a pair of crossed keys: the Medici coat of arms.

'I'm one of only a handful who have seen this object in five hundred years,' Sporani continued. 'And now it has disappeared from the face of the Earth.'

Jeff's sitting room was spectacular, a vast open space, furnished in a contemporary style, all brushed steel, dark woods, soft cream and white fabrics. The wall facing the doorway was taken up with massive windows looking out on to San Marco, the

Campanile and S. Giorgio Maggiore beyond. To the right of this room lay the kitchen, and to the left, a shadowy corridor led to the bedrooms.

Mario Sporani stood in the doorway taking it all in silently, his eyes glinting with appreciation. 'Beautiful,' he said simply, and Jeff indicated he should take a seat. The place was silent. Rose and Maria were apparently in bed.

Jeff went to the kitchen and started to make coffee. He kept an eye on Sporani who was gazing around the room and through the windows as if in a rapture. He watched him get up to admire the paintings and then to study a set of glass shelves containing a collection of artefacts.

A few minutes later, Jeff was standing beside him with a tray in his hands. Sporani was staring up at a painting of a reclining nude.

'At first glance I would have sworn this was Modigliani's *Nude Sdraiato*, but there's something wrong.'

Jeff appraised the old man. 'It's a very early work from his days in Venice at Istituto per le Belle Arti di Venezia; from about the time he first got into smoking hashish actually. Modigliani moved to Paris the following year and reworked this picture.'

Sporani shook his head slowly. 'Fascinating.'

Jeff placed the tray on a stainless-steel table between two sofas close to the windows.

'OK,' he said, handing Sporani a cup. 'What's this all about?'

'Naturally you're sceptical, Mr Martin. I too would have reacted the same way forty years ago.' He took a sip of coffee. 'As I said, I was the warden of the Medici Chapel, until I retired a few years ago. I was in charge of the chapel when the terrible flood of November 1966 struck Florence and destroyed so many wonders.'

Jeff watched him in silence. He guessed that Sporani was probably about seventy but he looked older than his years.

'The morning the waters broke the banks of the Arno and came into our district in a great torrent, I managed to struggle through the storm to reach the chapel. My worst fears were realised: the crypt had flooded and the bodies of the entombed Medici were in danger of being swept away.

'I was young and impulsive. Without a thought for my own safety, I rushed down into the burial chambers and was almost drowned, escaping by the skin of my teeth. I could do little to protect the crypt, but mercifully, although the waters caused immense damage, the worst of outcomes was avoided and, by that evening, the flood water in the district began to recede. While I was in the crypt scrambling to escape the rising water I happened upon a strange object, an ebony tube. I realised immediately from the crest that it had once belonged to the Medici, but I had no idea what it was. As I said, I was young. I should have handed it over to the authorities, but I could not, at least not straight away.'

He paused for a moment and took another sip of coffee. 'I broke the seal. Inside, I found a sheath of papers covered in tiny handwriting. It was written in a strange language. I've since concluded it was probably Greek, and of course, I couldn't understand a word of it.'

'Did you think of getting it translated?' Jeff asked.

'Well, I thought of it. Indeed, I mentioned my discovery to a couple of friends. This was probably a mistake. I should have just kept my mouth shut.'

Jeff looked puzzled.

'None of them could help, you see. Even those who knew a little of other languages could not translate more than the odd word. I learned one crucial thing however. The last page of the text bore a signature, that of Cosimo de' Medici, the great patron and leader of Florence. Although I said I couldn't understand a word of the document, it was clearly some sort of diary or journal because the text was separated into chunks with dates at the top of each section. I made a mental note of these. Later I discovered the dates were from the year 1410.'

'And did that prompt you to hand in your find?'

'It should have done,' Sporani said and placed his empty cup on the table. 'And, I would have done so. I'm no thief.'

'Would have?'

'Two nights after my discovery, there was a bang on the front door. My wife and baby were asleep in the back room. I went to answer it. I was pushed back into the hallway with a gun held to my head. There were two men. One of them was British I think, the other, Italian. He was the one who did most of the talking. Although, actually neither of them said very much. They wanted the Medici document.'

'How did they know about it?'

'I'm not certain. But I should have told no one about my discovery. I handed it over, of course. When the Italian guy noticed the seal had been broken I was sure he was going to kill me. I had to think fast. I told them it was broken when I found it.'

'And they believed you?'

'I don't know. I think the man with the gun was all for pulling the trigger, but the British one stopped him. He said something I'll never forget: "I will blow your baby's brains out if you ever tell another soul about this."'

From outside came the faint sound of a ship's horn.

'So, why are you here, now?'

Sporani was gazing out through the windows as if in a dream. Snapping out of his reverie, he turned his weary eyes to Jeff. 'Oh, they no longer have a hold over me, Mr Martin. My baby boy grew into a fine young man, but five years ago he was killed in a motorcycle accident in Bologna. And my wife, Sophia, she passed away last month. Breast cancer.'

'I am sorry.'

'Oh, you needn't be. We had a happy life, the three of us.'

Jeff poured them some more coffee. 'So, why have you come to see me?'

'I need your help. You're of course aware of the Medici Project, the team studying the remains in the chapel?'

'Yes.'

'Well, I believe they are in terrible danger.'

'Why do you think that?'

'Because of what I have just told you.'

'But that was over forty years ago . . .'

'When I first heard about the Medici Project, I voiced my opposition. I told the authorities at the University of Pisa who are funding the team that I believed someone or some group of people did not

38

want the bodies disturbed. No one would listen.'

'I can see why they might have been sceptical,' Jeff admitted.

'Indeed. At the time I could offer nothing to make them think me anything other than a crank.'

'But you've spoken to the team?'

'This is why I've come to see you, Mr Martin. Professor Mackenzie wouldn't even agree to see me. They have their daily fill of protestors – people like Father Baggio. You've heard of him?'

Jeff nodded.

Sporani gave him a piercing look. 'Your old friend, Edie Granger. You will know from her that Professor Mackenzie is an arrogant man, but he must be persuaded to reconsider his work in the chapel.'

Jeff and Edie went back a long way. Indeed, she was his closest and oldest friend. They had met at university, and although they had since travelled very different paths, they had remained close. When they first met, she had been an eighteen-year-old Goth who went on to win a first in chemistry and pathology before completing a DPhil specialising in palaeopathology. Her friends joked that she was carrying on the family business; both her parents had been archaeologists.

'I've only met Professor Mackenzie a handful of

times. I know him as much by reputation as anything else.'

'Yes, of course, the world-famous palaeopathologist, something of a household name these days, the man your *Times* newspaper dubbed "The Mummy Detective". Maybe he is too important to talk to me. Which is why I've come to see you. You're the only one who can convince them of the danger they face.'

Jeff stared at Sporani and shook his head slowly. 'I hate to disillusion you Mr Sporani, but you're quite wrong. There's nothing I could do. Besides, I'm not convinced your fears are justified.'

'You're not?'

'Well, no. I believe your story, but it was a long time ago. Maybe the two men who broke into your house were simply thieves, and they knew how to buy your silence.'

'Perhaps,' Sporani replied, fixing Jeff with an intense stare. 'But a year ago, before my Sophia died and soon after the planned disinterment was announced, I was sent this.'

Sporani handed an envelope to Jeff. He pulled out a single sheet of paper and read the short message: STOP YOUR FRIENDS. DO NOT DISTURB THE MEDICI TOMBS. YOUR SON MAY BE DEAD BUT YOUR WIFE STILL LIVES.

★

40

For most of the night sleep eluded Jeff, and before dawn, he was up and dressed. He was making a pot of strong coffee when Rose wandered in yawning, her hair a blonde mess.

'It's alive!' He smiled broadly.

She pulled a face and rubbed her eyes. 'Are you always up this early, Dad?'

'Only when I've been out clubbing all night.'

Rose looked startled for a moment before she realised her father was kidding. When she smiled she looked disarmingly like her mother, Jeff thought, and pushed aside the painful memories. From the hall, they could hear Maria plugging in the hoover. She popped her head around the door and said good morning before starting her work.

'I love this city the most when there's no one around, Rose,' Jeff said and took a large gulp of coffee. 'A psychiatrist might draw some alarming conclusions from that, but there it is.' He pulled on a brown flying jacket. 'Have some coffee, I've put a couple of croissants in the oven to warm.'

'Where're you going?'

'Chores to do.'

Leaving the elevator, Jeff crossed the marble-floored hallway, waved to the dozing concierge and emerged into the narrow passageway behind the building. As he turned the corner, he almost tripped over a body in the shadows. The man groaned and sat up with surprising speed.

'Ah, my friend Jeffrey.' His voice had a heavily accented rasp.

'Dino. This isn't your usual day around here.'

Dino rubbed his eyes. 'Changing my routine. Keeps the tourists on their toes,' he said with a lopsided grin.

Dino had lived on the streets for as long as Jeff had lived in San Marco. During the dark days when he first moved to Venice and left behind his old existence in England, Jeff had befriended the man, taking him for a coffee and a sandwich. There, Dino had revealed some of his life. How he had fled Kosovo after his wife and young daughter had been slaughtered. He had buried them with his bare hands and headed west with nothing but the clothes on his back. Before the war, he had been a maths teacher in Pristina. Now he lived on the few euros rich American tourists occasionally deigned to toss him.

Dino followed a routine in which he would show up in San Marco once a week having passed through a list of hot tourist spots on the other days, and Jeff would always offer him a few euros or take him for a coffee. In a peculiar way, they shared a bond; they were both exiles, men who had passed beyond the veil of normal life. Dino was deeply religious and he believed with all his heart that he was merely biding his time here on earth and that he would see his family again in a better world. Jeff, a committed atheist, kept his own counsel on the subject but he understood that the mere existence of his friend was a great help to him, a constant reminder that his own daughter, Rose, was very much alive and well.

'Here, Dino,' Jeff said, handing him some crisp new notes. 'Get a bite to eat. I have to go. Talk next time, yes?'

Dino took the money and shook Jeff's hand. 'God bless you,' he said with a smile.

An orange light was spreading across the eastern sky as Jeff strode into San Marco and long shadows stretched across the Piazza. At the Torre Dell' Orologio he followed a winding course along Calle Larga and then turned left into Calle dei Specchieri. The place was deserted, the shops closed up. Jeff could almost imagine the entire population of Earth had been exterminated and he was the last man left to wander these silent passageways alone. But soon he was crossing Rio di S. Zulian where he passed a woman with a tiny dog on a lead. Between her bright red lips she clasped a slender black cigarette holder, which she kept in her mouth as she remonstrated with the dog for dawdling at a lamppost. Cigarette ash fell on to cobbled stones. Behind her wandered two middle-aged women, their skin worn, eyes tired. They both looked extremely drab except for their multicoloured headscarves pulled low over their brows.

By the time he reached the Rialto, the sun was emerging, transforming the waters of the Grand Canal into a pastel palette. Under the bridge passed a vaporetto packed with early commuters. The bridge itself was almost deserted, gondola T-shirts and cheap carnival masks could be seen behind grilled glass.

Pausing for a moment, Jeff surveyed the view. He had seen it a thousand times but it still moved him deeply. Venice, he decided long ago, was what he liked to call an 'emotion amplifier'. If you felt happy, it made you happier, and if you were depressed, it could drag you further down. In one way or another, Venice had always been a special place for him and his ex-wife. They had come here when they were first married. Flushed with confidence and a buoyant share market, they had bought the apartment on San Marco. But here too was where he had learned of Imogen's infidelity.

They had left Rose in London with the nanny and flown to Venice for a two-night stay. The evening they arrived, they went straight out to dinner at The Danieli. It had been a typically extravagant affair, but at that time Jeff was revelling in the high life to which he had grown accustomed. Walking back along the Riva Degli they called into the piano bar at the Monaco, and Imogen had told him she had been seeing someone. The next morning, she flew back to England, but he had elected to stay on for a while. He had needed time to think, to try to take on board what he had learned.

Alone and bereft, for him, Venice transformed into a city of ghosts and he felt himself losing touch with reality. He lay in bed in their apartment and searched his mind and soul in an effort to discover what he had done wrong.

He felt sorry for himself, of course, but he was most concerned for Rose, and furious with Imogen for tearing their family apart. He got angry and his anger made him stoic, and he surprised himself with his ruthlessness. Returning to England, he immediately filed for divorce and anaesthetised any feelings he once had for his perfidious wife.

He sometimes wondered whether it had been a good idea to return to the city where his world had fallen apart. But he loved this place too much to let it go. He could not blame Venice for what his wife had done to him. During the early days, soon after the divorce, he had spent long nights walking through the empty maze of Venice listening to Samuel Barber and Tom Waits on his iPod and wondering if he would ever be happy again.

His oldest friend Edie had helped pull him through. She had taken time off work to stay in Venice with him. She had forced him out to restaurants, compelled him to talk, and rationed the booze he found too easy to pour down his throat. The bond between them grew stronger than ever. Jeff knew Edie did not care for Imogen. She never said a word against his ex-wife, but he knew Edie so well that at times they were almost telepathic. Imogen had certainly been jealous of their relationship, but it was misplaced. Edie was his dearest friend, they shared a brotherly–sisterly closeness; Imogen had been his wife and he had loved her, for a while.

Thinking of Edie led his mind back to the previous night and the strange figure of Mario Sporani. The man had been convinced Jeff could somehow talk Edie into influencing Carlin Mackenzie, and he was clearly convinced the team working at the Medici Chapel were in real danger. The old man had left soon after showing him the bizarre note, refusing the offer of a room for the night. Jeff had made a lame promise he would sleep on the idea of calling Edie. Sporani would be in Venice for a couple of days and Jeff had agreed to meet up with him for coffee during that time. Now he didn't know what to think. He couldn't help feeling concerned for Edie, but surely it was all nonsense? Only religious nuts believed there was anything wrong with disinterring the Medici. Surely Sporani was deluded, a fantasist. Perhaps the loss of his family had turned his mind.

Descending the northern side of the Rialto, he turned immediately right into the fish market, Mercato del Pesce. He loved this place, loved even the pungent smell of fish being gutted by men in white overalls and rubber boots. At the stalls, he could see trays filled with scores of squid like distended brains; crabs, their claws grasping the air trying to reach some place they would never find, and whole tuna stamped with the name of the fishmonger who would slice it up to accommodate thirty families. Beyond the fish stalls stood row upon row of counters laden with fruit and vegetables, and beside these, flower stalls, a riot of every colour in every shade.

Jeff loved to cook and this was his favourite place to buy fresh produce. The stall holders all called him by his first name. They joked with him, and during the past year they had taught him a thesaurus of colloquialisms and obscene phrases.

He wandered slowly around the stalls picking the best cut of fish he could find, trout fillets which he knew Rose would love. He then selected courgettes, aubergines, mushrooms and firm new potatoes. Fifteen minutes after entering the market, he was done, two plastic carrier bags were filled with everything he needed to cook that night.

Leaving the market, the day had blossomed. Now there were plenty of people around and the light had changed from its former moody ambience to the bleach of true morning. It was time for a coffee and maybe even an aperitif.

Dropping the plastic bags beside a table, Jeff called over the waiter and placed his order. Then he noticed the TV in the far corner, high up on a wooden shelf. The news was on with the sound low. An image of a tank exploding and the faces of newly dead soldiers. Then the newsreader in the studio mouthed almost silent words before the picture changed. The waiter arrived with the coffee, a pair of small biscuits on the saucer. Jeff returned his gaze to the screen, a coloured bar now stretched across the bottom of the picture and he could read the words: MEDICI CHAPEL, FIRENZE. Above this, the image of a dimly lit room. He soon realised it was the crypt of the chapel. Then the picture dissolved, replaced with a head shot of Professor Carlin Mackenzie.

Jeff felt a sudden spasm in the pit of his stomach. He was about to call over the waiter to get the volume turned up but already the image on the screen had vanished, replaced by a shot of Downing Street. He reached into his pocket and pulled out his phone. Punching the keys, his mind acting on autopilot, he found the BBC Internet News Service. Clicking again he pulled up 'Breaking News' and scanned the brief report. It was only as he finished reading the last line he realised his hands were shaking.

Chapter 4

Florence, 4 May 1410

Cosimo de' Medici considered his reflection in the small mirror in his bedchamber. He was an ugly young man and he knew it. Not for him the full blond curls of his best friend Ambrogio Tommasini; nor could he make claim to anything like Ambrogio's shapely nose, his large brown, sometimes fathomless eyes with their long lashes. Cosimo's face was an odd confection of mismatched features, a jutting chin, narrow lips and a wholly unappealing nose. Admittedly, his eyes were large and nicely shaped, but they were slightly different sizes and arranged either side of his nose without precision. Even though he had only just entered his twenty-second year, his hair was thin and wispy, his skin sallow. But then he smiled faintly and his face changed in an instant. He was still ugly, but a new light was revealed in his eyes, the sudden wrinkles around their sockets added a decade but they also offered warmth. He felt comfortable with the face that stared back at him, and at that moment he would not have exchanged his singular visage for Ambrogio's redoubtable beauty. Plucking from the bed his *lucco*, the rich crimson ankle-length coat he wore every day, he slipped his arms through the sleeves, letting the great folds of fabric drape luxuriantly around his wrists. A moment later, he was heading for the door.

Along the echoing corridor and down the broad, curving stone stairway, the house was silent, but as Cosimo stood in the hall he could hear the sound of people walking by on the road outside, and beyond this, the clatter of hooves on cobbles.

Cosimo found his mother, Piccarda, sitting in her sewing room situated close to the front of the house. The curtains had been drawn wide and sunlight spilled in through the shutters casting broad bands of lemon across the room. His six-year-old brother Lorenzo was playing with one of the cats. Olomo, the black slave boy, recently arrived from Lisbon, was cleaning ashes from the fireplace, sweeping them into a broad wooden pail tipped forward on to its rim. Waving a brush in a broad arc between sweeps of the dirt, he was trying to shoo away a brown and white kitten that was intent on demolishing and dispersing the pile of grey powder so carefully gathered from the grate.

'I'm to meet father at the eighth hour,' Cosimo said to his mother.

'But breakfast, Cosi.'

'I'll stop for some bread on the way. I'm late.' He kissed his mother on the cheek.

Lorenzo saw his brother and ran over to him. Cosimo ruffled the boy's hair. Then, lifting him high into the air, he whirled him around.

'Don't forget our ball game later, Cosi. Remember you promised,' Lorenzo exclaimed between squeals.

'How could I forget such an important engagement?' He placed his brother back on the rug, kissed the top of the boy's head, waved to his mother and was gone.

The Medicis lived in a large but rather plain house on the Piazza del Duomo, and the front windows on the upper floor offered a spectacular view across the city towards the Ponte Vecchio. The foreground was dominated by the unfinished colossus of the Duomo, in the distance the Cathedral of Santa Maria del Fiore could be seen encased in wooden scaffolding.

It was already busy on the streets close to the Duomo. Stepping out on to the piazza, Cosimo quickly dodged a man pulling a cart laden high with vegetables and turned south along Via dei Calzaiuoli towards the river and the banking district centred on Via Porta Rossa, where his father, Giovanni di Bicci had founded the Medici bank thirteen years earlier. The air was thick with a confusion of odours: an acidic tinge from the tanneries and the ammonia stench of fish guts clashed with the wonderful aroma of baking bread. But Cosimo was almost totally oblivious to the smells. He had been born just a few yards from here on a day when the same scents wafted all around. They were as natural to him as the spotless blue sky above the towers, the tiled roofs and the cobblestones of the street beneath his feet.

Looking up, he saw a matronly figure flapping a sheet as she pinned it to a length of thin rope above the balcony. From inside the house came the squeals of children, a crash and then an adult shouting. Cosimo smiled to himself and stepped up his pace; he was late after all.

A few yards on, and he could see the river glistening in the morning sun and directly ahead was the Ponte Vecchio with its huddled shops and houses, the tanners, purse-makers and a clutch of butchers. The bridge was already crowded with people bartering and haggling over the price of a fine leather pouch or a side of venison. On the river itself a small barge was approaching the quay, a young boy dressed in a black felt cap and badly ripped hose leaned forward at the prow and swung a rope, expertly lassoing the mooring post on his first attempt. The boy shouted something unintelligible to a man at the helm then ran aft to secure that end of the boat.

Cosimo turned right into Via Porta Rossa and saw immediately the grand façade of the banking house. A small crowd milled around outside just as it did on most days. At small wooden tables topped with green baize sat men in formal black jackets buttoned up tight to the neck. Around each table, a small crowd jostled, making it difficult for the men at the front to hold a proper discourse with the seated officials. On the tables could be seen quills and ink bottles, clusters of promissory notes and small piles of coins. Beside each table stood an armed guard, each clutching a pike, watching the eager faces and itching for some action.

Cosimo strode past the tables and the customers gathered there, climbed six stone steps at the front of the bank, nodded to the guards at the doors and was ushered into the grand entrance hall that lay beyond.

It was cool inside. His feet echoed on the smooth stone floor. To each side stood more tables, these were larger and the smartly dressed figures presiding over them looked more important than the men doing a similar job outside. Cosimo passed between the tables without looking at the customers and walked up another small flight of stairs to a mezzanine floor. At the top, he turned right and followed a corridor to a pair of heavy wooden doors. He knocked but after receiving no response he knocked again.

'Who is it?'

'Your son, Father.'

'Come.'

Cosimo pushed the door and entered a large, low-ceilinged room empty except for a heavy wooden desk and two chairs, a large one behind the desk and a smaller one facing it. Cosimo's father, Giovanni di Bicci was walking towards him, his arms extended. He wore the formal red gown and cap of his guild.

'Come my boy,' he said, his voice warm and gentle. 'Have you eaten? Can I get you anything?'

Cosimo looked into his father's face. He had recently turned fifty but seemed older, more weathered. His was a crooked face. As with his eldest son, nothing matched properly; each feature was slightly misplaced, creating an unappealing asymmetry. But Giovanni's intense black eyes, a concerned frown, the line of his jaw, each expressed different aspects of his character with unusual clarity.

'No thank you, Father,' Cosimo replied and as Giovanni retreated behind the desk, the younger man took the other chair. Placing his hands in his lap he looked intently at his father and waited for him to speak.

Giovanni had a half-finished bowl of fruit on the desk in front of him. He had placed the bowl on a pile of papers and juice had slurped across what looked to Cosimo like official documents of some kind. Before speaking again, the older man stabbed at a piece of orange with a silver fork and brought the oozing fruit to his mouth, wiping his moist chin with the back of his hand.

'I expect you're wondering why I've asked you here today, Cosimo,' he intoned slowly, fixing his son with his black eyes. Leaning forward, he found a piece of crisp pale green pear with his fork.

'Well, I finished my studies two weeks ago, Father. I imagine you would like me to pull my weight here at the bank.'

Giovanni smiled warmly. 'You make me sound like a dragon. Two weeks and then you are enslaved!'

Cosimo returned the smile, but he felt disturbed. His father might make a joke of it, but he knew that his time of freedom was about to end and that he was to lose for ever the life of study and contemplation he had enjoyed.

'Actually I have some news I thought might excite you.'

'Oh?'

'I have arranged for you to begin a tour of branches of our bank.'

'A tour?'

'Yes, obviously not encompassing all thirty-nine banks, but a trip that will allow you to visit the branches in Italy. It will take you to Genoa, Venice and Rome. It will be a marvellous way for you to learn more about the Medici business.'

Cosimo made a show of appreciating the gesture, but he could feel his mood sinking.

'You seem displeased, Cosi.'

Cosimo was staring into space, seeing his new life, his pre-planned career flashing before his eyes.

'Cosimo?'

'Sorry, Father. Yes, a tour.'

'I said you seem displeased.'

Cosimo paused for a second too long before answering. In that time it was clear that whatever he was to say would have little effect, other than to complicate things. 'I'm not displeased, Father, I just feel a little, well, a little . . . rushed?'

Giovanni laid his fork in the bowl and sat back in his chair. Again, he fixed his son with his keen black eyes. Cosimo knew his father to be a caring and warm-hearted man. He knew that all those who did business with him respected and admired this man who had risen from humble beginnings to become one of the most successful bankers in Italy. But Cosimo also knew his father had a will of iron, and what he wanted, he made happen. He believed he knew what was best for his family and for the future of the dynasty he had founded. Cosimo had enjoyed freedom and the exuberance of youth, now it was time for him to assume the heavy mantle of manhood and responsibility. For his part, Giovanni did not entirely approve of the group of friends Cosimo had gathered around him during the past year or two. To him, such figures as Ambrogio Tommasini and that other fellow with whom his son seemed particularly tight, Niccolò Niccoli, exuded a distinct whiff of subversion. Giovanni did not hold with many of the new humanist ideas of the younger generation.

'I believe it is time, Cosimo. It is time for you to adopt the role that has been prepared for you. You are a Medici, you are my eldest son. You have proven your worth as a scholar, now you must begin to show the world your many other qualities.'

'But Father, I had hoped . . .'

'You wished to spend the summer in the pleasure gardens or with your friends idling the time away?'

'Not idling, father, discussing and debating. Surely . . .'

'My boy,' Giovanni replied, keeping his patience

but only just. 'I understand these impulses. I once craved the world of the intellect as you do now, but responsibilities came upon me fast, and I have to say, thirty years on, I do not regret the path I followed. Do you not wish for a wife, a family? Do you not wish for independence and to play your part in the growth of the family business . . . this great bank? I thought you would.'

Cosimo knew his father was manipulating him and he had no illusions about who would win this argument. Give him the literary importance of Dante to discuss over wine and he would have stood a chance, but on this subject and against his father's iron will he withered like a flower in the frost.

'Naturally, Father. I just thought . . .'

'Very well then, I will make the appropriate arrangements,' Giovanni jumped in and made a show of rifling through the papers on his desk. 'I think you will find this a most enriching experience, my boy.'

Chapter 5

London, June 2003

Sean Clifton, Sotheby's Early Italian Renaissance specialist, descended in the security lift to the subterranean vaults beneath the auction house's Mayfair offices. Following the guard in silence along the over-lit and echoing concrete-floored corridor, he reached the door of the air-conditioned document room and waited as his security number was punched into the electronic locking system. Next, the guard told him to put his computer and briefcase through the security check before he swung open the heavy steel door to let Clifton start his work.

Once inside and alone, Clifton relaxed and prepared himself for the task ahead. His job frequently required him to authenticate and value a wide range of old manuscripts. Before him on the table was a unique find, a recently discovered collection of rare scrolls belonging to the great Renaissance humanist, Niccolò Niccoli.

Before starting, Clifton pulled on a pair of white linen gloves, coughed quietly and settled himself into his seat. Then he examined the collection. It stood in two separate piles. On the left, a stack of unbound loose papers, on the right, a set of scrolls rolled up and tied with narrow, red ribbon. He leaned forward and moved aside the stack of unbound sheaves and began to tease open the first of the pile of neatly tied scrolls.

He sat in total silence. The only sound in the room came from him as he inhaled and exhaled, moved papers and rearranged himself in the chair or occasionally tapped at his laptop, writing his report on the Niccoli archive, assessing its value at auction.

He had to read slowly, the handwriting was idiosyncratic, and in places it was barely legible. He had gone through six pages of closely packed text and had begun to slip into the world of six hundred years past and the thoughts of one of the most adventurous travellers of the fifteenth century when the revelation came. Later, he recalled it like a slow motion action replay of a great sporting moment. The core of the collection consisted of three volumes of journals and diaries, hand-written and dated 1410, in which Niccolò Niccoli gave a detailed account of a journey from Florence east to Macedonia. It was a romping adventure full of colour and excitement, but the journey seemed to have little purpose. Then, turning a page, Clifton's heart gave a leap. Confused, he paused for a moment, then began to read as quickly as he could.

It was as if the author had become bored with his own story and changed gear suddenly. Or perhaps he had slipped into a delirium and had begun describing a fantasy. This was something quite extraordinary. Niccoli was famed for his rationality and his devotion to learning and the Arts. So what was this all about? Had the scholar temporarily lost his mind? What he had suddenly started to describe bore no relationship to fifteenth-century reality.

The surprise lasted only a few moments before it was swamped by a far stronger emotion, one Clifton would never have imagined. During his fifteen years handling priceless documents and previously unseen antiquities, he had never once been tempted to stray. But now, looking at these extraordinary pages, he felt completely overwhelmed.

He reached for the scanner attached to his laptop and quickly swept it over each of the pages in front of him, storing the information on disk. Without considering for a moment what he was doing, he returned the documents to their former positions, switched off his computer and left the room. Outside the door to the vault, Clifton passed through the X-ray security check, followed the guard to the surface and left the building, numb with excitement and anticipation.

Chapter 6

Venice, present day

The afternoon train to Florence was packed and Jeff was lucky to get a seat, even in first-class. Squeezed against the window by a huge woman in the aisle seat, he contemplated the countryside speeding past. Maria had been happy to look after Rose and Jeff had promised he would make it up to his daughter when he returned; he expected to be back in Venice the next day.

Even though he had met Mackenzie only two or three times, he was still finding it hard to believe the man was dead. He hadn't seen Edie for nearly three months. She had promised to visit him in Venice while she was working so close by in Florence, but she was always too busy and he had not felt inclined to intrude on her. But this news, combined with what he had learned from the mysterious Mario Sporani, had propelled him to do something. He had phoned her straight away and now here he was on the first train to Florence.

Mackenzie, he knew, was an abrasive character with plenty of enemies and few real friends. He was respected for his knowledge and his huge experience, but many of his colleagues considered him an overbearing egomaniac who believed his own publicity a little too much. He was certainly not popular with other academics, but Jeff found it hard to believe he could have been murdered for his character failings.

He opened the *Corriere della Sera* he had bought at the station, and on page three he found a full report on the murder. Mackenzie had been garrotted. One of the team had found his body at around 8 a.m. yesterday. The Florentine police were being predictably tight-lipped about the details. Jeff noticed next to the main feature a report on the fanatical group, Workers For God, who had been protesting outside the Medici Chapel since the arrival of Mackenzie's team. He read it with growing interest.

Florence, 17 February

With yesterday's shock news of the murder of one of the world's most renowned science popularisers, Professor Carlin Mackenzie,

Florentine police have cracked down hard on the Workers For God organisation. For three months now this group, led by the charismatic but elusive Dominican priest Father Giuseppe Baggio, has held daily vigils outside the Medici Chapel, but yesterday morning the protestors were asked to disband immediately. According to official reports, Father Baggio instructed his followers to ignore a police request to leave the vicinity, which prompted immediate intervention by the authorities. Fortunately, the group then made no further efforts to resist and the protestors were escorted away while Father Baggio was held for questioning. The priest left police headquarters before lunchtime yesterday but refused to talk to reporters who had gathered outside, claiming he would only speak to a local Catholic magazine, THE VOICE.

Father Baggio and his group have been vocal in their insistence that the bodies of the Medici should not be tampered with. The leader of the group recently told THE VOICE, 'I believe Professor Mackenzie and his team are risking their very souls by doing this ungodly work. They are working for the Devil and they will pay for their sins.'

Father Baggio is famous for his fundamentalist outbursts from the pulpit, and there have been claims that his extreme remarks and protestations have drawn reproof from his superiors. The priest has made it clear to all who would listen that he sees himself as a latter-day Savonarola, the fanatical Dominican cleric who ruled Florence briefly at the end of the fifteenth century before being burned at the stake in the Piazza della Signoria in 1498. Baggio makes no secret of his ambition to, as he has put it, 'scourge modern Italy of demonic forces'. In recent years he has protested against gay groups, attacked local television stations for broadcasting what he calls 'pornography', and most notoriously, he and his followers made a failed attempt to vandalise several pieces on display at a recent Robert Mapplethorpe retrospective. Now, with the man who Baggio claims is 'working for the Devil' murdered in his own laboratory just yards from where Workers For God have been protesting, some are starting to point the finger of suspicion in the direction of Baggio's organisation.

Emerging with the crowd through the gates at

Stazione di Santa Maria Novella, Jeff paused and surveyed the main concourse, a rather scruffy place with a grimy ticket office to one side and newspaper stalls lining the other. It was a railway station that offered no clue about the splendours of the ancient city beyond. He and Edie saw each other at the same moment.

They hugged and it felt to Jeff as though she didn't want to let him go. When they pulled apart, Jeff could see she was putting on a brave face. 'It's been far too long,' she said simply.

Jeff followed her out to the car park. He threw his bag into the boot of Edie's tiny Fiat and squeezed into the passenger seat.

'God, it's good to see you again.' Jeff smiled at Edie as she drove down the long slope from the station and on to the road.

It was busy, the streets choked with cars. Edie headed down Via Sant' Antonino. Jeff looked at the ancient buildings, office workers, tourists, street hawkers, shopkeepers and tradesmen, a medley of human activity that had been pursued in Florence with little change for more than a thousand years.

'I guess it's been pretty rough,' Jeff said.

'A lot of people despised my uncle, and to be honest, he could be a real pain in the arse, but this has come as a terrible shock.'

'Why didn't you call me?'

'I thought to, several times, but I don't know . . . I didn't think you could help and I didn't want to worry you unnecessarily. Besides, I was stuck in the police station with my lawyer until late last night. The police have questioned the whole team at least once and none of us is allowed to leave Italy until they've completed their inquiries.'

She swung the car into a space behind the Medici Chapel and then led the way into the building through a side door. Jeff followed Edie down the steps into the burial chamber. The lights were low and it was eerily quiet. In a room off the main chamber, they could see a man slowly removing his lab coat.

'Have you met Jack Cartwright?' Edie asked.

Cartwright offered Jeff his hand. 'Nice to see you again,' he said rather stiffly.

Jeff looked puzzled.

'We met at Edie's thirtieth birthday . . . in London.'

'Yes, yes, of course,' Jeff replied. 'That was so long ago.' He grinned at Edie. She gave him a false smile.

'I'm sorry to hear of your loss,' Jeff added seriously. Jack Cartwright, a man in his early forties, was a highly regarded specialist in the study of ancient DNA. Although much admired in academic circles, for years he had lived in his stepfather's shadow.

'Thank you. It's hit all of us very hard.' Cartwright had a deep, booming voice and a soft, amiable face. He plucked his coat from a hook and started to pull it on. 'Now, I'm afraid I have to dash. I have a meeting at the university. Hope to catch up with you later, Jeff.'

Edie turned to Jeff and placed a hand on his arm. 'Come into the lab, let's sit down.'

She pulled a chair over for Jeff and lowered herself into another. 'You said on the phone you had something important to tell me.'

'Last night I had a visit from an elderly man who told me he had tried to warn Mackenzie that he was in some sort of danger.'

Edie sighed and shook her head slowly. 'I imagine you're talking about Mr Sporani?'

Jeff nodded.

'He's been here a few times. He's convinced he found a Medici artefact sometime back in the sixties. But he can't support the claim with any hard evidence.'

'He told me he was visited by some people who threatened his family. And he really was the warden here, wasn't he?'

'Yeah, until about five years ago. To be honest, Jeff, I think he's lost it a bit.'

Suddenly Jeff felt a little foolish. 'I must say, Sporani struck me as quite together,' he said. 'I thought he was the genuine article.'

Edie took his hands in hers. 'I really appreciate your concern,' she said. Then standing up, she added. 'Now you're here, would you like a look around?'

'I'd like that very much.'

Edie led the way into the burial chamber. 'There are fifty-four members of the Medici buried here,' she said. 'Just before Carlin died . . . was murdered, we had started work on a body my uncle believed was Cosimo the Elder.' She indicated a table with a white plastic sheet covering a lumpy object.

'Believed?'

'It's a long story.'

'You're still working here?'

'Jack and I came back early this morning. I find it helps to keep busy. The others have been given some time off.'

Jeff glanced into the other room where Mackenzie had his office.

'The police have almost emptied it,' Edie said.

The computers had gone, as had many of the folders once housed on shelves over the desk. The remaining papers on the late professor's desk had been arranged in neat piles.

'Do you have any idea what all this is about?' Jeff asked and perched himself on a vacant dissection table just beyond the entrance to Mackenzie's office. He caught something odd in her expression. 'You know something.'

'My uncle had received at least one death threat,' she said simply.

'When?'

'The first was a few weeks ago. He didn't know I knew, but not much gets past me here. I was in his office searching for a lab report and came across a note. One of those ridiculous cut-up newspaper messages. Such a bloody cliché. It said something like: Stop work, or . . . or there will be consequences.'

'So when Sporani came along?'

'Well I couldn't let on I had seen the letter.'

'No, quite. You must be scared out of your wits.'

'I am.'

'Does Jack know about this?'

'He and I have never been close and I couldn't say anything about the letter, he would think I'd been snooping.'

'What do the police say?'

'Not much, actually. One of the lab assistants has a brother in the force and we've gleaned a little from her. They're working on the assumption it was simply an opportunistic murder. We have no real security here, as you can see.'

He looked into her eyes. 'There's more though, isn't there?'

'Yes,' she said quietly and told him about the object they had found inside the body only a few hours before Mackenzie was murdered, and how it had since vanished.

'And you've told the police about this?'

'Of course. But it means little to them. We didn't have time to properly analyse the artefact and it appeared to be completely featureless.'

'Appeared to be?'

She sighed. 'My uncle called me late the evening he died. I was at a function in Pisa. He left a message on my mobile, which I only picked up the next morning, just after Jack called to tell me Carlin had died.'

'The last time I saw my uncle alive he was sitting in that chair studying the tablet under a desk light. He was still irritated with me over a silly disagreement hours earlier and he hardly acknowledged me when I wished him goodnight. That was about seven o'clock. The police think he died not long after that, no later than ten o'clock. His message was left just before nine.'

'What did he say?'

'This.' Edie produced her mobile, flicked to 'messages in' and put it on speaker.

The dead scientist's voice emerged from the phone. 'Edie. I don't have long. I . . .' Mackenzie sounded both excited and nervous, his voice pitched higher than Jeff remembered it. 'I'm looking at the tablet and lines have just started to appear on the surface. It's extraordinary. I can only conclude the chemical structure is changing as the tablet absorbs moisture. In the body it must have been coated in a thin layer of embalming fluid which sealed it against the atmosphere. When we took it out and washed the surface, the tablet began to hydrate again. The lines are appearing with amazing speed now, fluorescent green against the black. Must be some odd sulphurous compound.

'I can see some sort of animal and below that a few lines of writing. Let me see.' They could hear his chair scrape on the floor as he repositioned himself under the lamp. 'The animal is a lion. It's strange though . . . Hang on, it's a winged lion. Yes, I see it now. Below that . . . writing, Italian, a verse by the look of it. "Sull'isola dei morti / i seguici di 'geographus incomparabilis' / progettato qualcosa nessuno ha desiderato / Sarà ancora là / Al centro del mondo."

74

'Haven't a clue what that means . . .' Then, 'Hang on . . . I can just see a couple of centimetres from the bottom . . . two, no three evenly spaced wavy lines. Now listen Edie . . .'

There was a bleep to indicate the phone's memory had expired.

Edie locked up the lab and they left through the upper level of the crypt. The Via dei Pucci was busy as they made their way to a small café across from the chapel. It had red awnings and plastic screens protecting customers from the winter wind. Inside, only a few tables were occupied. A waiter who recognised Edie showed them to a table close to an open log fire and they ordered coffees.

Jeff picked up a napkin. Taking a pen from his top pocket, he drew a rough representation of a winged lion. 'What was the verse?'

She played the message again.

'It sounds archaic, and my Italian is far from perfect,' Jeff said. 'But I think it translates as: "On the Island of the Dead, the followers of the 'geographus incomparabilis'" . . . What the hell is that?'

Edie shrugged, '"Great geographer", I guess.'

Jeff looked at her blankly. 'OK, so, "On the Island of the Dead, the followers of . . . the great geographer

. . . made, no, *designed* something no one wanted."
Can you play it again?'

As he listened he wrote the verse out on a napkin:

> On the Island of the Dead,
> the followers of the great geographer
> designed something no one wanted.
> It will be there still,
> At the centre of the world.

Edie looked at the napkin. 'What does it mean?'

'Well, the winged lion is the symbol for Venice, obviously.'

'The Island of the Dead? The centre of the world?'

'Search me.'

The coffees arrived and Edie stirred hers absent-mindedly.

'Your uncle sounded scared.'

'That was my immediate impression too.'

'Which would imply he had taken the death threats more seriously than he let on.'

'He had no shortage of enemies, he knew that.'

'But you think it goes further; that the artefact you discovered is directly linked to his murder? What about this character Baggio?'

Edie looked angry. 'Don't think I haven't considered him,' she said. 'But the police have drawn a blank. The good Father has a perfect alibi. He was taking a late night mass in front of some seventy people when Carlin was believed to have been killed. Then he was in a prayer group until midnight. He's just what he appears to be: a nut, but not a murderer. Even so, I'm totally convinced my uncle died because of the tablet we found. It's too much of a coincidence otherwise.'

'In that case, why haven't you told the police about the mobile phone message?'

'Because I don't see how it can help, and . . .'

'And what?'

'I don't know, some instinct. Maybe it's silly . . .'

He gave her a quizzical look.

'I feel I can't trust anyone.'

The sun hung low in the sky as they left the café and returned to Edie's car. She pulled out on to Via del Giglio heading south-west towards the Ponte alla Carraia and her apartment across the river. The Arno was a blazing orange, the stone of the bridge had turned grey-black and was flecked with the red tail lights of hundreds of cars. Edie took them on to the bridge and they were immediately gridlocked.

She leaned on the horn in a futile effort to shift the cars ahead of them. A tiny opening appeared and she sped into it before swinging left off the bridge. They drove beside the river towards Piazza Frescobaldi. There they turned right before doubling back and taking another right into a narrower street relatively free of traffic.

Jeff peered into his side mirror and glanced through the back window. 'This may sound a bit ridiculous,' he said, 'But I think we're being followed. Look in the mirror. A grey Mercedes with darkened windows, two cars back. It took off after us on the bridge.'

Edie took the next left, then, without indicating, turned a sharp right into a side street. A few seconds later, the grey Mercedes reappeared and accelerated towards them.

'Shit,' Edie exclaimed and put her foot down.

At the end of the street they turned left on to a major road, Via Romana and headed south towards a broad piazza. There they hit traffic again. It gave them a moment to think, and, as soon as they started moving, Edie took the first turning off the main road. She sped along the street and swung left at the end, skirting the Piazzale di Porta Romana.

Jeff looked back and his heart sank as he saw their pursuer turn into the same street no more than twenty metres behind them.

'We can't go to the apartment,' Edie said. 'I've got to lose them.'

She was about to accelerate when a woman pushing a pram stepped out on to the road. Edie slammed on the brakes. The woman pulled back with phenomenal speed and cursed them as Edie changed down to second and shot away.

'Head for the motorway,' Jeff said.

The A1 was just a few miles south along a broad road. They slipped into the traffic, and for a moment they lost sight of the grey Mercedes. Edie drove fast and Jeff found himself gripping the plastic dashboard every few moments. 'Can you try not to enjoy this quite so much?'

'Believe me, this is not my idea of fun,' she snapped back.

As they approached the motorway, they caught sight of the car with the darkened windows again. It was dodging between slower cars and gaining on them.

They took the Rome exit on to the A1 and headed east.

'Perhaps this was a bad idea. We can't outrun that thing,' Jeff said.

Edie ignored him and floored the accelerator, shooting past the cars in the inside lane. The dark fields flashed past. Far off to their left they could see the lights of Florence. 'If you have any ideas, this would be a good time,' she said.

Jeff saw a sign for a service station 200 metres ahead. 'Turn off there.'

She slowed a fraction and left it to the last second before swinging the wheel. Tyres screeched as they careened off the motorway.

It was darker here, but ahead and to their left they could see a multicoloured glow: a gas station and food hall.

Edie killed the headlights and they were suddenly thrown into a tunnel of darkness as trees obscured the service station. Barely slowing, she took a hard left and then dodged between two lanes of parked cars. Jeff looked back. There was no sign now of the other car. Edie spun the wheel and they skidded through a sharp bend with a line of parked trucks to their right. She brought the car to a halt. Between the trucks they could see the Mercedes speeding along the stretch of road they had just left. It shot past the narrow turning.

'What now?' Edie's face was cast in deep shadow. Just a sliver of light came through the window.

'Leave the car here. We can't risk going back to the motorway without being seen. Head for the service station. We've probably only bought ourselves a couple of minutes.'

The entrance to the food hall was no more than ten metres away up a covered stairway. It was busy and they blended in with early evening travellers, families and people stopping off for a quick coffee on the commute home.

Upstairs, a small galleria consisting of a pharmacy, a bar, a café and some toilets formed a bridge across the motorway. The whole place stank of cigarettes and fast food. They kept looking behind them, but they had no idea who their pursuer was or what he looked like. They walked quickly across the bridge trying not to attract attention. On the far side, they descended the stairs and found themselves in a lorry park. An articulated truck turned slowly right in front of them and they had to step back. The air was rank with diesel fumes.

Around a corner, they saw a white van. The driver, a man in jeans and a sheepskin jacket with a cigarette dangling from his lips, was pulling shut the back door and they glimpsed stacks of cardboard boxes inside. Jeff ran up to the driver and Edie waited on the pavement staring around anxiously and pulling her coat tight about her. The temperature had dropped and she could see her breath in the air. She watched Jeff take out his wallet and fish out a couple of notes. A moment later, he was waving to Edie to join them and the driver was sliding the door up a few feet. They climbed in and the driver pulled down the door. The van accelerated away.

*

The man was on his way to Bologna and had agreed to take them as far as Galluzzo a few miles south of Florence just off the motorway. From there they caught a taxi back into the city. Edie's apartment was on Via Sant' Agostino. They directed the taxi driver to drop them at Piazza S. Spirito, a short walk away. It was seven o'clock and the bars were filling up, the piazza flooded with a rainbow of colours from the shop fronts and eateries.

Edie led the way and they slowed as they approached the apartment. The street was busy with cars and people on the pavements window shopping. Edie's place, above a smart shop selling personalised wrapping paper and exclusive stationery, was accessed through a door set back under an archway. She lived in an ancient, three-storey building that was darkened with pollution from the busy street.

A light came on automatically in the hall as they entered, and Edie quickly closed the door behind them. A broad, stone staircase led to two apartments on each level. Edie's was on the second floor.

It was only when they reached the door that they realised something was wrong. It was open a crack.

'Wait here,' Jeff said and eased the door inwards. With exaggerated care he stepped forward, then paused to listen. All they could hear was the traffic from the street below. Edie looked scared and Jeff raised a finger to his lips before taking two careful steps into the hallway of the apartment. At the end of the passageway he paused again, stood against the far wall, then moved quickly into the main living area. Edie joined him and they both stared in disbelief at the devastation.

The floor was strewn with papers. Edie's computer lay in pieces, parts scattered across the carpet, the screen smashed. Disks, books, papers and files had been thrown around and bookcases overturned.

Without saying a word, Edie picked up the chair to her desk and sat down, burying her head in her hands. After a moment, she looked up, her eyes were watery, her face very pale.

'Who would do such a thing?' she demanded.

Jeff placed a gentle hand on her shoulder then turned towards the tiny kitchenette, which was almost untouched. In a moment, he had found a bottle of brandy. He poured two large measures into a couple of teacups and handed one to Edie.

'Here. I think you could do with this.'

Edie stared at it listlessly then downed it in one. 'Thanks.'

'I don't mean to sound insensitive,' Jeff said after a moment. 'But I don't think we should hang around here too long.'

Edie said nothing.

'Whoever followed us obviously knows where you live. They'll quickly put two and two together.'

'And what do you expect me to do?' Edie snapped.

Jeff looked away. 'I just think . . .'

'I'm not going anywhere, Jeff.' Edie's face was a mask of fury, all the pain and anger bursting to the surface. Crouching down, she picked up a silver-framed photograph of her dead parents. The glass was shattered. She gingerly pulled out the remaining shards, touched the image gently with the tip of one finger and brought it over, placing it on the kitchen counter.

'What the hell is all this about?' Her face was flushed and Jeff could tell she was barely in control. She collapsed into the chair and burst into tears.

He wasn't quite sure what to do, but then as quickly as the tears had come, they stopped, and she looked up at him, her eyes red, her cheeks damp. She wiped her face with the back of her hand and sniffed.

'Where am I supposed to go? Should I call the police?'

Jeff pulled a chair over and sat close to her, putting an arm around her shoulders. 'I don't think the police will be able to protect you . . . and you haven't told them about the mobile message. At best, they'll believe you've been deceitful. At worst, they could suspect you of being complicit in the murder of your uncle.'

'This sort of thing doesn't happen to people like us,' she said after a moment. 'We're usually left alone to get on with our quiet lives. Car chases and murder don't figure.'

Jeff raised his eyebrows.

'So what do you suggest?' She looked around at the mess, feeling lost.

'If you want to know who killed your uncle, the tablet offers the first clue, and that is clearly telling us to go to Venice.'

Chapter 7

Florence, 4 May 1410

It was a cloudless, starry night, perfect for walking, perfect for contemplating one's place in the scheme of things. Cosimo arrived late at the home of his friend, the former condotierre Niccolò Niccoli. Built during the thirteenth century, the house was fine and old, situated close to the church of Santa Croce in the south-east of Florence, not far from where the city walls came down to meet the Arno. Stretching back behind the house in the direction of the centre of Florence was an expansive, luxuriant garden, and it was here Niccoli hosted most of the gatherings of Cosimo and his friends who had recently dubbed themselves, not too seriously, the Humanist League.

A servant met Cosimo at the door and escorted him silently through the house, traversing a cavernous marble-floored hall before passing through a series of interconnecting rooms and on into the garden. As Cosimo passed through a grand doorway, he could hear voices and laughter. His companions had assembled close to a fountain depicting Icarus soaring towards the sun. They were regulars at these gatherings of Florentine humanists, and good friends of Cosimo's. As he approached, Cosimo saw Ambrogio. He wanted to speak with him before the end of the night as his friend was leaving the very next day to work for the Doge in Venice. But then his attention was drawn to an elderly man he had never seen before who was addressing the small gathering. He was exceptionally tall, bird-thin and dressed in a rather old-fashioned black lucco. His grey beard was trimmed close, his cheekbones protruded and he had large, dark, animated eyes.

Cosimo took the few steps to the paved area, and as he reached his friends, the stranger concluded his story and a couple of the men laughed good-naturedly.

'Ah, here he is,' Niccoli said as Cosimo came into view. Dressed in the red toga he always wore on such occasions, Niccoli took a few steps away from the gathering and embraced the young Medici. With an arm around his shoulder, his host drew him towards the others.

'Cosimo. I would like to introduce you to Francesco Valiani, our guest of honour this evening, who only four days ago arrived in Florence from his travels in far-off lands.'

'It is a pleasure to meet you, sir,' Valiani declared. 'I've heard so very much about you . . . and all of it good.'

Cosimo gave a small laugh. 'Well that is a relief.' And he turned to Niccoli. 'So sorry I'm late, it has been a most perplexing day.'

Niccoli was about to ask why when he was distracted by a servant at his elbow. Turning to the gathering, he said. 'I'm reliably informed we are required at table. If you would, gentlemen,' and he signalled that they should follow him into the house.

The dining room was vast and the performance put on by Niccoli was characteristically over-the-top, even for Cosimo's circle of friends, who each tried to outdo one another as hosts for such gatherings. The room was lit solely by candles in a huge silver chandelier hanging low over the table. A small group of musicians played in a corner: a lutist, a beautiful young harpist and an older man on the flute.

After the guests were shown to their seats, a massive gilded pie on a silver dish was brought out. It took four slaves to carry it and to hoist it into the centre of the table. A middle-aged servant in a green uniform, his white hair cut close to his head, leaned forward, and with great ceremony, sliced through the pastry. As a crack opened in the pie, the pastry seemed to bubble up and a bright yellow bird pushed through the crust and flew bewildered into the room. A dozen more birds emerged from the pie, circled the room, and in a few moments they had found the doors opening on to the gardens.

The guests burst into spontaneous applause. The pie was filled with dates and pine nuts (along with a few bird droppings). Dissected by two slaves, it was quickly piled on to silver dishes.

As soon as this was finished, the silver was removed and fresh plates appeared. On these were placed a breast of capon in jelly. When that had been consumed, it was followed by twelve more courses, including pigeon, venison, swan and specially imported figs wrapped in fantastically thin gold foil.

The men ate noisily, talking with their mouths full, at times laughing uproariously, at others arguing fiercely, before coming to agreements and slapping each other on the back then returning to the feast to consume another course. They quaffed excellent local wines, as well as vintages from France.

It was a feast to remember and Cosimo was finding a special enjoyment in tonight's events because he knew it would be the last such gathering he would attend for some time. Perhaps, he thought, this could even be the very last night of such revelry with this particular group of friends. He would still see these men, still enjoy their company occasionally, but soon, such youthful and exuberant affairs would be substituted by banquets laid on for and by new friends and associates within the world of banking, his father's friends and those men whom Giovanni had arranged to associate with his son.

The guests dallied over a collection of sweetmeats and milk pudding accompanied by strong spirits and a sugary dessert wine from Normandy. Cosimo was about to move around the table to talk to Ambrogio when Niccoli stood up at the head of the table and asked the gathering to adjourn to another room where Francesco Valiani would address them.

The noblemen sat on soft couches and Valiani settled himself into a chair in front of them. Servants provided the men with more drinks, and a hush fell over the proceedings.

'I tarried in Turkey for two years,' the old man began. 'For much of that time I was a guest of Mehmet, the charismatic son of the former Sultan, Bayazid the first, who, as you may know, was called "The Thunderbolt". Bayazid was a most learned man as well as a fierce warrior, and his son, who throughout my stay was busy trying to prevent his country falling into civil war, followed in his footsteps. The Sultan's library is a place of priceless wonders which could have kept me there a lifetime, rather than a mere two years.

'The library is a wonder not simply because of the incredible collection of books it contains, but also for the references I was able to find there, references to still more arcane sources kept far beyond the sight of normal men. I was greatly honoured by the Sultan who had heard of my modest works, and I was granted permission to study at my leisure. In this library, I found original manuscripts of Greek playwrights, a tome handwritten by a disciple of Plato, as well as a host of volumes composed in strange languages I had never before seen. I was told by the librarian that some of these books had originated in the great empire of the Egyptians and date back many thousands of years. They are written in a lost hieroglyphic language no living man understands.'

Valiani looked around the room at the rapt faces. 'But, as I say, for all the magnificence of these things, more exciting still is the promise that greater treasures are to be found in remote parts of the land of the Turk. My biggest regret is that I could not take advantage of this information, for within days of making these discoveries in the library of the Sultan, my very life was threatened.

'Mehmet finally lost control of his country. He escaped Constantinople and lives to fight another day. He has many resources and most of his people are on his side. For me, things became dangerous because of the simple fact of my nationality and because I had enjoyed the special protection of the Sultan, who was now in fear of his own life. I quickly made preparations to leave the city. It was then that fate, I believe, took a hand.

'Two of my travelling companions, Michelangelo Gabatini and Piero de' Marco were murdered on their way to the harbour where they had secured passage across the Aegean. One of their slaves survived the attack and escaped to warn me. The harbour was now too dangerous. I had no choice but to turn my eyes north and hope to escape to Adrianople, and from there cross the border into northern Greece.

'I will not bore you with the details of my journey, suffice it to say the four weeks it took me to reach Adrianople were perhaps the longest of my life. One of my slaves died from fever on the way, another fled our camp one evening and was found the next morning at the bottom of a ravine.

'Now, sitting here in the comfort of this beautiful palazzo, I can say it was all worth it, but it did not seem so at the time. Most importantly though, my greatest discovery was awaiting me in Adrianople. I was given shelter at a monastery just beyond the city walls. The kind monks fed and watered us. They even found a room for the slaves to share, and those brave souls who had escaped with me were treated by the holy men as equals. I confess I was very ill, and, as soon as I arrived I fell into a dark fever from which I believed I would never recover. The monks attended me and gradually I regained my strength. There were rumours that the civil unrest in the capital was spreading and that even life behind these hallowed walls would not always remain safe. The monks, though, showed no fear and had placed their fate in God's hands.

'When I was well, I explained to the monks something of my mission in this country and told them of the wonders I had found in the library of the Sultan in Constantinople. One particular monk, Brother Aliye, was fascinated with what I had to say and we formed a particularly strong bond. He was young and thirsty for knowledge. He had lived in the monastery since the age of ten, but he had been born in the nearby village. His parents had died and he had been cared for by the holy men before being initiated into the Order.

'One evening, just before I planned to leave to continue my escape into Greece, Aliye came to see me after Vespers. He seemed agitated. I asked him what troubled him. At first, he was not keen to speak, but then he opened up and recounted a most peculiar tale. He said that when he was a boy, late one night, a stranger had visited his parents at their home in the village. Aliye had pretended to be asleep, but through barely opened lids he had seen his parents talking to the stranger. The man had given them a small package and then left without another word. Brother Aliye had then seen his father hide the package under the floor of the hut in which they lived. The next day, both his parents were killed. No one could speak of how they had died and he had been too young to be told the details of their last walk home from working in the fields and how their mutilated bodies had been found in a ditch nearby.

'Aliye told me that just moments before the monks arrived to take him to the monastery he had recovered the package his parents had been given. Even as a young boy he had known there was some connection between the parcel and the death of his parents and that the package had to be of special significance. Soon after he had settled at the monastery, Aliye had opened the package left to him. Inside, he had found a map. On this evening, just hours before I was due to leave Adrianople, he showed the map to me.

'He had treasured this secret all his life, he told me. It was the only remaining link with his parents.

He could not part with it, but he told me he would be happy for me to copy it in the time I had left in the company of the monks, and he hoped it would be of some use in my travels and schemes.'

Valiani stopped for a moment to catch his breath and to take a sip of wine. 'I was staggered by what I discovered. Aliye's map described a route to another monastery, high up on the mountain of Golem Korab in the north-west of Macedonia. The monastery is hidden from the world, a secret bolthole for monks who fled Muslim forces hundreds of years ago. To one side of the map there was a block of text which related how the monastery contained great literary and Hermetic wonders. It claimed the librarian of the monastery had kept safe irreplaceable volumes thought lost in the destruction of the library of Alexandria: originals of Greek scholarship and the texts of Egyptian and Hellenic magi, a world of science, magic and lost knowledge.'

Valiani stood up and a slave walked over to him. He was holding an ornate box and had opened it so his master could retrieve an item inside. The old man took a step towards his audience.

'And now I must deviate from convention.' In his hand he held a scroll tied with a black silk ribbon. He tugged at the bow and let the silk fall to the floor. With great ceremony, he opened the scroll. 'My friends, here is the copy I made. I knew when I left the monastery and the kindness of Aliye and his brethren that I could not make the journey to Macedonia myself. I am too old, and the flight from Constantinople has sapped my strength irredeemably. Indeed, I do not expect to live very long and I know I will never again travel beyond this land. I have no family, no heirs, no students. Instead, I have resolved to bring this to Italy and to bequeath it to those who deserve it and whose views I respect and admire. In my correspondence with Lord Niccoli before tonight and from the many things I have heard about you all, I have grown convinced I should leave in your hands, this treasure, to do with what you will. I know you will act wisely and with honour.'

His audience was stunned into silence. Niccoli stood up and walked over to the old man. 'Are you sure of this, Master Valiani?'

'I am sure,' the scholar replied. 'But there is great need for secrecy. There are many who would wish to lay their hands on this treasure. So I have built in some safeguards to my offer.' He scrutinised each of the men.

'Safeguards?' Cosimo asked.

'This map is incomplete,' Valiani said. 'You will have noticed this.' And he indicated a circular blank patch about three inches in diameter in the middle of the map. 'A crucial fragment is missing from the centre, here. The missing piece is in Venice. If you wish to discover the secrets of Golem Korab you must first travel to the Most Serene Republic. Upon your arrival, send a brief message to one Luigi at a guest house called I Cinque Canali. Luigi is a most unusual man, but I would trust him with my life. He will lead you to the missing section of map.'

He pulled a ring from his finger. Walking over, he handed it to Cosimo. It was a silver band holding a large rectangular garnet. 'Give this to Luigi as proof of who you are. Once you have the missing section, you must protect the map with everything you have, and then leave Venice without delay. If you need help there are very few you may trust. Garnet is my family stone and a secret sign to my friends. The final thing you will need is this,' he added, and handed Cosimo a small gold key. 'The rest is up to you.'

Valiani left soon after making his unexpected offer, but a few of Niccoli's guests stayed on to discuss it. Cosimo was fired up and could not stop thinking about Valiani until the small hours found him still talking it through with his closest friend, Ambrogio Tommasini, and their host, Niccolò Niccoli.

'Can we trust him?' Cosimo asked, turning over in his hands the golden key Valiani had given them.

'He is an honest man,' Niccoli assured them. 'He has no reason to lie about what he has stumbled upon. I did not say earlier, but when I was a young man Francesco Valiani was my teacher. I owe him much. He was always noble and true and his heart is pure. I will happily vouch for him.'

Cosimo looked into his friend's eyes. 'That is enough for me,' he said. 'Now this map.'

Niccoli unfurled it on the table between them. It was a well-drawn copy, wrinkled and stained after the long journey that had brought it to Florence. It showed a mountain range running diagonally across the scroll, and around it, a web of place names. Weaving its way through the mountains was a path drawn in red, the beginning of the road to Golem Korab and the remote monastery described by Valiani. In the centre was a hole where the monastery and surrounding mountains would have been located, making the map all but useless.

'It is rugged country,' Niccoli said. 'I have not travelled that far East, but it looks like a hazardous mountain path, especially here,' and he pointed to the edge of the hole in the map. 'Lord knows what the terrain is like nearer the monastery.'

'Great rewards never come to the faint-hearted,' Cosimo replied.

'No, indeed they do not my friend. But I fear you'll have to possess a very sturdy heart if you plan to visit Golem Korab.'

As the tangerine sun rose over the distant hills, Cosimo and Ambrogio passed in silence through the gates to their friend's estate and took the dust track back to the city. Cosimo was lost in thought trying to resolve the clashing emotions Niccoli's strange house guest had conjured up in his mind.

'I know that silence,' Ambrogio said.

'You do?'

'It's your faraway silence, the one that shrouds you when you are trying to resolve a seemingly insoluble problem.'

Cosimo laughed. 'Well put, my friend, for I am indeed shrouded in thought.'

'Valiani offers a tempting challenge, I can't deny that.'

'It's a dream come true, is it not, Ambrogio?'

'Almost too good to be true might be another way of putting it.'

Cosimo turned to look at him as they entered a small copse of spruce. 'You do not trust the man?'

'Oh, I didn't say that. It's just . . .'

'What?'

'I think none of us, with the exception of Niccolò

of course, has any concept of the dangers involved if we accept Valiani's offer.'

'Oh come now, Ambrogio, we flatter our egos in the study of esoteric ideas and we feel relaxed in the presence of lofty thoughts, but I believe we are all made of sterner stuff than many may imagine.'

Ambrogio smiled. 'I did not mean to insult you my dear Cosi. Perhaps I was thinking of myself.'

'Then you were insulting yourself, Ambrogio. If I can entertain the thought of a great adventure then so too could you.' He clapped his friend on the back prompting him to overreact and stagger forward, pretending to be mortally wounded. They both laughed.

'Perhaps I could,' Ambrogio said. 'But have you forgotten? I'm leaving for Venice today.'

'No, I have not forgotten my friend, and to be truthful, it grieves me. We would make good travelling companions.'

'We would, but I fear it is not to be.' And he clamped his arm about Cosimo's shoulder.

Reaching home on the Piazza del Duomo, Cosimo was exhausted, but he could not sleep. His mind was still racing, but he now knew what he had to do. Washing quickly, he was shaved and dressed by his manservant. Then, alone in his room, with the early morning sounds of the street drifting up to his window, he sat at his desk, trying to focus enough to write.

It was a simple note, a message for his love, Contessina de' Bardi, asking her to meet him that evening. He needed to talk to her. Folding the note and sealing it with the Medici coat-of-arms, he called Olomo and gave him his instructions.

The day passed slowly. He played with his young brother, Lorenzo; he wrote in his diary; and he wandered the streets of Florence.

He arrived early at his suggested meeting point, the garden of Niccoli's house where he knew no one would spy on them. Cosimo was seated on a stone bench under a flower-laden archway, and before she noticed him, he saw Contessina sweeping down four recessed steps, her green velvet gown brushing the stone. Tall and willowy with jet black hair, her high cheekbones and full lips made her the embodiment of Athenian perfection.

'Cosi, you look troubled,' she said taking both his hands in hers and sitting beside him on the bench.

He gazed into her ebony eyes. 'I can hide nothing from you, Contessina.'

She did not interrupt once as he told her Valiani's story. 'So, you feel you must go and see this place and unravel these secrets for yourself, yes?' she said when he had finished. 'But Cosimo, what of us?'

'It changes nothing, my Contessina. I will return in a few months and we shall continue with our wedding plans.'

'And your father, Cosi? He knows nothing of this?'

'Nothing.'

She held his gaze. 'I want to come with you.'

Cosimo smiled. 'That would be a thought I could cherish, my love, but we both know it is not possible.'

'Why?' Contessina asked. 'I have studied the masters as fully as you, and I too have a burning desire to know more.'

'But your family would never . . .'

'And I suppose yours would.'

Cosimo conceded the point. 'It will be immensely dangerous.'

'I know.'

'And I would be accused of abducting you. It would destroy the relationship between our two families.'

'That's being a little melodramatic, don't you think, Cosi?'

'No, I don't think it is, my Contessina,' Cosimo replied gently. And then, with steel in his voice. 'Contessina, I will have to do this without you.'

She looked at the darkening sky beyond the

archway and the roses silhouetted in the amber dusk. 'Clearly you have made up your mind. Is there nothing I can say?'

'You could wish me luck.'

He looked at her hands clasped together in her lap and noticed the whiteness of her knuckles. Then fixing Cosimo with her black eyes, she said. 'Cosimo, my love. I dread the thought of you embarking on this journey, but I know that once you have set your mind to a thing there is no turning back. It is one of the many things I adore about you. I will wish you luck, of course I will; but more than anything, I offer you my eternal love,' and she kissed him softly on the cheek.

Chapter 8

Holy Father, as always you were entirely right and my years here have not been wasted, as I worried they might have been. Tonight, the most extraordinary news reached my ears. A messenger from the East has related a discovery which I believe could bear significant fruit. There is a certain map describing the route to a secluded monastery in the mountains of Macedonia.

I believe this may be the place we have heard about, for news of it has been imparted by a well-known scholar named Francesco Valiani. The man has not been able to travel to the monastery himself but he believes a great treasure is to be found there. No mention was made of the specific object Your Holiness seeks, but I am hopeful.

Holy Father, I am ready for your thoughts and await whatever instructions you wish to impart to your most loving and humble servant . . .

Chapter 9

London, June 2003

Several venues had been booked then rejected before
the meeting had finally taken place in a small hotel in
Bayswater. There were three men in the room: Sean
Clifton, Professor Arnold Rossiter, an Oxford don
and expert consultant, and Patrick McNeill, Senior
Vice-President of Vitax, a division of Fournier
Holdings Inc., a vast corporation owned by a French-
Canadian billionaire art collector named Luc
Fournier; McNeill was also Luc Fournier's chief
aide. Rossiter, a consultant for hire, had been
selected for the job by Fournier himself because the
businessman knew so much about the professor's
murky private life he could trust the man almost
unconditionally.

It was hot and there was no air-conditioning in the
hotel. Clifton was nervous and sweating so profusely
dark rings had appeared at the armpits of his shirt.

Mopping his brow with an off-white cotton handkerchief, he eyed the other two silently and removed a rectangular clear-plastic document wallet from his briefcase. He had not met Rossiter but knew him by reputation. The scholar was a man in his late-sixties, his face mottled, veins clearly visible through the pale skin of his bald head. He was little more than five foot six and his shapeless linen suit completed the image of the crumpled intellectual.

Clifton handed the wallet to McNeill. 'These are copies of course.' His nerves belied the coolness it had taken to walk past the guard in Sotheby's vault two weeks earlier.

McNeill removed the photocopies from the wallet. There were about forty pages, double-sided, handwritten. He read the first few pages in fascinated silence.

'And your family inherited these recently?'

Clifton nodded and walked over to the window, eyeing the street below with suspicion. Turning back to the room, he lit a cigarette.

'I'll obviously need some time to read through . . .' Rossiter said.

'Ten minutes.' Clifton replied squinting through the smoke. 'You have ten minutes.'

McNeill gave Rossiter an amused look. 'You'd better get cracking,' he said and settled into a sofa.

Rossiter sat at a table near the door and began reading.

'I suggest you look at the marked pages,' Clifton said.

Rossiter turned the pages slowly, his excitement mounting. He had never seen this document before, although academics had long discussed the possibility of its existence. The originals, he knew, had been presumed lost years earlier, and rumours spoke of copies of fragments that might still survive, vanished perhaps into the attics of the unsuspecting or lying at the back of cupboards in dusty storerooms. As a consequence, very few had seen this document since it had first been composed some six centuries earlier. And so, as he read he began to realise why Sean Clifton was so keen to strike a deal with Fournier. One of the few things known by the media about the head of Fournier Holdings was that he was the world's wealthiest and most enthusiastic collector of early Renaissance documents and artefacts. And this was a most remarkable find.

Clifton walked over to the table and began picking up the photocopied pages. 'Time's up.'

Rossiter made to protest but McNeill silenced him with a wave of his hand. 'Has our time been wasted, Professor?'

'No. These are copies of a genuine manuscript in the hand of Niccolò Niccoli.'

'Thank you. That's all I wanted to know. Now, I wonder if you might leave us.'

Rossiter looked surprised for a moment, then he turned and left.

'So,' McNeill said as the door closed. 'You want ten million pounds, is that correct?'

'It is.'

'Quite out of the question.'

For a second Clifton looked deflated. 'Why?'

'Because my boss is offering four million. One hundred thousand now, the rest in two stages after other . . . requirements have been met.'

'Ridiculous!'

'In that case, I'm afraid we cannot do business.' He turned to leave.

McNeill had taken only two paces and was reaching for the handle when Clifton said, 'OK, OK. Eight, with a million up front.'

McNeill didn't even break his stride and started to pull the door open.

Clifton sighed and took a couple of steps towards him. 'All right . . . six.'

McNeill stopped and returned to the room. Standing so close to Clifton that he made sure the man could feel his breath on his face, he said slowly and deliberately 'Four and a half with two fifty now. That's our final offer.'

Clifton took a step back and lit another cigarette. 'Five million and it's yours.'

McNeill gazed across the room to the window. The only sound was coming from the traffic below. 'Very well. Five million. But, these are our conditions.'

Clifton took a deep drag on his cigarette.

'For our £250,000 we have the copies for two weeks. If my boss likes what he sees, one of our people will retrieve the originals from the Sotheby vault. Only then will you receive the rest of the money.'

'No!'

'Take them elsewhere then.'

Clifton bit his lip. 'And the money?'

'£250,000 will be placed in a Swiss account by noon Monday. You must have the documents in another specified account by 10 a.m. the same day. The transfer of funds to your account will automatically decode a six-digit security sequence of your own choosing which will then be transmitted through the Internet to my representative. This code will enable us to access the document. No money, no code and vice versa. My people will email the details.'

Chapter 10

Venice, present day

'No matter how many times I see this view, I still find it breathtaking,' Edie said as she gazed out of the windows of Jeff's sitting room. He was standing beside her with a hand on her shoulder; they had arrived in Venice only an hour earlier. It was approaching lunchtime and the crowds were already filling San Marco. Across the square, a small ensemble on a raised stage was playing a selection of Vivaldi and Mozart pieces. Closer to the Ducal Palace, clowns on stilts tottered around on the uneven paving stones handing out balloons to children, and clusters of masked pedestrians paraded about, some in ornate costumes. Carnivale was in full swing.

There was a commotion at the door to the apartment. Turning, they saw Rose and Maria laden down with bags.

Edie raised an eyebrow.

'I gave her my credit card,' Jeff explained. 'I felt bad about abandoning her yesterday.'

Edie gave him a sceptical look. 'Not over-compensating at all then?' She beamed at Rose. 'Well, hello there, young lady. I haven't seen you for . . . God, how long is it?'

Rose stopped fussing with her bags and looked coldly at Edie. Puzzled, Jeff was just about to say something when they heard a cough and saw a tall man dressed entirely in black leaning against the door to the apartment, a slight smile playing across his lips.

'We find Signor Roberto as we go in building,' Maria declared in broken English and bustled out past Roberto, making him stand up straight in the doorway. She was shaking her head and tutting as she waddled along the corridor towards the bed-rooms.

Roberto stepped forward and took Edie's hand and kissed it theatrically. She flushed.

Behind Roberto, Jeff caught sight of Rose, her face like thunder.

'You two get acquainted,' Jeff said, and strode over to Rose.

He led her into the hall. 'What the hell was all that about?'

She looked at the floor.

'Well?'

'You really don't know, do you?' Rose said. Her eyes were filling with tears. Jeff walked forward to embrace her, but she turned on her heel and ran down the corridor.

'Rose . . .' he said. But her bedroom door slammed shut. He would have to deal with this later. Feeling terrible, he returned to the sitting room.

Without taking his eyes from Edie, Roberto said to Jeff, 'How have you managed to keep us from meeting before now?'

'Oh, it's quite deliberate,' Jeff replied trying to sound jolly. Edie seemed completely at ease with all the attention and was appraising Roberto just as overtly. 'What brings you here anyway?' Jeff said.

'We have lunch booked at the Gritti, remember?'

'So we do. I'd completely forgotten.'

'But if you . . .'

'Roberto, come with me.' Slightly red-eyed, Rose was standing at the opening into the hall. She had a bag held up in front of her. 'I want your honest opinion of this jacket.' She walked over and snatched hold of his hand, looking daggers at Edie.

When the two had left the room, Jeff let out a heavy sigh. 'I'm sorry,' he said.

Edie shrugged. 'Just her age, I guess, but I've

obviously done something to offend her, even if I haven't seen her for over a year.'

'And Roberto has just made it worse. Rose has a huge crush on him.'

'Who *is* he?' Edie's eyes were sparkling.

'Roberto? He's just about my best mate here, an amazing guy. In fact, I think he might be able to help us. Would you mind if I told him about what's happened?'

'Why do you think he can help?'

'Roberto's the closest thing to a genius I've ever met. And I trust him implicitly.'

Edie shrugged. 'OK.'

They turned to see Rose in her new jacket holding Roberto's hand.

'Lovely,' Jeff said.

'Isn't it,' Rose replied darkly and sat at the far end of the sofa to look over the rest of her purchases.

'Actually Roberto, you're just the person I needed to see.' Jeff led him to a table and handed him a copy of Mackenzie's phone message. As he read it, Edie related how they had found the tablet and how she had received the call from her uncle the night he was murdered.

'So you're thinking he was murdered because of what you found?'

'It seems likely, yes,' Edie answered.

'Well, it's obvious why you've come to Venice,' Roberto said. 'But the three wavy lines makes it much more interesting. Together with the lion they make up the symbol of I Seguicamme.'

'Which is . . .?'

'Quite literally it means "The Followers". They were a group who broke off from the Rosicrucians. They met in Venice on a regular basis; their members travelled here from all parts of Europe. They first cropped up sometime in the mid-fifteenth century. The last anyone heard of them was sometime in the late eighteenth century.'

'What did they do, these followers?'

'No one knows exactly. Marsilio Ficino mentioned them in his *De vita libri tres*, and Giordano Bruno alluded to the group in his book *The Ash Wednesday Supper*, but these references are mostly mystical, barely comprehensible.'

'Ficino?' Jeff said. 'The mystic? He worked for Cosimo de' Medici, didn't he?'

'He translated a manuscript for him just before Cosimo died, *Corpus hermeticum*, a famous collection that described the ancient foundations of magic.'

'But what's this got to do with the verse?' Edie asked.

'Well, that's the mystery isn't it? Jeff, this translation? It's accurate?'

Edie played the message again for Roberto's benefit.

'But what do you make of "the *geographus incomparabilis*"?' he asked, frowning.

Rose approached the table and stood beside Roberto. 'What are you doing?' she asked. 'Did I hear you mention the *geographus incomparabilis*?'

'You did,' Roberto replied.

'That's what they called Father Mauro, the great map-maker. I've just done a class project about him.'

'Well, thank you, Rose,' Roberto said. 'Perfect taste, and a diligent student.'

Rose beamed.

'Father Mauro was a Venetian; well more correctly, he was from Murano. He worked in the convent of San Michele . . .' Roberto explained.

'On the Island of the Dead,' Jeff exclaimed. 'Of course.' They both could see Edie was confused.

'San Michele is the cemetery of Venice.'

'And the verse says whatever Mauro designed is there still.'

'I don't know much about Mauro, but he's most famous for his mappamundi, his map of the world. It was completed just before his death in, when was it? 1465, 1470?'

'1459,' Roberto corrected.

'But the map is in the Biblioteca Marciana, just

over there,' Jeff added, and pointed towards the Piazetta.

'Well, whatever this verse is referring to, it's not the Mauro map in the museum,' Edie pointed out.

'Maybe, except, we don't know when the inscription on the tablet was made, do we? So, it could refer to something that *was* on the Island of the Dead some five centuries ago but has since been moved.'

'Good point. Had the body in the crypt been tampered with at all?' Roberto asked.

'If you mean had it been dissected before we exhumed it, then, no,' said Edie.

'So the tablet you found must have been put there at the time of burial or just before.'

'Definitely.'

'In that case, Jeff is right. If the person who wrote this verse is referring to Mauro's famous map then it could be in the Biblioteca Marciana and it would be almost impossible to get a close look at it.'

'Is it easy to get to San Michele?' Edie asked. 'Can we take a vaporetto?'

Roberto smiled. 'Don't be silly.'

Roberto's liveried chauffeur, Antonio, a remarkably handsome man with jet black hair and finely chiselled features, met them at the quay close to the Royal Gardens. He escorted them to Roberto's launch, a beautiful blue, steel and teak speedboat, which had been built around 1930. Jeff and Edie were helped aboard while Roberto stayed up front for a few moments explaining to Antonio where he was to take them. When he returned to the rear of the launch he was carrying a small wicker hamper.

'Antonio managed to get cook to rustle up a little something on his way out,' he explained.

Jeff rolled his eyes. 'You old smoothie.'

Edie gave Roberto the most radiant smile.

A few moments later, he was pouring Dom Perignon '96 into exquisite champagne flutes and the launch was swinging west out on to the Grand Canal. They swept past gorgeous palazzi on either side and glided under the Ponte dell' Accademia before following the curve of the waterway. Just before reaching San Samuele on their right, Jeff pointed to a beautiful russet-coloured palazzo a short way ahead on the same side of the canal.

'That's Roberto's pad,' he said, before biting into a savoury pastry.

'What a dump,' Edie grinned.

Around the Rialto, the canal was busy with vaporetti and along the banks the restaurants were crowded with foreign visitors here for the Carnivale.

A little further on, just beyond the magnificent façade of the Ca' d'Oro, they came to a major tributary that led to the northern edge of Venice and the Canale delle Fondamenta Nuove. This waterway narrowed to little more than the width of a barge and the launch had to slow to a crawl. After they had passed under a succession of crumbling bridges, the canal widened again and they picked up speed. A few minutes later, they emerged into the Sacca della Misericordia, the private docking area where hundreds of boats lay moored. From here they swept east into open water.

Directly ahead of them they could see the walled island of San Michele. Antonio opened the throttle and they sliced through the icy grey water passing parallel to the Fondamenta, the north-eastern edge of the city and around the southern tip of the Island of the Dead. The wind was fierce here and the air very cold. Edie pulled her coat about her and lifted the collar to shield her ears. She could feel the crisp sea air burning her cheeks and she began to long for the trip to end.

The chauffeur slowed the launch as they approached a corner of the almost square island and they caught their first glimpse of its impressive northern face with amber walls ten metres high. A little way ahead, they could see the tower of the church of San Michele and the domed bell tower. A vaporetto glided slowly into view, and docked. A large group of figures emerged on to the quay. They were widows visiting graves. The black cloth that covered them almost head-to-toe contrasted sharply with the bright reds and yellows of the flowers they carried.

'We are entering the kingdom of the illustrious dead,' Jeff said to Edie, clutching her arm and pulling a mock-horror face.

'Well I know all about them.'

'Indeed you do, but this place is pretty special, the final resting place of people like Ezra Pound, Stravinsky, Sergei Diaghilev and Joseph Brodsky.'

The launch curved away from the quay and entered a narrow inlet that ran almost to the centre of the island. About a hundred metres along the waterway, Antonio pulled the launch over to the bank and snapped off the engine. A few moments later, Roberto was leading them ashore. He pointed to the bell tower. 'The monastery where Mauro lived and worked is over there,' he said. 'It's not far.'

The archivist of the monastery met them at the entrance to the cloisters. He was a tall man in monk's habit. Although he was entirely bald, he looked exceptionally youthful and fresh-faced. But his eyes possessed a certain indefinable serenity incongruous with one so young.

'Maestro,' he said softly, offering his hand to

Roberto. 'I am Father Pascini. The Prior sends his apologies for not meeting you personally and has asked me to help you in any way I can.'

'That's most gracious of him,' Roberto replied. 'These are my friends, Jeff Martin and Edie Granger.'

The monk gave them a slight bow. 'Welcome.'

'Roberto knows everyone in Venice,' Jeff whispered in Edie's ear as Father Pascini gestured for them to follow him through the ancient cloister.

'How exactly may I help you?'

'We're interested in the work of Father Mauro.'

'Ah, our most illustrious brother. It seems suddenly everyone is interested in his maps.'

'Oh?' Jeff said. 'Who else has been making enquiries?'

'I had a phone call only this morning,' Father Pascini said. 'A historian in London, would you believe?'

They entered a small chapel. Crossing the marble floor, the monk led them through a doorway, down a flight of wide stairs into a long, dark, narrow room lined with ebony shelves stacked with ancient tomes.

'So what do you want to know about Father Mauro?'

'You mentioned maps,' Jeff said. 'The plural. I

thought his mappamundi was in the Marciana in the city.'

'It is. But Mauro produced more than one map in his career. We keep a lesser example of a mappamundi here in this library. It's on display to the public.' He led them a few paces towards a free-standing glass cabinet positioned in the centre of the room.

The map had been beautifully preserved. It was about six feet square. A circle filled most of the area, and at first glance it seemed to be crammed with random images, huge crenulated biscuit-coloured shapes skirted in blue. The blue intruded into the lighter regions like ink spreading its fingers into water. But then, as they looked closely at the stunning object, the shapes seemed to shift, becoming slowly recognisable as a contorted map of Europe, Africa and Asia. Gradually, the map became less a piece of abstract art and more a scientifically designed work of craftsmanship.

'So how is this different to the map in the Marciana?' Edie asked.

'This was completed after Mauro's death,' Father Pascini replied. 'By his best pupils.'

'"The followers of the *geographus incomparabilis*",' Jeff quoted from the verse.

The monk looked puzzled. 'Why this sudden

fascination with Mauro? My caller today was most interested in this particular map. We have at least a dozen others here, but it was just this one he wanted to know about.'

'Is it too much to expect he left a name or anything?' Edie asked.

'He said he was calling from the History Department of University College, London. But gave no other details.'

'So, why is this map here?'

The monk turned to Jeff. 'It was considered inferior to the famous map now in the Marciana. It was commissioned by King Casimir IV of Poland, but he returned it, saying he was dissatisfied with it. In truth though, he had hit financial trouble, and to cover his embarrassment he claimed the map was substandard. So, we kept it here.'

'Good for you,' Edie said.

'Would it be possible to remove the map from the case?' Roberto asked hopefully.

Father Pascini shook his head. 'I'm afraid that is impossible, Signor Armatovani, but I could set up a magnifying lens for you, if you wish.'

'That would be splendid.'

Father Pascini disappeared and returned a few moments later with a large lens on a floor stand. He pushed the stand to the midpoint on one of the long sides of the glass cabinet and manoeuvred the lens over the top. 'I'll leave you to study,' he said and retreated to a desk at the other end of the room.

'It's absolutely beautiful,' Edie said.

'An amazing piece of workmanship; incredibly detailed. Look at the writing. There's hardly a scrap of space between captions.'

The illustrations depicted castles and towers, some topped with magnificent multicoloured flags; knights in armour on powerful steeds; strange beasts, serpents, gryphons; abstract patterns and strips of rainbow colours. The more closely one looked, the more detail there appeared to be; it was a microcosm of exquisite beauty and staggering artistry.

'The verse says "At the centre of the world,"' Jeff said, positioning the lens to a point approximating the centre of the map. 'But all I can see is a tangle of words and images. Where would this be on a modern map?'

Edie peered through the magnifying lens. 'Somewhere around Turkey? Iraq, maybe?'

'Any idea what we're looking for?'

'None at all.'

'May I?' Roberto and leaned forward to survey the critical area.

'Anything?'

'Nothing other than labels for regions. It is Persia,

by the look of it. I can see the Euphrates and the mountains of the South. It was a region the Venetians knew quite well, even in the mid-fifteenth century, thanks to Marco Polo and others.'

'But there's nothing unusual on the map there?'

'Doesn't appear to be.' Roberto stepped back, frowning. Then suddenly his face brightened. 'Of course.'

'What?' Edie and Jeff asked in unison.

'The centre of the world. It isn't meant literally. To the people of the fifteenth century, the centre of the world was the Holy City . . . Jerusalem.'

Roberto pushed the magnifying lens to the left. Here the map was covered in writing and illustrations that were even more densely packed and elaborate than in the region of Persia. There seemed to be a subtle but unmistakable glow to the parchment in the region of the Holy City; Jerusalem was represented with shining towers and domes surrounded by men at arms. It was clear the creators of the map wanted to honour this place above all others.

'I can't see anything unusual here,' Roberto said after a long pause. 'Take a look.'

But Edie too drew a blank. Stepping back, she watched Jeff take his turn.

'No, it's hopeless,' he said, straightening up. 'This must be the map, it fits perfectly with the verse; made by "the followers of the *geographus incom-parabilis*". And then there's the fact that Casimir returned it; the followers: "designed something no one wanted". But, we don't have a clue what we're looking for, and without being able to take the map out . . .'

'Success?' Father Pascini appeared at his elbow.

'Not a glimmer,' Roberto said.

'There is one other mappamundi.'

'There is?'

'It's a very poor example, a practice piece you might say. And it has been damaged in places. It too was rejected by the person who commissioned it.'

'May we?'

'Of course, follow me.'

Father Pascini led them along a corridor to a locked door. 'This is one of the archives,' he said as they entered. 'We keep our documents in these special boxes.' He pointed to metal shelving built into the wall. 'Each document is kept in an acid-free, humidity and temperature-controlled environment. To view the map you'll have to go into this room.' He waved to a glass enclosure in the corner. 'I'll supply you with gloves and tweezers.'

A few minutes later the three of them were sitting at a table in the viewing room with the map between them. It had been covered with a protective transparent plastic sheet, over which Father Pascini had positioned another large magnifying lens.

The edges were ragged and it was badly torn, a jagged line ran across about a third of the map and the illustrations were far less detailed than the mappamundi in the main room.

Edie examined an area approximating to the Middle East and manoeuvred the lens a little closer to the map until she found an illustration representing the Holy Land. 'Well, how about that,' she exclaimed and stood aside to allow Jeff and Roberto to take a look.

Immediately beneath an image of a citadel with blazing red flags atop a pair of towers, they could see tiny, faded handwriting that did not match the other markers and labels across the map. The nature of the caption was also quite incongruous, a five-line verse in Italian. Roberto translated as he read it aloud, 'Reaching across the water, / the man with the perfect name: / a sad man, deceived by the Devil. / It is hidden there with the lines, / Beyond the water, behind the hand of the architect.'

By the time they left the monastery it had grown dark, and a dense fog had descended on the Island of the Dead. Walking along the path to the monastery earlier in the afternoon, the sun and the crisp seaward air had made San Michele seem very much like any other part of Venice, but now, in the inky darkness it had been transformed into a place of shadows and nameless fears.

Gazing back as they passed through the outer wall and headed along the cobbled path en route to the launch, the monastery looked like a cut-out in black card. There were very few lights in this part of San Michele, and those close by cast almost no illumination. Indeed, the brightest light came from the pinpricks of countless stars, the Milky Way, a trail of glitter scribbled across the moonless firmament.

Edie had never been here before, and even though she worked with the deceased almost every day, she had found the Gothic character of the place quite overbearing, even in daylight. Now, all she could do was think of the countless dead all around her, the famous and the ordinary who had lived and died and been forgotten by all but the worms. Every cheap horror flick and prurient fairy tale seemed to have a home here in the dark. The wind had dropped, but the soft lapping of the lagoon was ever-present. It sounded like a lament.

The launch lay in deep shadow, bobbing gently in the water hard up against the wall of the cutting. Without wasting a moment, they stepped into the boat. The driver fired up the engine and flicked on the headlights sending two splashes of lemon into the water.

'Take us straight home please, Antonio,' Roberto called, and he threw himself into the soft leather upholstery of one of the aft passenger seats. A moment later they felt the boat accelerate and swing round in the channel before speeding off towards the open water.

They sat in silence, each mulling over what they had learned, each content to watch the shadows of San Michele dissolve into the water. For a few minutes they headed directly south towards Fondamenta Nuove and the lights of the city; but then, without warning they felt the launch veer to port. For a second, Roberto didn't react, then Edie and Jeff saw him go forward to talk to Antonio. As he did so, the driver spun round to face them. He had his cap low over his brow and was wearing dark glasses. In the opaque night they could barely make out his features, but it was clear that it wasn't Antonio. The man was holding a gun, pointed directly at Roberto.

'Please sit down, Signor Armatovani.'

Roberto paused for a moment.

'Sit down. I will not repeat this. I only need one of you. I am not famed for my patience, and believe me, shooting two of you would make this journey so much easier.'

'What's happened to Antonio?' Roberto demanded.

'Oh, he went for a refreshing swim.'

The launch slowed and they headed for a point further south along Fondamenta Nuove, away from the main route to the Grand Canal. The driver kept the gun trained on them and appeared to have little difficulty steering the launch with one hand and glancing ahead only occasionally.

Within a few moments they were approaching the quayside. Directly ahead ran a grey stone wall, a narrow path and a row of houses. On the path they could see a few people hurrying along, collars turned up, breath streaming from their nostrils into the cold night.

'Now, I'll ask you to keep still and quiet,' the driver hissed.

Edie was looking ahead at the approaching canal wall when she spotted Roberto easing something out from under his seat with his feet. With startling speed, he lifted a black cylinder. There was a sharp crack and a stab of orange light. Roberto fell to the floor, knocked off his feet by the recoil, and the flare shot the length of the launch, ricocheted off the control panel at the helm and zigzagged erratically over the prow.

An intense flash of light cut through the darkness as the flare exploded just a few feet away and the stunned gunman was propelled backwards against the throttle. His gun fell behind him and slid across the polished wood of the prow and into the canal. The launch almost leapt out of the water as the engines roared. Edie and Jeff tried to steady themselves, but they were flung forward against the chairs in front of them. Jeff was sent sprawling across the bottom of the boat, his knee striking Roberto's head.

Out of control, with the throttle open, the launch span round and bucked in the water before it smashed sidelong into the quay, sending chunks of teak and brass into the air. The last thing Jeff heard before feeling the freezing cloak of water envelop him was the grinding of metal against stone, and in the distance, the sound of Edie screaming.

Strong arms were pulling him on to the quay; rough stone pressed against his abdomen. He gasped for breath. Rubbing the water from his eyes, he could see Edie kneeling beside Roberto, dabbing his head with a bloodied cloth. She turned to Jeff, a look of relief on her face. He crouched down beside her trying to catch his breath.

Roberto grimaced up at him. 'I'm OK.'

Off to their right they heard cries coming from the quayside.

Jeff straightened up to see a mutilated body

bobbing in the water; one blackened leg knocked against the stone wall of the quay. It was Antonio, the chauffeur. He had been tied to the stern of the launch. A rope was still knotted around his wrists, the other end attached to a cleat.

Jeff suddenly became aware of just how cold it was. He shivered and averted his eyes from the hideous sight, feeling outraged and impotent. A police launch and an ambulance sliced through the freezing water towards them, and came to a dead stop, covering the final few metres with the engines stilled. There was no sign of Antonio's murderer.

'Hi Rose. Yes, I'm so sorry, darling. We had a little accident . . . No, nothing serious . . . we're all OK. I'm at Roberto's place, but I'll be home later. Look . . . No, listen. Don't stay up. We'll have a day out together tomorrow, I promise. Yes, yes . . . Maria is up watching it with you, is she? Yes, that's good. OK sweetie . . . I'll make you breakfast in the morning and I'll show you the sights . . . OK, bye.'

It had been an exhausting night. Roberto's head wound was treated at the scene then all three of them were escorted to the police station, an ugly, squat building on Ponte della Liberta, the causeway linking Venice to the mainland. There, they had been separated. Jeff had answered questions and made a detailed statement, and was about to ask for a lawyer when he was led from the interrogation suite to a conference room where he found Roberto and Edie talking to a man in a very natty police uniform. They had left the station soon afterwards.

The officer was the Chief of Venice police, Aldo Candotti, and he was now sitting at one end of a parcel-gilt eighteenth-century settee, holding the stem of an empty Schott Zwiesel sherry glass. He was a powerfully built man; a former rowing international gone to seed thanks to his love of fine wines and too much tender venison. He had ruddy cheeks and a broad nose upon which was perched a pair of Dior spectacles.

At the other end of the settee sat Roberto. He had showered and changed. But his hair was still wet, and a piece of gauze covered the cut he had sustained earlier. Edie was swirling a single malt in a tumbler. They were in the ground floor library of Palazzo Baglioni, the Venetian home of the Armatovani family since the fifteenth century. Facing the Grand Canal, the palazzo was the epitome of faded grandeur. Four storeys high, rows of Byzantine windows and crumbling colonnades made it as beautiful as a Titian or a Byrd motet. Inside, each room was filled with antique furniture, some of which had been in the building since their purchase centuries earlier. The library was a vast, high-ceilinged room, lined on all sides, floor to ceiling with rosewood shelves containing thousands of books, a collection that had grown with each generation. The books ranged from a priceless seventeenth-century edition of Hobbes' *Leviathan* to signed, leather-bound first editions of Hemingway. Several of Roberto's antecedents had been flamboyant bibliophiles and the Armatovani library was considered one of the finest in private hands.

'Well, I'll leave you and your guests now, Roberto,' Candotti said, pushing himself up from the settee and placing his glass carefully on a marble-topped occasional table. 'One of my men will call on you tomorrow to give you an update. Tonight I shall begin the search for the mysterious stranger. You will speak to the unfortunate Antonio's family?'

Roberto nodded. Aldo Candotti shook hands with each of them and was then led away along the wide hallway by Vincent, the rake-thin and extremely distinguished butler who had served Roberto's parents and came with the house.

'An eventful evening,' Roberto said. 'And what have we learned, apart from the fact that our lives really are in danger?'

'You can remember the exact wording of the

inscription on the map?' Edie asked, sitting in the place vacated by Candotti.

'I can do better than that,' Roberto replied. 'A little frayed and smudged perhaps, but just about legible.'

And he unfolded a crumpled and soiled piece of paper, smoothed it down as best he could and read aloud the lines of verse he had transcribed from the map on San Michele:

> Reaching across the water,
> the man with the perfect name:
> a sad man, deceived by the Devil.
> It is hidden there with the lines,
> Beyond the water, behind the hand of the architect.

'What do you make of it?' Jeff asked his friend.

'That's all I've been thinking about between answering police questions and trying to be nice to the Chief of Police.'

'And?' Edie asked.

'The first part is quite obvious, but the last two lines are a little more enigmatic.' Roberto looked at their puzzled faces and smiled. 'The man with the perfect name? It must be Andrea Da Ponte.'

'The man who designed the Rialto? Of course.'

'Reaching across the water, the man with the

perfect name,' Edie said half to herself. 'Ponte, bridge . . . neat. But, why "a sad man, deceived by the Devil"?'

'Ah, well, that's a little less obvious,' Roberto leaned over to offer Edie a refill before passing the bottle to Jeff. 'Late in 1591, as Da Ponte's deadline for the commission approached, cracks kept appearing in the main structure of the bridge and it was only the scaffolding that saved the whole thing from crashing into the Grand Canal. Legend has it that one night, the designer was walking alone beside the canal when the Devil appeared before him. The terrified Da Ponte froze to the spot and the Devil smiled cruelly before telling him that he could help solve all his problems with the bridge. The designer was so desperate he listened to what the Devil had to offer.'

'No doubt, he wanted his soul?' Edie interrupted.

'No, he didn't actually. He wanted the soul of the first person to cross the bridge.' Roberto took a sip of his drink. 'Da Ponte obviously thought this was a great offer and he quickly accepted. A few weeks later, the bridge was completed successfully. The night before the official opening, Da Ponte was putting the finishing touches to an ornamental stone at one end of the bridge while at home his pregnant wife Chiara was waiting for him to return. There came a knock at the door of Da Ponte's house. His wife answered and was confronted by a young builder from the site who told her that she must come quickly, her husband had been hurt. Chiara Da Ponte rushed from the house, and thinking that Andrea was on the far side of the canal, she stepped on to the Rialto and ran as fast as she could towards the other side. It was only after she had traversed the bridge that her husband saw her and at the same moment he heard a terrible, cold laugh from behind him. He turned, but no one was there. Terrified for his wife and unborn child, he rushed on to the bridge and took Chiara home.'

'A month later, Chiara was struck down by plague and she and the baby died. Da Ponte was inconsolable, and it is said that to this day, on the anniversary of Chiara Da Ponte's death, her ghost and that of her baby may be seen wandering over the bridge, lost, looking for rest that will for ever elude them.'

Edie drained her glass. 'Nice story, Roberto.'

'Thank you.' He smiled and held Edie's eye for a moment.

'So, that explains "the sad man", etc. But what about the rest? You don't seriously think the next clue is really hidden in the bridge itself, do you?'

Roberto shrugged.

'I suppose, "with the lines" might refer to the lines of mortar between the stones that support the bridge,' Jeff said. 'But what about "beyond the water, behind the hand of the architect"?'

'Only one way to find out,' Roberto said, standing up.

At 2 a.m., the banks of the Grand Canal around the Rialto were almost silent. Approaching the bridge in a rowboat, Jeff, Roberto and Edie saw a solitary drunk swaying his way home. Past the bridge and further along the canal were brightly lit windows, and from far off came the faint throb of a bass drum drifting through the night.

Roberto guided the boat slowly along the canal. The traffic had fallen away to nothing and the vaporetti had stopped running. They passed slowly under the bridge and Jeff helped Roberto manoeuvre them towards the point where the wet stone met the water of the canal. Jeff took over steering the small boat. Roberto held a powerful flashlight and Edie helped to search the walls. They saw broken stones, ancient hooks and rusted iron, but nothing that resembled a hand or the mark of the man who had constructed the bridge over four centuries earlier.

After doubling back once, Jeff rowed them across the canal towards the far wall. It arched over their heads in the gloomy night. There they repeated the search, and one third of the way along the wall on the south-eastern end of the bridge, they found it, a small brass plaque, no more than a few inches square. It contained a single, simple image, a human hand, held palm outwards.

Jeff kept the boat steady by clinging on to a large iron ring a few feet to one side of the plaque and Roberto held the torch level with the image.

'The hand of the architect,' Edie said.

'Fascinating. I've never even noticed it before and I must have passed under this bridge a thousand times.'

'But I don't see what good it does us,' Jeff said. 'It's been built into solid stone. We can hardly start chipping away at the Rialto, can we?'

'No,' Roberto sighed.

'So what now?' Edie stifled a yawn.

'There's nothing more we can do tonight. I suggest we all get some rest. We need to sleep on this. I think we're going to need a little lateral thinking to solve this puzzle.' And Roberto turned to Jeff. 'I'll drop you guys back at your place.'

Chapter 11

THE TIMES, June 2003

Little remains today of room 16 of Sotheby's vault sixty feet beneath their London offices. The fire which yesterday destroyed several collections of near-priceless documents some dating from the fourteenth and fifteenth centuries was thought to have been started by an electrical fault in the computerised security system. A spokesman for Sotheby's said, 'The loss is tragic. Many of the documents stored there were irreplaceable. Room 16 was a holding vault for prospective auctions, and from here the documents were microfilmed and stored on a database.'

It is believed insurers will be liable for a multi-million pound claim from Sotheby's. The greatest loss appears to be a unique collection of Renaissance manuscripts written by a prominent member of a Humanist movement linked to the Medici of Florence. Reports suggest that at the time of the fire experts at Sotheby's had been authenticating the authorship of these papers. Independent experts today placed the value of this collection alone at a figure in excess of five million pounds.

Chapter 12

London, June 2003

It was approaching 7 p.m. and Sean Clifton was thinking about his earlier meeting with the estate agent in which he had concluded negotiations over the eight-bedroomed house he had chosen close to Sevenoaks. Emerging from Highgate tube station, he considered with pleasure the fact that he would not have to make this journey many more times. Soon, he would be bidding farewell to his scruffy rented flat just off the High Street.

Rush hour had passed and it was quietening down, most of the shops were closing. The street lights had come on and it had started to rain, windscreen wipers beating to the urban rhythm. But Sean Clifton was barely aware of anything around him. In his mind he was already the lord of the manor, sipping a G & T in his elegant drawing room with views across perfectly manicured lawns.

He turned off the High Street into a quieter road as the rain grew heavier. Quickening his pace, he crossed over, his head down, collar up. At the end of the street, he turned right. It was empty except for a young couple walking away from him on the other side. Without pausing to look, he stepped off the pavement and into the road.

A silver Lexus pulled away from the curb.

He reached the mid-point of the road and turned just in time to catch a glimpse of the two men in the car and the huge hands of the driver, a sovereign ring on the middle finger of his right hand.

The car smashed into him, tossing him into the air. Landing on the bonnet, Clifton slithered beneath the wheels and the car drove on, crushing him. A faint hiss came from his mouth, and he died on the cold, wet tarmac.

Chapter 13

London, present day

Luc Fournier sat in an apartment once owned by the Rockefellers who had financed the construction of this Beaux Arts building overlooking Green Park almost a century earlier. Now the entire building was part of his multi-billion pound property portfolio.

Little was known of Fournier's past; he lived in the shadows but enjoyed the finest the world could offer. Flitting between homes on five continents, travelling by private jet, he was very rarely seen in public, and even then, few people knew who he was.

As he slowly stirred his peppermint tea, he reclined in a George Newton chair and glanced through a wall of windows to his immediate left. It offered a spectacular vista: Green Park was spread out before him like the baize of a billiard table, and in the distance, Buckingham Palace, The Mall and St James. On the wall behind him hung his favourite de

Kooning, a mess of yellow, orange and turquoise which Fournier liked because, for him, it represented the world beyond the air-tight bubble he had created for himself.

He would soon be seventy. He didn't feel it, and he knew he looked twenty years younger thanks to a rigorous exercise and dietary regimen he had followed conscientiously since his thirties. Fair enough, he had been born into money, but he had seen this inheritance grow a hundredfold and at the same time he felt that he had contributed greatly to the world. Luc Fournier perceived himself as a warrior, or better still, a leader of warriors: a man who made things happen.

He took a sip of his tea and thought back over his many successes and his occasional failures. He had been in this industry for forty-five years. Using his intelligence and natural talents, and what had developed into a huge clandestine network of contacts, he supplied arms and other materiel to any anti-Western group who could afford him. A percentage of his earnings was reserved to maintain his lavish lifestyle, but a portion of every deal was used to finance his hobby, a hobby that was more like an obsession: a vast and growing collection of ancient artefacts mostly dating from the early renaissance. The beauty of this life was that every aspect of it brought him rewards. With the money he earned he could buy the things he desired and at the same time he could attack the thing he most hated: modern Western society.

Luc Fournier's loathing for the twenty-first century created by the West had not dissipated with age. No matter how much effort he devoted to insulating himself from the world, each new McDonald's that sprang up caused him real, physical pain. Every time he happened to catch a snatch of some ghastly pop song, his stomach turned. The edifice the West had created was, he believed, a deadly cancer that was spreading disease through what had once been a pure and noble body, metastasising into new and ever more repellent forms. One of his most vivid and cherished memories had been the day two passenger jets crashed into the twin towers. He had known of the mission in advance, of course, but the thrill of seeing the destruction of such iconic monuments to all that he abhorred was unmatched and surely unmatchable.

His career had begun in the early 1960s. Some of his earliest work had been supplying munitions to the Vietcong. In those days he had also dabbled in selling strategic information, but those were simpler times. With the rewards he had earned from the early days of that war, he had financed the operation to retrieve Cosimo de' Medici's journal from the chapel in Florence. But, in spite of all his efforts and the assistance of a team of experts, he had lost the prize. The fool who had found the journal in the flood waters had broken the seal and the precious contents were crumbled to dust.

The Western powers were never short of enemies and, as a consequence, Fournier had never been short of work. He had made hundreds of millions from Contra rebels, South American dictators, from Havana, from Moscow and latterly from the 'new' terrorist groups of the Middle East. And then, a few years earlier, he learned of the greatest treasure he could wish for. One of his many contacts informed him of a priceless document written by none other than Niccolò Niccoli, a close friend of Cosimo de' Medici. But more extraordinary revelations were to come, for apparently this document described the most unimaginable things, clues to great mysteries, remarkable secrets. Soon this document was his.

Placing his cup on a glass-topped table, he picked up a remote and depressed two buttons. A moment later, a large plasma screen was filled with images of the Niccoli document. Each page was frayed and a few had been torn, but the original was in remarkably good condition. He had had each page carefully photographed and stored on a drive for which only he had the password. He flicked through the pages, rereading his favourite passages.

Then after a few minutes Fournier clicked forward to the end section, the part that always produced the greatest thrill. He had read this section so many times he knew it almost off by heart. And now, as he read it for perhaps the hundredth time, he felt again a strange sensation of prescience, almost déjà vu. But as always, comprehension lay just beyond his reach.

Chapter 14

Florence, 9 May 1410

It was the third hour after sunset when the two men and their servants met at the San Miniato gate to the east of Florence. Cosimo arrived mounted on a grey gelding, accompanied by three men on horseback, servants hooded and wrapped up against the unseasonable chill of the night. Niccolò Niccoli, sitting on a white mare, had eschewed his usual red toga for the sake of discretion and was wearing a green coat and an anonymous black hat. It was six days since the meeting at his home and during that time he and Cosimo had organised everything in secret for the journey that now lay ahead of them.

'We will make for Fiesole and stay there the night,' Niccoli said. 'It is a mere league distant, but I would like to make sure we are away from prying eyes.'

Niccoli led them through the gate and on to the

road that took them around the city wall. From there they followed a broad track north-east, a road hemmed by dense woodland stretching as far as the eye could see.

The road was deserted but travel was always dangerous. Cutpurses and bandits made a healthy living prying on careless city folk who stayed beyond the walls. These men had no compunction in slitting throats for a few coins, often stripping naked the corpses to make a little extra.

But this was a sizeable group and, with Niccoli they had a man who not only knew how to handle himself in a fight but who seemed to possess a sixth sense for danger. He had a tracker's instinct and a nose for the slightest whiff of trouble.

It took them only an hour to reach Fiesole, a small, ancient town that had become a possession of Florence centuries earlier. It was colder now and very dark. And it had begun to rain. The town looked lifeless. Reaching the gate, they had their first surprise. The keeper refused to open the grill and would only communicate by shouting through the oak gate.

'What brings you here at this hour?' he yelled.

'We have travelled from Florence on business.'

'What business?'

'That is of concern only to us,' Cosimo replied.

'You cannot enter the town tonight. We've heard of plague not an hour's ride from here. My orders are to bolt the gate and to allow no one in.'

'We are healthy merchants from the city. We present no danger.'

'I have my orders,' the voice boomed, hard and resolute.

Cosimo turned to Niccoli. 'What now?'

'We could ride on to Borgo San Lorenzo. We'd make it before dawn. But this is an inauspicious beginning.'

'The gatekeeper will not budge.'

'I agree.'

'What about the old amphitheatre?' Cosimo said suddenly. 'I recall there are chambers under the auditorium. It will be dry and secure there.'

A few minutes' ride later, they made out the sharp silhouette of the amphitheatre against the night sky. Circling the eastern side, they entered the level ground close to where performers once took the stage. It appeared to be utterly deserted and as silent as the grave. Sodden from the unrelenting rain, they dismounted and tethered the horses. Cosimo led the group into the semi-circular auditorium.

It was an ancient and once-hallowed place built more than a thousand years earlier when Rome was basking in all its glory. Actors and showmen from across the empire had travelled here to perform. Emperors and noblemen led the audience in rapturous applause if the gods had blessed the performance. Cosimo had visited this relic when he was a child and had explored the cavernous chambers that lay beneath the stone steps of the auditorium. This was where the performers changed costumes, where circus troupes with their lions and performing monkeys had been housed. Here also slept the slaves who kept the amphitheatre running and manned the huge mechanical devices used to manoeuvre elaborate stage sets. It was a labyrinth of chambers and passageways now barren and lifeless, but with a little imagination, you could still hear the voices of a millennium past, the screams of delight from the thousands gathered on the stone steps of the auditorium, and the moans of exhaustion from the slaves. A little more imagination and you could smell the animals and the rank odour of blood.

Cosimo pushed a creaking door inward and they entered a broad passageway. Small dark chambers opened to the left and right. He lit a small lantern dangling from the end of a pole and handed it to Niccoli. Rats scurried away into the shadows beyond the puddle of light around the travellers.

'Well, it's not quite the comfort you're used to, Niccolò,' Cosimo joked. 'But at least it's dry.'

The servants were sent back to the horses to feed them and to collect the bed rolls and blankets. Two of them took the first hour on watch while the rest of the party tried to get as comfortable as the hard stone floor would allow. They found an old lantern in a wall bracket, filled it with an oil-soaked rag and lit it.

Cosimo had no idea what time it was when he was awakened by screams coming from the passageway. Then he heard the slither of steel close to his ear as Niccolò unsheathed his blade and sprang to his feet in a single fluid movement. In the dim brown light of the chamber he could see nothing at first, but then came the sound of heavy breathing. A bleached-white face appeared in the doorway. It was one of the watchmen.

'Wolves,' he croaked and fell on his face. Cosimo and Niccoli crouched down; the man's back was shredded and streaked with red. Through his ripped tunic they could see the lacerated flesh.

Before they could reach the door two black shapes appeared in the opening. Cosimo caught a flash of white teeth and a red lolling tongue. Niccoli reacted with lightning speed. There was a whoosh of tempered steel then a sickening squelch as Niccoli found the throat of the lead animal, sliced it open, withdrew his sword and slid it into the mouth of the other wolf; driving it home so hard it emerged through the back of the beast's head.

Cosimo had his sword unsheathed and fell in behind Niccoli who edged his way to the door. 'Stay here!' he shouted to the unarmed servants. 'And bolt the door.'

Niccoli pulled the torch from the bracket and edged into the passageway. Ahead lay a bend in the corridor which opened on to a passage leading to the outside. Niccoli took the lead, moving forward silently, his back pressed up against the cold stone wall. He peered around the corner and then dashed forward.

The other watchman was dead, sprawled on the floor on his back. One arm lay half-eaten a metre away. A wolf was bent over him gnawing at the man's face. As Niccoli appeared, the animal looked up. Its eyes were yellow, its fur matted with blood; a scar ran down one side of its face from eye to lower jaw. Raising its huge head, it let out a blood-curdling howl and two more wolves appeared from behind a column to their left.

'Back to back!' Niccoli yelled. 'Now!'

Cosimo obeyed immediately. Niccoli thrust the torch forward with his left hand and swept it through the air in a great orange arc. In his right hand, his sword glinted in the light.

The animal that had been devouring the servant

was the first to react. It sprang straight for Niccoli's throat. Its back legs had hardly left the ground before a sword slashed down on to its head, splitting its cranium in two. The wolf fell, dead, its huge paws splayed on the stone floor.

One of the other wolves was caught by a glancing blow from Cosimo's sword. The blade slid down the animal's cheek slicing open its left eye and cutting a deep trench into its snout. It crumpled to the floor, writhing in agony before Cosimo stepped forward and decapitated it.

The third wolf, one of the pair to emerge from the chamber further along the corridor, had suddenly turned on Cosimo. Niccoli span round in time to see a flash of white fangs and a massive black shape flying through the air. Then he heard Cosimo scream in agony. Swinging his sword over his head, Niccoli brought it down with pinpoint accuracy slicing off the creature's head.

Cosimo dropped to one knee, blood pouring from his arm, sweat running down his cheeks. Niccoli tore open the remainder of his friend's sleeve before ripping a length of material from his own tunic and binding the wound.

'It's not too deep. You were lucky,' he said, helping Cosimo to his feet. 'Get the servants. I'll watch the tunnels.'

A few moments later, Cosimo returned with the terrified men and the bags and Niccoli led the way out waving a burning torch in front of him.

Two of the horses were dead and two others had disappeared but, within a few minutes, they had found the remaining animals and calmed them down. It was agreed that two of the surviving servants should return on foot to Florence. Cosimo's arm had stopped bleeding and neither man could see any sense in again trying to persuade the gatekeeper at Fiesole to let them in. They would press on to Borgo San Lorenzo where Cosimo might receive medical attention and they could take stock.

Wearily, they clambered on to their horses and made their way back to the main track north, heading once more into the wilderness.

Dawn was breaking as they approached the small town of Borgo San Lorenzo. There was no trouble at the gate and they tarried only long enough to have Cosimo's arm cleaned and bound properly while two servants were dispatched with a bag of coins to find fresh horses. Even before the townsfolk were starting the business of the day, the riders were back on the road, heading north-east.

They travelled on, following the winding track road past the borders of Tuscany and into the

Romagna. Cosimo felt strangely elated. The fact that he had simply shrugged off his responsibilities and abandoned the role of dutiful son did not bother him. He felt thrilled by the journey and excited by the prospect of adventure. He recalled the many times he had ridden all day with Niccolò and Ambrogio Tommasini hunting and hawking in the woods surrounding Florence.

It was blisteringly hot, the sun dazzling in a perfect blue sky. A league beyond Borgo San Lorenzo, the road began to ascend into the hills. At times the route became hazardous with deep ravines dropping away on either side. The day was fading and the shadows growing long when they had their first view of Brisighella, a town spread over three tall peaks. The pinnacles rose out of the treeline like the blackened bones of a vast and long-dead monster that had rolled over and perished in some ancient time.

By the time they reached the inn on the edge of the town, they were exhausted. They were all boarded in one room with two straw mattresses for the noblemen, a stone floor for the servants. Cosimo and Niccoli decided to stretch their legs and take the mountain air before retiring.

Brisighella was a small but prosperous town that had done particularly well through recent turbulent times. A century earlier, a local nobleman had built a tower on the most southerly peak and the town had grown up around it. On one of the other two pinnacles stood a fortress, while the most easterly peak was home to a Marian Sanctuary. There were few people about and as the two men crossed the main square and walked through the charming cloistered street known as Via degli Asini, they found themselves alone with only the echo of their footfall to keep them company. The moon was bright in a cloudless sky.

'How are you feeling, Cosi?' Niccoli asked as they paced slowly across the uneven pathway with the stone roof of the cloister curving low over their heads.

Cosimo turned to him studying his face in the moon-glow. 'Why do you ask?'

'I have left nothing behind. But you . . .'

'It was my idea, remember Niccolò?' He paused watching a young mother shooing her small child into a house ahead of them. 'For my father, money and commerce are all there is. Not for me. But then, maybe it goes deeper than this. Maybe this need is a way in which I can negate death.'

'Acquiring knowledge is a noble aspiration, but no one can avoid the inevitable.'

'Maybe not. But it's like love. My love for

Contessina is my way of defying death. I know that one day all must turn to dust, our lovers leave us and forget us, and they die as we will. But by loving another we are making a stand. The seeking of knowledge, the unravelling of a mystery is the same, it allows me to say: I'm a man, I have some value in this world.'

'Sounds blasphemous to me.'

'Perhaps it is, but there you have it.'

They decided to follow the cloistered road back to the inn when they heard a sound behind them. Turning, they saw a young man approach. He was wearing a leather gilet and riding boots. On his left breast was the Medici coat of arms, five red balls on a gold shield with a pair of crossed keys in the background. Cosimo sighed.

The young man gave a cursory bow and held out a rolled-up scroll. 'Master Cosimo. My name is Captain Vincent Oratore from your father's guard. I apologise for disturbing you at this hour. At your father's bidding I have ridden long and hard from Florence. My master sends you this message. He would like an immediate reply.'

Cosimo broke the seal and read the letter.

My son. I am deeply saddened by your actions. First you decided to run off to pursue your muse, but worse, you did not deem it necessary to speak to me of your decision. Your mother and I are in great fear for your safety. If you return home now I will forget this aberration ever occurred. Please, for your mother's sake, do not disappoint us.

Leaning on the stone wall of the cloister, Cosimo looked out across the tops of hundreds of olive trees, shadows in the dark. The sky had filled with stars. Staring up at the overarching firmament he suddenly remembered a text he had read, a heretical piece of writing, composed by a madman for sure. The author had spoken of infinity, of space tumbling on and on endlessly, of how stars were suns like our own, suns so far distant they appeared to us as mere pinpricks of light, an endless, infinite universe. Perversely, he liked that idea. He wanted to be a small fish in a big pond, it gave him room to grow. He turned to Captain Oratore knowing exactly what reply he would send to his father.

Chapter 15

Venice, present day

Edie and Jeff were having a late breakfast at Jeff's apartment. Maria was off-duty for the day and Rose had refused to leave her room all morning. Jeff had barely seen her since returning from Roberto's. As they were polishing off the remnants of a full English breakfast the phone rang.

'It struck me early this morning,' Roberto said, 'we need to broaden our horizons a bit. Whoever killed Antonio and tried to abduct us is on the same trail as we are. We have to get a fresh perspective. That chap who came to see you . . . ?'

'Mario Sporani? I'd forgotten about him, and I promised to call at his hotel. He's staying at The Becher.'

Edie looked up at the mention of the name Sporani and gave Jeff a questioning look.

'Shall we meet there?'

'No, I really can't this morning, Roberto. I promised Rose . . .'

'Of course you did, Jeff, and I don't want to come between a father and his daughter. Is Edie up?'

'She is. I'll put her on.'

'Hi.'

'Good morning. You are well rested, I trust?'

She laughed. 'I slept like the dead of San Michele.'

'We almost ended up there for real,' Roberto replied. 'So, what do you fancy? Traipsing around museums and galleries with Jeff or following leads with me? Plus lunch at the Gritti thrown in when we've had enough sleuthing?'

'I'll have to think about that,' Edie said and pulled a face at Jeff who was rolling his eyes.

Rose's mood of the previous afternoon had not lightened. As they crossed St Mark's Square, Jeff could feel the weight of her silent resentment, but he had no idea how to get her to talk. Their first stop was the Basilica of St Mark, a short walk from the apartment. Rose had been there before but she had been too young to really appreciate it. Now, things were different. Rose seemed to have matured ten years in the past two, and not for the first time, Jeff winced at the thought of what damage her parents' acrimonious break-up might have caused. Looking at her as she gazed sulkily at the tombs and the splendid domed ceiling, it began to dawn on him what her black mood was all about. She had been okay until Edie had turned up; but surely Rose couldn't think . . .? It was so easy to believe that everything was fine with his daughter and that she had managed to cope brilliantly with the trauma of recent years, but how was he to really know? Everyone locked away some secret pain. Why should Rose be any different?

At the altar, they studied the ornate stonework and the remarkable mosaics depicting how, in the ninth century the body of St Mark had been stolen from Alexandria by Venetian merchants and brought to the city. 'This basilica was built especially to house the bones of the saint,' Jeff said, trying to spark some interest.

Rose shrugged her shoulders. 'What's so special about a bunch of old bones?'

Jeff smiled. 'Yeah, I know what you mean. It does seem daft to us, but a thousand years ago people placed great significance in such things.'

'I don't see how they could have known they were the bones of St Mark anyway.'

'Well actually, they didn't, but they wanted to believe that they were. Besides, there was no way it could be disproved, was there?'

She shrugged again.

'Most relics were fakes. Indeed, there was a roaring trade in the bones of saints and other holy men. There used to be auctions in Byzantium. Sort of an eBay of the first millennium.'

Rose cracked a faint smile.

Jeff sighed. 'Come on. I think we need to talk.'

Following the crowds, they turned right outside the basilica and entered the maze of streets to the north of San Marco, past the designer clothes stores and shops selling souvenirs and trinkets mass-produced on Murano. From there they took a route back towards the Riva degli Schiavoni, the water-front to the lagoon close to the Ducal Palace. Reaching the water, they sat down on the high wall with the canal lapping under their feet and watched the gondolas bob on the tide.

'OK,' Jeff said softly. 'So, are you going to tell me what this is all about?'

'What?'

'Rose, please.'

She looked up suddenly. 'That woman.'

Jeff looked confused.

'Your girlfriend, Edie.'

'My? Oh, so that's it.'

'Oh Dad, please don't insult my intelligence. I know all about you and her. I've known about it for a long time.'

Jeff shook his head and smiled.

'Don't patronise me!' Rose exclaimed angrily.

'Rose stop, just stop. You've got it all wrong.' He grabbed her shoulder and she turned on him, her face distorted with fury.

'Oh really.'

'Yes, really. Edie and I, we're friends. That's all we've ever been.'

'That's not what I've heard.'

'From whom? Oh, I see . . .'

'She told me everything.'

'Look, whatever your mother has told you, it's simply not true.'

'She told me you wrecked the marriage, that you had an affair with Edie.'

Jeff didn't know what to say. He simply stared at his daughter and suddenly she knew with absolute certainty that she had been strung a line.

'Oh Dad,' and she reached for him. Jeff pulled her close and for a moment he was transported back in time to when Rose was a toddler weeping into his shoulder after a fall from her bike or having been scared by the neighbour's dog. He drew back and looked at her face, the large moist eyes and full lips. He felt incredibly angry, furious with his deceitful bitch of a wife, his ex-wife. The woman had absolutely no scruples. She had lied and cheated in their marriage and now . . . But he had to suppress the bitterness, at least for the moment. He put his arm around Rose and they sat for a moment silently watching the vaporetti.

'Why would Mum lie like that?' Rose asked.

It was an impossible question to answer. Jeff looked at his daughter and made a conscious effort to choose his words very carefully. 'I guess, well, I suppose Mum couldn't face the guilt she felt. We're all human, Rose. Your mother and I, we were under a lot of pressure. It was painful for us and painful for you. Maybe she just thought it would be the easiest thing to do. I don't really know . . .' His answer petered out.

'Why did you and Mummy ever have to break up?'

Jeff took a deep breath. 'You have to understand that it's hard to cope with infidelity. A relationship can never be quite the same after that.' He fixed her with a hard stare. 'Is everything all right? At home I mean?'

'With Mum? Yeah, of course. But, well, it's not like old times.'

'No. I'm sorry, darling.'

They fell silent again. Then Rose said, 'Do you miss her?'

'I miss some of the old times. Like you.'

'I don't care for Caspian much.'

'Oh?'

'He tries to tell me what to do. He thinks he's my dad.' She stared intently at the water.

'Well, he's a sort of stepfather now, and I'm sure he has your best interests at heart.'

'We did have some fun, though, didn't we, Daddy? I used to love coming here for long weekends and holidays – you, me and Mum. You'd both pick me up from school and we would go straight to the airport. I could never concentrate on work those days. When we got here we'd catch a water taxi from Marco Polo; that first glimpse of San Marco as we came across the lagoon was always so exciting.'

She didn't look at him, and continued to stare at the water. Finally, she said. 'Do you remember the hidey-hole?'

'Of course.'

When Rose was five, he and Imogen had remodelled the interior of the apartment on San Marco. The builders had put in a 'secret' little room especially for Rose. Hidden away at one end of the apartment, it could only be reached by a concealed door in the smallest bedroom. She had loved it.

'It's still there,' Jeff added. 'I will always keep it.'

Suddenly Rose burst into tears and threw her arms

around her father's neck. He let her cry and gently stroked her hair.

A few moments later, she pulled away, looking embarrassed, tears still streaming down her face. He put a finger under her chin and kissed her forehead. Then he wiped away the tears with the back of his hand.

She forced a smile.

'I know exactly what we need right now,' Jeff said, pulling Rose to her feet.

'What?'

'A super-duper, triple-decker chocolate chip gelato with all the extras. And I know just where to get them.'

They had just stepped out of the ice-cream parlour when Jeff's mobile rang.

'Hi, Edie,' he said, recognising the number on the screen.

'Jeff,' she sounded hyped up. 'You have to come here as soon as you can.'

'I'm out with Rose, Edie. Remember?'

'I know.'

'Where are you anyway?'

'Mario Sporani's hotel room. Please come now . . . alone.'

He looked at Rose who mouthed, 'It's OK.'

'All right,' he said wearily into the phone. 'I'll be there in fifteen minutes.'

Jeff dropped Rose at the apartment then raced to Sporani's hotel. The Becher in Campo San Fantin was a mid-price hotel, rough around the edges and claustrophobic. The front door was ajar. There were six uniformed policemen in the reception area. One was talking to the receptionist and taking copious notes in a small leather book. Two others were going through papers piled on to shelves on the rear wall behind the desk, a fourth stood at the entrance to the lift and two others were pacing at the foot of a narrow staircase. Jeff approached one of the officers at the stairs.

'What's going on?'

'And you are?'

'Jeff Martin. I had a call on my mobile to meet some friends here.'

'I'm afraid no one is allowed beyond this point, sir.'

Jeff was about to protest when he heard a voice booming down from the first floor landing. 'Let him up.'

Jeff took the stairs two at a time. Aldo Candotti met him just outside Room 6. The door opened on to a narrow, dark corridor leading to the room beyond. 'What's happened?' he asked Candotti.

'I was hoping you and your friends might enlighten me on that matter, Signor Martin,' he replied and placed his palm in the small of Jeff's back, gently guiding him inside.

A mean light seeped from the narrow window that looked out on to a rear yard dominated by a wall of grey plasterwork stained with water from a broken gutter. The room was packed with people. Close to the window stood Edie and Roberto, talking to two men in uniform. Next to the narrow bed was a hospital trolley. A body lay on it, covered by a sheet. But Jeff could see long white hair exposed above the sheet. Then he noticed a length of frayed rope dangling from a large hook high up on the wall above the bathroom door. On the floor close to the bed there was an upended chair.

Jeff felt his stomach turn. He stepped back as a paramedic almost ran over his toes with the trolley. The man eased it around the tight corner into the short corridor leading to the landing and quickly disappeared from view.

Edie came over, took Jeff's hand and led him across the room. He caught a brief glimpse of himself in the mirror of a cheap dressing table against the wall. His skin looked almost drained of blood. The floor was strewn with clothes and papers, Sporani's suitcase had been upended, everything ripped from the wardrobes. A bar of soap lay at the end of the bed and a bottle of brandy had been smashed, the shards scattered over the worn, heavily patterned carpet. The whole place stank.

'They think Sporani's been dead for at least twenty-four hours,' Edie said quietly. 'Roberto and I had come to see him. The concierge told us there'd been no sign of him since early yesterday. He brought us up here. When there was no reply, he used the house key. We called the police straight away.'

Roberto looked intently at Candotti. 'Deputy Prefect, do you have any idea who could have done this?'

Candotti signalled to the two officers to leave. When they were gone, he began to pace in the small space between the bed and the wall, hands clasped behind his back.

'Signor Armatovani, Roberto,' he began. 'I am beginning to worry about you and your friends here. Death seems to be stalking you. I have heard from colleagues in Florence that Dr Granger may be a witness to a murder in the Medici Chapel.'

'I'm not a witness . . .' Edie began, but Candotti raised his hand.

'Please, I'm not accusing anyone. I am simply commenting that wherever you go, people keep dying.'

'The murder victim in Florence was my uncle.'

'I'm well aware of that.'

'So what are you driving at exactly?' Roberto said, his voice uncharacteristically hard.

'I do not have the manpower to interrogate you or your friends,' Candotti said, 'and I have no evidence to implicate any of you in any of the sudden deaths that now occupy all my waking hours. I have known you, Roberto, for very many years, and I knew your father very well, but please do not abuse our relationship. If there is anything to link the deaths of Professor Mackenzie, your driver Antonio Chatonni, and Mario Sporani I will find it and I think it would be better for all of us if you, or your friends,' and he flicked his eyes towards Edie and Jeff, 'decided to pay me a visit first. You know where to find me.' He turned on his heel and left the room.

A moment later, the two uniformed officers returned to escort them out of the room to the stairs.

Roberto sat down between Jeff and Edie at a wooden table at the back of Bar Fenice, a small and quite empty wine bar close to The Becher. He slid a glass of red towards Edie and one of two Pinot Grigios to Jeff. 'I really wouldn't advise telling Candotti anything,' he said.

'God no,' Edie said quickly. 'He might be an old

172

friend of your family, Roberto, but he gives me the creeps.'

'I suspected Sporani knew a great deal more about this whole thing than he let on to me.' Jeff took a sip of wine.

'And the state of the room,' Roberto said. 'Why would he wreck the place before hanging himself? Candotti's forensics team will probably come up with some useful clues, but we won't hear about them, that's for sure. But we have one little advantage over the police.' Roberto pulled something from his pocket and placed it on the table. 'I liberated this before Candotti's boys got there.'

It was a Polaroid. Taken in the hotel room, Sporani was holding in his left hand a rectangle of white card approximately the size of a photograph. In his right hand was a strange pen-like object, which he was pointing at the card.

Edie clapped her hands together. 'How did you . . .?'

'When you went out with the concierge and called Jeff, I had a couple of minutes to myself. I put on my gloves and had a quick poke around. This was in Sporani's jacket pocket. Whoever killed him missed it.'

'What's that thing in his right hand?' Jeff picked up the Polaroid.

'Do you see what it says along the side?'

'Penna Ultra Violetto? It's a kid's toy. I remember Rose had something like this years ago. But what . . .?'

'He's telling us to use ultraviolet light. Those toy pens show up invisible ink, don't they?' Edie said.

Roberto drained his glass and stood up. 'I'll be back in five.'

It actually took him twenty minutes. Striding into the bar, he slapped a garish purple and pink object on the table. 'I had to go to four different toy shops to track down that bloody thing!'

It looked like a fat pen for a ten-year-old girl, but, when Edie picked it up and twisted its base, a puddle of purple light appeared on the surface of the table. 'Cool,' she said.

'Can I have the Polaroid, Jeff? ' Roberto asked.

Jeff took it out of his pocket and placed it face down on the table. Holding the pen a few centimetres above the surface of the photo, Roberto flicked it on and there, in tiny writing in the middle of the picture, they could see two lines of handwriting:

msporani.com.it
Thethreeofus

On the way back to Roberto's palazzo, they stopped

to pick up Rose. They were taking no chances. Someone had tried to kill them. It was obvious Mario Sporani had been murdered, perhaps by the same person. Rose was happy to watch TV in the drawing room while the three adults gathered in the library.

Edie and Jeff stood either side of Roberto, who sat at his Mac, typing in the web address from the back of the photograph. A moment later, a password request appeared. He keyed in 'Thethreeofus' and two folders appeared, labelled simply '1' and '2'. Clicking on '1' a file named 'notes' was displayed. Opening this produced a page of Italian text. Roberto translated as he read:

NOTES:

COSIMO DE' MEDICI: I've learned very little from journal. I know Cosimo travelled east in 1410. Destination: Greece, or perhaps Macedonia. I know he found something of great significance there. What exactly, remains a mystery.

CONTESSINA DE' MEDICI: Cosimo's wife. Visited San Michele soon after her husband's death. I think it was to speak with Father Mauro's disciples and to arrange for a map to be designed.

GIORDANO BRUNO: The great mystic and occultist spent some time in Venice and Padua during 1592. He had been travelling throughout Europe and must have heard something important about Cosimo de' Medici and his circle. I think he formed a group in Venice to conceal this information, this 'Medici Secret'. Bruno's group was somehow connected with the early Rosicrucians, an occult group well known in Europe by this time. I'm quite sure Bruno tampered with Contessina's clue and planted a second. It's in the city archives and makes illuminating reading.

THE MEDICI CHAPEL: The nexus. I believe there is something there, but I don't know what it is. The secrets of Venice lead to the secrets of Florence which lead to the secrets of where? Macedonia? It is something very important – important enough to kill for.

'You were right, Jeff, he was several steps ahead of us,' Edie said. 'He knew something about the secret the clues are protecting.'

'Which makes sense. Finding the Medici journal in the crypt forty-odd years ago was the pivotal moment in Sporani's life. It was obvious whatever he had found was important; why else would anyone send a couple of thugs after him and threaten to kill his family?'

'So you think he's been trying to unravel this mystery all these years?'

'Why not?'

'I think Sporani was following a similar trail to us,' said Roberto. 'He didn't have the clue on the tablet found in Florence; in fact he didn't even know about that, but he somehow knew something about the Mauro map.'

'How could he have?'

Roberto shrugged. 'As you said yourself Jeff, Sporani's discovery in the crypt, Cosimo's journal, was a pivotal moment in the man's life. He obviously did his research, and followed a trail that convinced him that Cosimo's wife came to Venice and called in on Mauro's apprentices in 1464. He must have inferred from this that she planted a clue on San Michele to keep hidden what he calls the "Medici Secret".'

Jeff nodded. 'Yeah, but hold on. Cosimo died in 1464, and the clue refers to the Rialto Bridge, finished in 1591.'

'So,' Edie responded, 'either we have the clue all wrong, or the version we read in the library on San Michele is not the original.'

'I don't think we have the clue wrong,' Roberto said. 'It's just that the story isn't as straightforward as it seemed to be at first. Contessina may well have visited Mauro's disciples and she may have left a clue, but years later, Giordano Bruno learned of a mystery surrounding Cosimo de' Medici. He formed a group to protect whatever this secret might be. For some reason, he took it upon himself to replace the clue Contessina left, and according to Sporani at least, Bruno's clue leads to another created deliberately by him too.'

'Why would Bruno do that? Why change the clue?' Edie asked.

'It's typical of the man. Giordano Bruno was an egomaniac. He thought he was some sort of prophet, fancied himself as the founder of a new religion. He was planning to set one up when he was captured in Venice. It doesn't surprise me at all that he would interfere, he probably loved the idea he had gone one better than a Medici.'

'So what exactly is Sporani telling us?' Jeff asked.

'It's there in the section about Bruno. If Sporani knew about the clue on San Michele, he would have the same verse as us. He says Giordano Bruno tampered with it and planted the second. Clearly the clue on San Michele was Bruno's because of the timeframe. As we know, the Rialto was completed in

1591, not long before Bruno was in Venice. We know that's true because he was arrested here in May 1592 and tried by the Inquisition.'

'So, we were barking up the wrong tree going to the bridge itself,' Jeff interjected. 'The clue is in the city archives.'

'"It is hidden there with the lines, beyond the water, behind the hand of the architect",' Edie quoted. 'It must mean the architect's drawings. How cunning!'

'And the plaque in the wall of the bridge was a red herring.' Jeff looked at his watch. 'Will the archives still be open?'

'We don't need them,' Roberto said. 'I think Mario Sporani is our guardian angel and has already done the leg work.' He flicked back to the original screen and opened the folder marked '2'. Two more documents appeared. They were scanned-in pages of parchment covered in tightly written text. Beneath these they could see a typed version in Italian and English. The first document began:

Friday, 2 May, The Year of Our Lord 1592. Palazzo Mocenigo, Campo San Samuele.

I am Giordano Bruno, who some men refer to as 'The Nolan'. This is for my brothers of I Seguicamme, and this is my story.

I am now in the house of the nobleman Giovanni Mocenigo, a most loathsome man. Against my better judgement, Mocenigo persuaded me to return to Italy. I have been hounded by the Roman Inquisition for many years. Mocenigo, my patron of noble blood, promised me protection, but I know the forces against me are moving in for the kill, and my days of freedom are numbered. I fear I shall not leave Venice alive. Mocenigo wished to learn the Secret Arts of which I am an Adept (as I have proven in my many acclaimed works). But now, this man, who it transpires has no mind for the Hermetic Arts and is a fraud, has trapped me here in his palazzo and all the borders of this city are watched. My enemies are waiting for me to attempt an escape.

This then is a message to the future, a message of hope.

Twenty years ago I came by a most intriguing document. The details of how I acquired it do little for my reputation but I must confess all. I won the treasure playing cards in the backroom of a tavern in Verona. My card-playing adversary had lost all his money and insisted the parchment he was offering me was a genuine antique and that it had been handwritten by no less a figure than Contessina de' Medici, the wife of the great Florentine ruler, Cosimo the Elder. At first, I believed that the parchment was entirely without value. I almost threw it back at him, but when I looked a little closer I became intrigued and accepted his token.

Later, I managed to study the document in great detail. It was a fragment of a personal letter which alluded to the presence of a great treasure. At the end there were two lines of a riddle. At first, the clue made little sense, but gradually I managed to fathom some of its meaning and this revelation took me to Venice; more specifically, it took me to the home of the monks of San Michele, the Island of the Dead. There I found a map revered by the monks of the island, and again, after exhaustive effort and employing all my scholarship, I found another clue, a verse that led me to the next stage.

But all my efforts were in vain. The document, although genuine, led only to a blind alley. The clue in the letter and the others I unearthed on San Michele directed me to a tomb at the exact centre of the island. There, with the aid of my trusted servant Albertus, I unearthed a large leather casket. Inside lay just one thing, a metal plate on which had been etched the words: ALL MEN ARE TREACHEROUS.

At first, I assumed that this was some sort of elaborate hoax. But as time passed and I learned more (about which I dare not speak even now). I came to understand that although I had failed in my efforts, Contessina de' Medici really had hidden a great secret. Quite simply, I had not been wise enough to find it. For twenty long years I have continued my search. I have learned much, but not the core truth. My failure causes me so much pain I am barely able to countenance the thought of anyone else succeeding in the quest. To this end, I will hide the letter of Contessina de' Medici. Only the most determined may discover the hidden truth. I have just sufficient humility to say that whosoever does succeed in discovering the nature of the Medici Secret is a truly great man. May he also be honest and wise.

The second document was shorter. It read:

Thursday, 28 February, The Year of Our Lord 1593, Venice.

I am Albertus Jacobi. My master, the great

scholar Giordano Bruno has been transported to Rome in chains and I fear that soon he will die. My master entrusted me with many documents and papers, including a manuscript of his latest work. Most valued however is a document he discovered some two decades ago, about the time I began my association with him. Only the great shall be able to see this thing, and only the great will unlock its secrets.

The twins, the founding fathers.
In the street where they dispose of men like me,
Five windows over a balcony.
The point that touches the sky;
a hemisphere above, and a hemisphere below.

Edie, Jeff and Rose stayed the night at Roberto's. Rose had fallen asleep in front of the TV. Jeff woke her gently and escorted her to a room prepared for her on the first floor. Vincent then led Jeff and Edie to their rooms along the corridor, a grand galleried area at the top of a broad flight of marble stairs. Roberto stayed in the library to see what he could unearth.

From the windows of her room Edie had a magnificent view along the Grand Canal, The water looked like treacle. On her left, the canal curved away to the south. A gondola lit up with lanterns slid silently into the shadows. A fog was descending on the scene. Soon, she thought, Venice would be enveloped in a damp shroud, contorting light and quickening sounds.

Edie found it hard to believe anyone still lived in such opulent style. The bed was a huge four-poster, with silk drapes. A log fire blazed in the grate, ancient rugs lay across the stone floor, each positioned with perfect carelessness. Glass globes hung from the walls casting a gentle light. The ceiling was high and covered in hand-wrought mouldings and coving.

She ran a hot bath and lay in the bubbles for a long time, soaking up the romance of it all. After she was dry she put on a silk nightdress and kimono that had been laid out for her on the bed. Sitting on the floor in front of the fire, she stared into the flames and let her mind drift. So much had happened to her during the past few days, and there had been so little time in which to assimilate it all.

Less than four days earlier she had been working in the crypt of the Medici Chapel conducting the kind of research she loved doing. Then, abruptly, everything had spun out of control. She was scared. They had almost been killed. And then there was the poor old man, Mario Sporani, and Antonio. And what did she make of Roberto? He was brilliant and handsome, rich and charming. Too good to be true, really. But he was also Jeff's friend; Jeff trusted him and Jeff was as close as a brother to her. Jumping up, she tightened the belt of the kimono and headed for the door.

Out on the landing, it was dark, but there was a faint glow coming from the library, and she could hear the strains of a piano sonata. Roberto was sitting at a leather-topped desk poring over a massive, ancient-looking book. Edie gave a small cough and he turned round.

'A night owl, like me?' His look of surprise quickly turned to a warm smile.

'Not usually,' she said. 'What are you reading?' She peered over his shoulder at a leather-bound tome, the pages covered in fine print in a strange font. The paper was dry and yellowed.

'Trying to work out what the hell Giordano Bruno was going on about. I could do with some help. Would you care to join me in a brandy?'

'Only if it's Paulet Lallique,' Edie smiled.

Roberto's expression did not even flicker.

A few moments later, Vincent deposited two huge globes and a bottle of one of the most expensive cognacs in the world on the round table beside the desk.

'What's the book?' Edie asked, while Roberto poured.

'It's one of seven volumes, *Records of the Venetian Inquisition Between 1500 and 1770.* They've been in the family for a long time. I was just reading about Andrea di Ugoni, a writer friend of Titian's who was tried for heresy in 1565 and escaped punishment. Then there's the case of Casanova who was arrested almost two hundred years later and imprisoned for "contempt of religion". I thought we might find something to help explain what Bruno meant in his clue.'

'Bruno was put on trial by the Venetian Inquisition then?'

'His message must have been written immediately before he was arrested. Mocenigo certainly did betray him. He was snatched in the middle of the night from his room in the palazzo by hired thugs, and thrown in the Doge's prison.'

'I thought he was imprisoned in Rome. Isn't that where they executed him?'

'But he was first interrogated in Venice. The Venetian Inquisition was far more liberal than their Roman counterpart. The head of the Roman Inquisition, the Pope's right-hand man, was a radical cardinal named Robert Bellarmine, he had the nickname: Hammer of Heretics.'

'To the Hammer of Heretics.' Edie raised her glass, and took an appreciative sip of her brandy. It was deliciously smooth and warmed her whole being. 'So were the Venetians going to let Bruno off?' she asked.

'I don't know if they would have gone that far. They didn't like the Pope interfering in their more liberal society. In fact, the entire city was excommunicated several times over the centuries. The Venetian Inquisition were far more tolerant of occultists like Bruno. But unfortunately for him, the Doge bowed to pressure from the Pope, and after a few months in Venice, the authorities here extradited him to Rome where he was eventually burned at the stake.'

'So when Bruno says: "In the street where they dispose of men like me",' you think he's talking about the place where subversives were executed?'

Roberto flicked carefully through a few pages. 'Curiously, during the two centuries of the witch trials fewer than two hundred cases were brought before the Inquisition here and only nine people were prosecuted, none of them was executed. There were other sorts of subversives: spies, political activists, seditionists. From what I gather from this record, there were two places in Venice where executions of "undesirables" took place. Look.'

Edie leaned in and Roberto showed her a selection of reports. Between 1550 and 1750, six hundred and seven citizens labelled as 'dangerous' by the state police, the Council of Ten, were executed. They were hanged, away from public gaze, in one of two places: Calle della Morte, 'The Street of Death', or in Calle Santi.

Edie shuddered involuntarily.

'You're cold,' Roberto said putting an arm around her shoulders. 'Come, let's sit nearer to the fire.'

They sat down facing each other cross-legged on an ancient Khotan rug. Through the broad leadlight window tendrils of fog were drifting on to the Grand Canal.

'I don't suppose anyone has ever told you that you have quite a place here,' Edie said.

Roberto laughed. 'It's all in the genes,' Roberto said. 'I gather your parents were archaeologists.'

'Good old Jeff,' replied Edie.

'I wouldn't take offence. He's a great admirer of yours.'

'So did he tell you they were killed on a dig, in Egypt? I was there.'

'I'm sorry.'

'It was a long time ago.' She took an appreciative sip of her brandy. 'He hasn't told me much about you. How did you and Jeff meet?'

'About five years ago, he was still at Cambridge. He had come over on his own for a couple of weeks to research a book. He knocked a drink out of my hand at The Cipriani.'

Edie laughed.

'We started chatting, we got on, and well . . . And you?'

'At college. Jeff was a year ahead of me at King's and already quite a star. I was eighteen and totally in awe of him . . . I still am.'

'So, did you . . .?' Roberto asked after a moment.

Edie grinned. 'Jeff had a girlfriend when we met. By the time they broke up, I had a boyfriend. Then Jeff met Imogen and, I don't know, it never crosses my mind now. It would be like having a sexual relationship with your brother. Anyway, what about you, Roberto? You must have the ladies lining up.'

He looked embarrassed.

'Wow!' Edie said. 'You're actually blushing! Well?'

'Well what?'

'The ladies.'

'I've been in love twice. Both times it ended in tears.'

'Such is life.'

Roberto caressed her cheek. Edie leaned forward and brushed her lips against his. Neither of them saw

189

Rose in the doorway, watching them. But both of them heard the front door slam.

The tall, black-haired man lit a cigarette with the faint red stub of the previous one, then flattened it on the marble floor, and peered into the binoculars he had mounted on a sturdy tripod.

The vista from the window was one of extraordinary beauty, views that could be seen across the globe on postcards, chocolate boxes and in the windows of travel agents, but he was not interested in these. He was focused on a building across the Grand Canal, a russet-coloured palazzo, the home of Roberto Armatovani. He had seen someone arrive by barge and offload groceries, a cable repairman had been and gone. And that was about it. Three hours had dragged past very slowly indeed. He was growing tired and increasingly frustrated. The day before he had almost got lucky on the launch, but in the end he had barely escaped with his own life. It had taught him a very important lesson. These people might seem like amateurs, but he could not afford to underestimate them.

Suddenly the front door of the palazzo flew open and the girl, Rose Martin, rushed out of the building. A moment later, Armantovani appeared. But in Venice a person can vanish in the blink of an eye.

Roberto went back inside. However, the black-haired man had seen where the girl had gone and followed her with his binoculars. In a few moments she reached Ponte Dell' Accademia, and – he could hardly believe it – she was crossing the bridge to his side of the river.

'Rose must have seen us,' Edie said to Jeff. She flopped into a chair positioned under a gigantic gilded mirror and stared at the dark marble floor. 'We were kissing.'

'Brilliant.' Jeff's face was grim.

'I'll send out some people,' Roberto said. 'Vincent can help. Do you think she might have gone back to the apartment?'

'Christ knows. Call Maria, but I have to get out there.'

The night air was freezing. Jeff ran along the path beside the canal and then turned left into the maze of passageways clustered around San Samuele. The fog had become thick and heavy, blotting out everything more than a few metres in front of him. The torch Roberto had given him offered little help. Exiting from a passageway that opened out on to Campo Francesco Morosini, to his left, he knew, lay Campo Sant' Angelo. To the right was Ponte dell' Accademia. He stopped, took several deep breaths and tried not to let the sense of total panic overwhelm him.

The black-haired man saw the girl turn away from the Grand Canal and take a left skirting the Gallerie. He had left his lookout point and was following her, keeping his distance, conscious of how every sound was magnified in the fog.

He saw her duck into an alley. She slowed for a minute, unsure of the way. Then she stopped to get her bearings. He slipped into a doorway as she swept her eyes across the campo and then he almost lost her in the gloom when she suddenly ran down a narrow passage. She was heading towards the tip of the Dorsoduro, a spit of land that curved round to almost meet up with the San Marco district where the most southerly part of the Grand Canal opened out into the Basino di San Marco.

The fog was thicker here and he almost lost her again as they emerged on to Dogana E La Salute, a broad path that ran along the southerly edge of Dorsoduro. To their left lay the workshops where gondolas were built. They were all shuttered now and the place was deserted.

To their right, water slapped against stone. A gutter running along the low roof of a workshop had snapped and water had frozen into a treacherous sheet of thin ice across the entire width of the path. The girl slowed and negotiated the obstacle, then sped off the other side disappearing around the bend at the very tip of the peninsula, at Dogana di Mare, the Old Customs House, a severe colonnaded building, topped by two huge Atlases each holding aloft a golden globe.

He crept along, watching her slow as she turned back around the other side of the building. She stopped suddenly and sat down on the edge of the path, wrapping her arms about herself, and peering out into the fog across the expanse of water towards San Marco. He was so close he could hear her sob. As he took a silent step forward he felt the familiar, delicious thrill of anticipation.

Running past the amorphous Guggenheim Museum, Jeff weaved his way along the quickest route he could find, ignoring the ache in his chest. He was pretty sure now that he knew where Rose might be going. It was a place she had loved, a place they always returned to. To his left, Palazzo Dario tumbled into the fog, and he emerged on to Campo Salute, its northern edge providing one of the last sections of canal bank before the Grand Canal opened out into the Bacino. Another hundred yards and the steps of the Church of Santa Maria della

Salute materialised out of the grey gloom. And then he was there. The billowing fog girdled the colonnades of the Old Customs House. And his heartbeat slowed as he saw Rose sitting crossed-legged staring out towards San Marco.

'Hey.'

She spun round, her eyes filled with terror. But seeing her father, her whole body relaxed.

Jeff sat down beside her. For a moment he couldn't talk, he was gasping for air. Then suddenly he felt Rose fling her arms around him and she buried her head against his chest and cried as though her heart would break.

'This isn't really about Edie, is it Rose?' Jeff said after a while.

She pulled away so she could see her father's face.

'You're angry with Edie, but she's really a scapegoat.'

Rose shook her head. 'I don't . . .'

'You're setting Edie up as the baddie, but really you're just angry with your mother and me. You blame us for messing up your life, and you're right. People shouldn't have children if they're not mature enough to keep a marriage going. I'm sorry, darling, I've let you down terribly.'

'Oh, Daddy . . .' Rose started to cry again.

For a second, Jeff looked away to the shrouded

splendour. Venice lay there somewhere. It could be reached, just as the memories of what had once been could be reached, but only through a dense fog.

'Come on. Let's head back, yeah?' Jeff got to his feet.

The black-haired man slipped the gun from the holster and moved away from the column. One step on to the quayside and he sensed rather than saw someone approach along the path. Spitting a curse, he slipped back silently as Jeff came into view. He watched him greet his daughter then settle down beside her.

The fury took him by surprise. He had been trained to kill without compunction and knew how to pull back with clinical detachment when the situation demanded it. Closing his eyes for a second, he took several deep breaths. His finger tightened on the trigger.

A hazy white beam of light probed through the murk as a police launch came into view. Diving behind a column, he watched in disbelief as it pulled up against the canal bank and two officers leapt on to the quay.

Roberto was waiting on the steps of his palazzo. Jeff carried Rose, wrapped in a blanket and took her straight to her room. She was asleep almost before her head hit the pillow. Downstairs, he accepted gratefully a large balloon of cognac from his host.

'Jeff, I'm really sorry . . .' Edie said.

He lifted a hand to stop her. 'There's nothing to be sorry about. I think we're all right,' he said.

'God, I'm glad I'll never be fourteen again.'

'Ditto.'

'Changing the subject,' Roberto said. 'Edie and I made something of a breakthrough.'

'That's what they call it these days is it?' Jeff asked.

Roberto ignored the joke and turned to the page from *Records of the Venetian Inquisition Between 1500 and 1770*. 'I'm glad Rose is safe,' he said. 'She could not be dearer to me. But we three still have work to do. And I feel time is running out.'

'OK, Roberto. I'm listening.'

'There were two main sites for executions,' Roberto explained. 'Calle Santi, which is not far from here, close to the Accademia, and Calle della Morte, the Street of Death, which is to the east of the Ducal Palace, just off Campo de la Bragora.'

'Can I interrupt?' Jeff said. 'When I was searching for Rose, the only thing in my conscious mind was finding her. But I remember catching a glimpse of the top of the Old Customs House breaking through the fog – two figures of Atlas holding a golden globe.'

'What's that got to do with anything?' Edie asked.

'Some people say the figures of Atlas are twins. The line in the Bruno verse. "The twins, the founding fathers" . . . it must mean Castor and Pollux, the twins from Greek mythology, offspring of Leda and the god, Jupiter.'

'Why? What's that got to do with Venice for God's sake?' Edie sounded exasperated.

'Quite a lot. The earliest settlers in the lagoon were refugees from Rome, who were fleeing the invading Barbarians. They brought with them many archaic Roman religious rituals, including the traditional worship of Jupiter and his offspring, Castor and Pollux. There was a cult of the twins centred on a pair of islands that saw some of the earliest settlements here in the fourth or fifth century. There are images of twins all over the city, including the twinned Atlases.'

'So you think the verse refers to Calle Santi? It's a stone's throw from the Old Customs House.' Roberto said.

'No, I don't. I think it's the other place, Calle della Morte. It all came back to me in the launch. I visited a church in the area years ago. It's called San

Giovanni and it's located on the Campo de la Bragora; and "Bragora" derives from the word "b'ragal" which means "two men".'

'That's brilliant.' Roberto shook his head. 'Or completely crazy!'

Jeff was on to his second coffee when Edie walked into the breakfast room.

'Sleep well?' she asked.

'Surprisingly. You?'

She stifled a yawn. 'Hardly a wink.'

'Here, this will perk you up.' He poured her a cup of strong coffee. 'Listen Edie,' Jeff began and stopped as Roberto was preceded into the room by Vincent who was carrying a tray holding two tall silver jugs and a cup and saucer.

'I was about to say to Edie,' Jeff said. 'After last night, I think I should stay with Rose today.'

'Of course.'

'I disagree,' Edie said. 'I think you two should follow up the clue and I should stay with Rose.'

'But . . .'

'No buts, Jeff. I've already spoken to her.'

'You have?'

'Don't look so surprised. She and I were friends once, remember. I'd like to get things back on an even keel.'

Jeff raised his eyebrows and shrugged. 'Fine with me.'

The temperature had plummeted overnight and the campo was cold and deserted. A few straggly trees lined one side of the square and the odd pigeon, far from the hungry flock in San Marco, waddled over the uneven paving stones. Jeff and Roberto stood in the centre of the campo wrapped up in thick winter coats and scarves.

'Although this was indeed a site for executions, there is a lighter side to its history,' Roberto said. 'Vivaldi was baptised in the church over there, the church of San Giovanni.' He pointed to a façade that had clearly evolved through a succession of muddled renovations and extensions. 'And there,' he went on, 'is the most interesting building in the campo, the Palazzo Gritti Badoer; or as we know it now, Hotel La Residenza.'

'Which has five windows over a balcony,' Jeff observed and repeated the second part of Bruno's clue: ' "Five windows over a balcony. The point that touches the sky; a hemisphere above, and a hemisphere below." And this was here in the 1590s?'

'Most definitely. It's fourteenth century. You can tell by the shape of the windows and the design of the loggia. So your idea wasn't crazy after all.'

Jeff was looking up to the roof. 'Never doubted it for a second. But there's no "point that touches the sky" though, is there?'

'Unfortunately not,' Roberto replied.

They walked across the campo towards the palazzo. On the wall of a narrow passageway they could see a sign that read Calle della Morte.

The entrance to the hotel led directly into a vast echoing hall. There was a large reception area to the left, with heavy plasterwork around the tops of the walls; seventeenth-century paintings, all brooding dark colours and ravaged figures; clusters of antique chairs and tables. At the far end of the room stood a group of workmen arranging lights and hanging decorations. One of the men was perched precariously on a wooden stepladder. He was reaching up to the high ceiling attempting to attach a string of small white lights.

A middle-aged man in a dark green concierge's uniform appeared. He had dyed, jet black hair and was wearing pince-nez. 'May I help you?' he asked.

'Good morning,' Jeff said. 'You're hosting a function?'

'Indeed we are, sir. Tonight in fact. May I assist . . .?'

'We were just passing. My friend, Roberto Armatovani here, remarked how lovely the façade of the building is and that he had never been inside.'

'Signor Armatovani?' The concierge's back straightened. 'Of course. My apologies for the mess, the decorations should have been up hours ago. May I offer you both coffee?'

'That's kind, but no thank you,' Roberto responded. 'May I ask the nature of the function?'

'Certainly, signor. It's a gala carnival evening organised by the Vivaldi Society. It's a private function, but I'm sure I could have a word with the president.'

'That's very kind of you, er . . . ?'

'Gianfrancesco . . . Francesco.'

'Francesco . . . I know the president, Giovanni Tafani, well. I'll get one of my people to call him.'

The concierge gave a slight bow and they turned to leave.

Outside, they stood together looking up at the beautiful rococo stucco over the main entrance.

'You really do know everyone in Venice, don't you?' Jeff exclaimed.

'Don't knock it, it comes in very handy.'

'So what now?'

'Well, we obviously have to get up on to the roof somehow and I'm rather hoping the charming president of the Vivaldi Society will assist us.'

★

When Jeff, Edie and Roberto arrived at the Palazzo Gritti Badoer, it was already bubbling with masked party-goers in their finery. A string ensemble was partway through a robust performance of Schubert's String Quartet No. 9 and liveried waiters glided around the room with trays of champagne.

Jeff had been concerned about leaving Rose behind, but she had promised not to step outside the palazzo under any circumstances. And Roberto had convinced him that Vincent would be no slouch as a bodyguard.

Roberto wore a classic Savile Row dress suit which he had inherited from his father. His mask was that of an eagle with black feathers and a short beak. Jeff, who was taller and broader, had hired a more modern tux from Roberto's regular tailor on Via XXII Marzo, and had chosen a plain, elegant silver mask. With Rose's help, Edie had tried on at least a dozen gowns in some of Venice's most exclusive shops before settling on a dark green silk sheath and an ornate gold mask.

An usher met them, asked their names and immediately led them to the host of the evening who was standing with a small group close to the musicians. Giovanni Tafani was a tall, broad-shouldered man in his mid-fifties wearing a tiny gold mask that did little to conceal his features. He took

Roberto's hand. 'I'm so glad you could make it, maestro,' he said.

'These are my friends, Jeff Martin, an eminent historian from England, and Edie Granger, a palaeopathologist of great repute.'

Tafani gave Jeff a slight bow, then took Edie's hand, brushing the back of it with his lips. '*Enchanté*.' Straightening, he added, 'Now, I must introduce you to some of my associates.'

It was almost an hour before Jeff and Edie found the opportunity to slip away, leaving Roberto to hold the fort as planned. After they had left the reception area, a short passageway led to a courtyard. Beyond that was a large, empty dining room cast in darkness. They skirted the edge of the room emerging unnoticed into a hallway. Ahead stood a flight of stairs.

Edie led the way but was struggling in her tight-fitting gown. 'Damn it,' she said after a moment. Slipping off her shoes she hitched the dress up around her hips.

'I say!' Jeff mocked.

'Eye on the ball, Jeff; eye on the ball.'

They reached the top floor without encountering another soul. It was oddly quiet. The noise of the party had drifted away. At the top of the stairs was a corridor with three doors on each side, presumably leading to bedrooms. They could see an emergency exit at the end.

The door was unlocked and opened on to a plain grey stairwell. A metal handrail spiralled down four floors to the basement. The faint echo of voices and the clang of metal told them they were almost directly above the kitchens. Looking up, the stairs took a final half turn to a door which opened on to the roof.

The cold hit them immediately. Jeff took off his jacket and put it around Edie's shoulders.

'We didn't plan this very well, did we?' she said as they picked their way along a narrow walkway between two elevations. Ahead, the path opened on to a square about ten metres on each side. In the centre stood an ancient weather vane.

It was about five metres high, bronze and discoloured with age. A central pole supported the vane itself, an arrow mounted on a disc. Halfway up the pole there was a metal hemisphere about the size of a large wok. Jeff stood on tiptoe to study the hemisphere. It too had tarnished and was covered in green oxide and streaks of black.

He walked slowly around the vane. On the far side he noticed a mark in the metal. 'There're some letters on the hemisphere,' he said, and with a tissue from his pocket he tried to clean away some of the stains, but they were deeply encrusted. Gingerly, he levered himself up on one of the supports at the base of the vane to get a closer look.

'Anything?' Edie asked.

'I can make out a large "V", a gap, another small "v" and then . . . no. Hang on.' He tried scratching the surface with a nail. 'A letter "i".'

'Vivaldi,' Edie intoned as Jeff stepped back down.

'Makes sense. This was the man's manor after all. But why?'

Edie shrugged. 'And there's only one hemisphere. If this is the one above, where's the one below?'

The moon appeared as a slither in the northern sky partially obscured by stringy clouds.

'Unless,' Jeff said suddenly and pushed himself up. 'That has to be it.'

'What?' Edie asked, but Jeff was already heading back to the door. 'Where are you . . .?'

'Follow me.'

He held the door open for Edie. 'This leads straight down to the basement,' Jeff said. 'I think we should check it out.'

As they approached the ground floor the sounds of the kitchen grew louder. Someone was calling out orders for the guests at the reception. Stealthily, they slipped down the final flight of stairs that led to a series of dark storerooms. To one side, double doors opened on to a broad passageway leading to a wooden jetty used for unloading supplies to the hotel.

Jeff quickly pushed Edie into a recess as one of the kitchen staff carrying a whole cheese appeared at the door to one of the larger storerooms.

'There must be another hemisphere down here somewhere,' he said, when the man had gone.

'If there is, it'll be directly below the weather vane. Where would that be?'

Jeff gazed along the passageway towards the doors leading out to the jetty, then back the other way. 'Down there, to the right.'

The last door directly off the passageway was unlocked. They eased it open and Edie found an old, chunky bakelite light switch. It was a large room, damp and malodorous. On the far wall a narrow, grimy window at head-height looked out on to a damp, mossy wall. Light filtered in from the campo above. On the left, rows of metal shelving held a collection of cases and crates. To the right were towers of boxes each with the image of a large toilet roll and bearing the brand name 'Dolce Vita' written in red, white and green.

Edie sat down on a pile of crates, hands on her knees, and surveyed the room.

Jeff sighed. 'It must be here somewhere.' He

grabbed a couple of boxes lying near the back window. Dumping them in the centre of the dirty concrete floor, he climbed up to reach a large, rectangular plastic cover in the ceiling. Holding two sides of the cover, he passed it down to Edie who tossed it on to one of the metal shelves. In the ceiling to one side of the light fixture protruding from the plaster, was the bottom section of a metal hemisphere.

'Hallelujah!' Jeff cried.

It was tarnished, but much cleaner than its twin that was exposed to the elements on the roof. Etched into the surface of the metal were two Roman numerals, IV and V. Just discernible below this there was a line of musical notation, a series of notes on a finely etched stave. And, at the bottom, a single word: SUNSET.

Footsteps echoed in the passageway. Jeff pulled a pen from his pocket and copied out the inscription on the palm of his hand, taking care to include all the musical directions.

'Quickly,' Edie hissed, grabbing his sleeve.

The door swung open shielding Jeff and Edie from view, and two men stepped into the room. The old door had a long, thin crack running from the top to a crosspiece at hip height, through which, Edie and Jeff could just see. One of the two men was a waiter, the other an older man in dirty, blue workman's overalls. The waiter was unhappy about something. He paced to the centre of the room and growled a barely audible instruction, then strode out.

The workman swore under his breath as he prised open a plastic container. Fumbling inside, he pulled out a sink plunger, and headed for the door.

'Did you get everything written on the hemisphere?' Edie asked after a moment or two.

'Yes, but it doesn't make any sense.'

'We'd better go back in separately,' Edie said when they had made their way back to the reception area. The sound of laughter bubbled up over the chamber music. Jeff looked at his palm. Beside him was an occasional table with some hotel stationery placed neatly in a leather presentation box. He snatched a sheet of headed paper from the box and quickly copied out what was written on his hand, folded the paper and shoved it into his breast pocket. A few moments later, he was squeezing through the throng looking for Roberto and Edie.

They made it outside as soon as they could without drawing attention to themselves. Roberto sent a short text message to his new driver, Antonio's replacement, and they headed towards a prearranged meeting point. It was very still. Hardly a sound broke the cold night.

'Success?' Roberto's breath was white and warm in the freezing air.

'Maybe,' said Jeff.

There was a sudden shuffling sound behind them. Spinning round, they caught sight of a figure darting into a doorway about ten yards away. Without a word, the three of them started to run.

A dark, covered passageway lay directly ahead. Jeff led the way. At the end they came to a T-junction. High up on the wall was a yellow sign, an arrow pointing west with 'S. Marco' written beneath it. The plan was to meet the launch on a narrow waterway called Rio San Martin.

Edie glanced back as they turned right. There was a dark shape, a man, his cloak flapping behind him. He was wearing a black mask that covered most of his face. Long black feathers swept back at the ears. He had a gun in his hand.

The three of them entered a small cobbled square. A single bedraggled tree stood in a small plot at its centre. Edie fell behind for a second as she kicked off her shoes and hitched up her dress. The gunman arrived at the entrance to the campo just as she caught up with Jeff and Roberto on the far side. He raised his gun and fired.

The shot was muffled by a silencer. The bullet smashed into the wall a few centimetres above

Roberto's head. It ricocheted along the passageway taking chunks of plaster with it. 'Come on . . . Not far now!' Roberto shouted.

The gunman fired off another a shot. A chunk of plaster hit Edie in the arm and she screamed but kept running, her head down. As they reached the path adjacent to the canal, another bullet whistled past Jeff's ear.

About a hundred yards ahead, a barge was travelling north. On the other side of the canal a small rowboat was heading towards a tributary; the oarsman had his back to them.

They sped along the path towards Ponte Arco where they were supposed to meet the launch. The gunman was gaining on them. There was another muffled shot, and Roberto lurched forward as though he had tripped on a cobblestone. Blood jetted from his left arm. A second shot spun him round. He crumpled in midair and tumbled into the canal.

'No!' Edie screamed, and faltered. But Jeff grabbed her and pushed her on. There was no time to think. He was acting on impulse, animal fear forcing him on.

They turned left, then left again . . . straight into a dead end.

Jeff tried to shield Edie behind him as the gunman slowed to a leisurely walk. He was tall and well built.

Even though he was in costume, there was no mistaking who he was. It was the same man who had killed Antonio and held them at gunpoint on the launch. He stopped and raised his gun to eye level, holding it steady with both hands.

'Give me the clue, now, or I'll shoot you. Give me the clue and I may shoot you anyway.'

Jeff reached into his pocket, stalling for time.

'Slowly.'

Jeff was about to bring out a piece of paper when he saw a tiny glint of light in the darkness of the alleyway, and then a black object appeared above the gunman's head. With a groan, he crumpled to the stones, his weapon clattering away from his out-stretched hand.

A short, heavyset figure in a ripped overcoat and old boots tied with string knelt down to see what damage he had done.

'Dino,' Jeff said, in total disbelief.

Chapter 16

Northern Italy, May 1410

The journey from Brisighella to Venice took six days. Many years later Cosimo could still remember the sense of foreboding that descended on the party as they travelled north. It seemed that as they rode further from Florence they were entering a brooding darkness that grew ever more oppressive with each passing mile. There were rumours of plague spreading its deadly tendrils across the countryside and reports of bandits controlling the main routes.

They spent a night outside the walls of Modena where they shared a camp with a group of travelling musicians and actors. They were a merry band, but it was clear they were fuelling their high spirits with mead and something else, some strange weed they had acquired from another party of performers whose paths they had crossed in Venice. They claimed the weed came from China. The leader of the troupe, a bear of a man named Trojan, showed Cosimo and his associates how to roll it in the palms of the hands and then chew the darkened and mangled leaves. It tasted like thyme but hit you with a great wave of euphoria that lasted several minutes.

The encounter with the performers was one of the few bright times they experienced during this part of the journey. When they waved farewell at a cross-roads north of Modena, the dark veil of anxiety returned.

After a long night's ride, they reached Copparo, a small town near Ferrara. The sun was rising over low hills lighting up the young green shoots of barley. A dusty track led to the centre of the town. Turning a bend, they came upon a church. A crowd had gathered, which cheered loudly as a pyre was lit. In a matter of seconds, the flames licked the hem of a habit worn by a priest tied to a rough stake. He was dressed in grey, his hands bound with rope, head shaved. His eyes were black with terror.

The prosecutor had deliberately used damp wood, so the fire took a long time to blaze. Cosimo and Niccolò Niccoli turned away as the priest began to scream. They learned later that the condemned man had been found guilty of impregnating three young women in the small town.

The party stayed just long enough to sleep away

the daylight in a tavern on the edge of the town, the air rank with the smell of burned flesh. They returned to the road an hour after sunset, eager to leave. The bones of the priest had already been pulverised and the townsfolk had scattered his ashes across a field of barley.

Cosimo and his little entourage were no strangers to death, but this familiarity did nothing to help numb the rising sense of dread each of them felt that morning. The sky was leaden, the land grey. Pestilence stalked the land but death also came easily from the hands of men. It wasn't until they entered the Veneto that their spirits rose. A little over twenty-four hours later, they reached Mestre, two hours before sunset.

A servant was sent ahead to report their imminent arrival to the Doge. An hour later, as they emerged on to the quayside, a small company of men approached in a galliot. One of them came ashore.

Cosimo slipped off his mount and ran forward to embrace him. 'Ambrogio. It's so good to see you again.'

Ambrogio Tommasini held his friend at arm's length and surveyed Cosimo's face with his intense brown eyes. 'You've had a hard journey.' He looked weary himself, older than his thirty years, but he possessed an infectious energy that communicated itself immediately. 'I'm relieved to see you, Cosi,' he continued, 'but you have arrived at a most inauspicious time.'

At that moment Niccolò Niccoli strode up and embraced Tommasini, kissing him on each cheek. Ambrogio was one of the most respected members of their circle. He was especially close to Cosimo, but he was liked and trusted by all the members of the Humanist League. Although he had been in Venice for little more than a week, he had an important role at court, acting as consultant to the Doge, the elderly Michele Steno. Renowned as a copyist and restorer of ancient documents, Tommasini had worked for the Curia in Rome, and only five years earlier, he had become famous within the academic community of Europe for his discovery of a short play by Homer, a document which until then most scholars believed had been lost to history. His services were expensive and highly sought after and he could take his pick of eager patrons.

'You look very serious Ambrogio,' Niccoli observed.

'I was about to explain to Cosi. Plague. It struck two days after I arrived here and it is worse than you could ever imagine. Perhaps a thousand have died already, hundreds perish each day. No one is allowed to enter the city. Ships are being held in quarantine at

San Lazaretto Nuovo. Your messenger was stopped before he could enter the city and the news of your arrival was forwarded to the Doge. The messenger is on my boat.'

'But . . .?'

Tommasini had a hand raised. 'Don't worry. I have arranged for a special dispensation from the Doge himself to allow the two of you through quarantine. Your servants will have to return to Florence.'

'This is bitter news indeed.'

'The Doge has invited you to stay in the palace. I have a small room there also. It is the safest place. He has said though that if you decide to turn round and return home he would understand. In fact, your father has been putting pressure on Michele Steno to refuse you entry anyway.'

Cosimo shook his head.

'I'm sure he is only thinking of your . . .'

'I'm sure he is, Ambrogio,' Cosimo snapped, staring away across the orange lagoon. Then he turned to Niccoli. 'I must go. I have no choice, but I do not expect you to come with me.'

'Cosimo, don't be absurd,' Niccoli said dismissively, and began to unload the bags from his horse.

★

After a mile or two, the black shapes of the city began to rise out of the water. Venice looked as though it were on fire, the light from the sun setting behind them reflected off the old stone and glinted from a score of spires and crosses. Cosimo stood by the helm lost in thought. How terrible if he had wasted his time and alienated his father into the bargain. For all he knew their only contact in Venice, the strange Luigi whom Francesco Valiani had told them to seek out, could be dead, taken by plague. If that were so, how could they possibly find the missing section of the map and reach the monastery of Golem Korab?

They came ashore some distance from Piazza San Marco along a quiet stretch of canal that ran behind the Doge's palace. Their luggage was taken by servants, and a man in a long, fur-lined coat approached the quay. He was accompanied by four guards wearing burnished metal helmets and carrying pikes. The man introduced himself as Servo Zamboldi, personal assistant to the Doge. He bowed low but did not come close, nor did he shake hands with any of the travellers. Zamboldi escorted them along a narrow stone pathway running parallel to the canal and on into a courtyard.

The palace exuded a dull, mournful atmosphere. As they passed through a doorway, Zamboldi nodded to the guards and they snapped to attention. Ascending a great curved arc of marble staircase, Cosimo and his companions followed the Doge's personal assistant along a grand, galleried corridor. The walls were adored with rich tapestries and the floor of the corridor itself was inlaid with beautiful tiles of complex design; exquisite marble figures and sculptures of mythical beasts lined the corridor. This was Cosimo's first visit to Venice, and he had heard of its many splendours, but he was quite taken aback by the magnificence of the place.

Doge Michele Steno was a tall, muscular man now in his eighth decade. His face was narrow and deeply lined, his skin oyster-grey, long white hair hung to his shoulders beneath a blue velvet cap. He wore a long black and gold coat with gold buttons that ran from throat to ankle. Steno had been a much-honoured soldier and had become a powerful political figure who had dominated Venetian politics for more than a decade. Seated on a stone throne under a red canopy bearing the lion of Venice, he watched the visitors approach, and rose to greet them at the foot of the dais. But he was careful not to shake hands or embrace the new arrivals.

'Cosimo de' Medici,' he said, fixing the young man with his steel grey eyes. 'You have the bearing and dignity of your illustrious father. That is good.'

Cosimo smiled and bowed before introducing his friends. The Doge had met Niccolò Niccoli on more than one occasion.

'I was aware, of course, that you were coming,' said the Doge.

'So I understand,' Cosimo replied, glancing at Ambrogio.

'But you obviously have no intention of obeying your father's wishes. Your journey must be a matter of great importance.'

'It is,' Cosimo replied simply. 'And we are most grateful for your hospitality.'

'Don't assume anything, young man,' the Doge replied softly. 'We may wish to offer you our finest, but you have arrived at a very bad time.' His face was grave. 'The Great Pestilence is every bit as fierce as I remember when I was a young man, almost half a century ago. I learned this evening that more than a thousand souls have perished. We have tried everything: aromatic oils, ringing all the church bells in the republic and firing every available cannon at the arsenal; all to no avail.'

'I am sorry to hear of your plight, my Lord. And our business here will be as brief as possible. Indeed, we wish to travel on to Ragusa at the earliest opportunity.'

'Ragusa?' The Doge held Cosimo's gaze for a

moment and then he looked away. 'You and your companions are most welcome. Rooms have been prepared for you in the palace. I will help you with whatever you need to make your stay as comfortable as possible and I'll have my people arrange a ship for you. But we are as you find us. I do not need to remind you that for your own well-being you must act with extreme circumspection. Please, do not leave the environs of the palace without one of my personal assistants as a guide. I bid you good evening.'

After the three Florentines had been ushered from the chamber, the Doge resumed his throne and beckoned Zamboldi closer. Guards were dotted around the room, well out of earshot.

'I want to know their whereabouts at every moment,' Steno said. 'And that includes Tommasini.'

'Of course, My Lord. But I still do not understand why you have taken the risk of allowing these men into the city.'

'Men like the young Medici and his friends do not travel so far without good reason. Especially to a city riddled with plague. He needs something here and, although I have asked him not to leave the palace without a guide, he will of course do precisely that, and at the very earliest opportunity.'

Zamboldi conceded the point with a brief nod. 'But how do we know they are not infected? How do we know they will not make things worse for us?'

'We don't.' The Doge smiled humourlessly. 'But then . . . could things get any worse? I don't think so. Sometimes, risks are necessary.'

'But . . .'

Steno glared at his servant. 'Enough. Now do as I ask. If one of the party so much as farts, I want to be informed of it immediately. You understand?'

Zamboldi nodded.

'Now go.'

'So, what's the plan, Cosi?'

Cosimo and Niccolò Niccoli were seated at a table in a sumptuous apartment in a secluded wing of the palace. The floor was bare except for a beautiful red rug in the centre of the room. Through a doorway a short passage led to a vast bedchamber.

There was a light tap at the door.

'Come.'

Ambrogio Tommasini strode in.

'Ah, excellent timing. Niccolò has just asked me to propose a plan.'

Tommasini joined them at the table, pushing his chair back and relaxing with his long legs outstretched.

'I think you will agree, gentlemen,' Cosimo went on, 'that we should fulfil our mission here with all haste.'

'The good Doge has placed guards at the end of the corridor,' Tommasini said.

'Quite naturally he is worried we may endanger those sealed up in the palace,' Cosimo replied.

'On the other hand . . .' said Niccoli.

Cosimo grinned. 'I think it wise to assume the Doge is curious at least about our mission. Why else would he risk exempting us from quarantine? Anyway, a messenger arrived a few minutes ago. It appears our contact, Luigi, is alive and well and awaiting me.'

'Awaiting you?'

'He insists I meet him alone.'

'But Cosimo . . .' Niccoli exclaimed.

'I appreciate your concern, Niccolò, but there can be no compromise. If I do not comply with Luigi's terms, he will not lead us to the rest of the map. Without that, we will have wasted our time and risked our lives for nothing. Now listen, it should be a simple enough task. Ambrogio, I know you've only been here a short while, but I imagine after the meeting with Valiani you made it your business to find out where I Cinque Canali might be.'

Tommasini nodded. 'I can draw you a map.'

'Good man. Niccolò, you must distract the guards so I can slip out of the palace. Allow me precisely two hours to join you at a predesignated meeting point. You'll need to find us a suitable vessel and crew to set sail for Ragusa before dawn. It is a short sea voyage, but an extremely hazardous one. If I do not meet you by the end of the third hour of the night, you must retrace my steps as best you can.'

'I'll be coming to Ragusa too,' Tommasini said, surprising the other two.

'But, you have no reason . . .'

'Cosimo, I'm as curious as you are. Besides, I want to get out of this godforsaken place.'

Cosimo nodded. 'Of course.'

Tightening a scarf soaked in juniper across his mouth and nose, Cosimo emerged into the night. He was wearing a long plain cloak over a tunic, breeches and stout leather boots. Under his cloak he carried a one-handed arming sword. He took a swig from a small china bottle Ambrogio had pressed into his palm as he left his room. 'It's *Triaca*,' the scholar had told him. 'Amber and oriental spices. It may provide some small defence against the pestilence.'

The open space of San Marco was too exposed even in the relative darkness of a moonless night, so Cosimo crept along a narrow lane that brought him to the northern edge of the square. I Cinque Canali was close to Campo St Luca equidistant from San Marco and the Grand Canal and he made his way slowly along a path running beside a ribbon of grey water.

The buildings were blacked out and gave the impression that all human life had seeped out from them. In many cases it had. A number of houses carried on their doors a roughly painted white cross, and boards had been nailed across these doors sealing the buildings, imprisoning those inside to fester and die.

The lane opened on to a small square in the middle of which stood a brazier. Logs burned orange and pink with incense, filling the air with a pungent aroma and casting a mournful hue along the dark walls of the surrounding buildings. Cosimo heard a sound behind him. Startled, he spun round in time to see a phantasmagorial figure emerge from the lane he had just left. It was a tall man in a gown that reached the floor. He was wearing a white mask that covered his entire face. The nose of the mask was huge and modelled as a beak, curved downward. On his head was a black hat with flaps at the sides and back. His hands were gloved and he was carrying a large black leather bag. He was a plague doctor, a rare breed of men who had been forced to stay by order of the Doge to treat the sick. The man rushed past Cosimo in silence and plunged into a corridor at the southern end of the square.

Ambrogio had instructed Cosimo to take the northern exit from the campo. He walked quickly, keeping to the shadows. He was breathing fast, and the scarf around his face was prickly with sweat. Eventually, he stopped before a tall, narrow building, the stone of its façade streaked with stains, the upper windows shuttered tight. Over the door was a sign bearing the legend I Cinque Canali.

As Cosimo approached he could hear strains of music and the sound of human voices. Pushing on the door, he found himself in a long narrow room. A small counter stood at the far end. On it was a row of candles in metal trays, which offered a dim, creamy light. Two men stood at the counter drinking, a third sat in the corner playing a lute. They turned to the stranger as he entered, their expressions wary.

Cosimo was about to speak when a dishevelled figure appeared from behind the counter.

'You'll be looking for me.' The light from the candles threw jagged white patches across his face. He was a tiny man with straggly, white hair, no more than four feet tall, dressed in what appeared to be rags and leaning on a knotty wooden staff. Cosimo was startled to see that his eyes were mere white discs.

'You seem surprised,' Luigi chuckled. 'I can tell from the movement of your body, the sound of your feet moving slightly on the floor.' He gazed sightlessly at Cosimo's leather boots.

'You know the man who gave me your name?'

'I have known Francesco for many years,' Luigi replied. 'We have journeyed many miles together. I was not always blind.' The old man laughed, his face wrinkled like a decaying apple, his toothless mouth, dark red.

Cosimo rubbed his brow. 'My apologies,' he said. 'Our mutual friend told me you could help me.'

'And indeed I can,' Luigi replied, and walked straight past Cosimo to the door of the inn. 'Well, come along then.'

For a blind man, Luigi moved with surprising speed and agility. He trotted along the passageways and across squares with the confidence of a sighted man in broad daylight. He seemed to have some sixth sense, or was it that having lost completely the use of one sense, the others were heightened?

Cosimo struggled to keep up. They passed along darkened alleyways, the houses pressing in on either side, all as silent as the grave. Suddenly, in the distance, came a long scream, a sound that seemed to emanate from the very caverns of hell.

Luigi turned to him without slowing his pace. 'We are all dying, one by one,' he said.

They crossed over a narrow wooden bridge and plunged into a small campo. This too was lit by a brazier. The logs were burning low, giving off a hazy glow and smelling of beech and lemon. Hundreds of mosquitoes and moths buzzed around the dying flames. Directly ahead of them stood a chapel.

'The thing you seek is inside this building.' Luigi intoned. 'Come.'

He turned a heavy iron ring in the door and pulled. They slipped through the opening and the door slammed shut behind them. The interior of the chapel was awash with light from hundreds of candles placed randomly in holders about the nave and perched on shallow dishes and in stone alcoves. Luigi paced slowly down the aisle and Cosimo followed, the sound of his boots echoing around the walls. Directly ahead an ornate screen depicted the crucifixion. It was new and vivid. The blood dripping from Christ's palms looked almost real.

They heard a slight movement from behind the screen and a priest emerged. He was a tall, emaciated man, his clerical robes almost comically oversized for his narrow frame. His face was drawn, his eyes very tired.

'My Lord, Cosimo de' Medici,' the priest said and

bowed awkwardly. 'I am Father Enrico. Our mutual friend Francesco Valiani has left instructions.' He ignored Luigi altogether. 'If you would follow me.'

'I too have my instructions, priest,' Luigi declared.

'That was not . . .'

'I shall accompany Lord Cosimo.'

'There's really no need . . .' Cosimo began.

'I shall accompany you, Lord Cosimo,' Luigi repeated and he placed a firm hand on the nobleman's arm.

The priest hesitated for a moment, but, before he could reply, Luigi gave him a toothless smile. 'Then we are agreed.'

Father Enrico led the way through a door to one side of the nave and down a narrow staircase barely wider than a man's shoulders. At the bottom, the priest unlocked a heavy wooden door and Cosimo and Luigi followed him through. They stood in a long passageway lit by a single oil lamp suspended from the ceiling. The place smelt of damp and dead earth.

'This passageway leads to the original chapel,' the priest said. 'It was one of the first buildings constructed in Venice a thousand years ago and consecrated by the great Church Father, Bishop Athenasius himself. The present chapel was built on top of it. My associates and I use this place for special services.'

It was a small chamber. The roof, a series of stone canopies, was supported by four thick pillars. An intricate mosaic about a metre wide stretched the length of the room. Light came from a score of candles placed in stone alcoves around the perimeter of the room.

'It's beautiful,' Cosimo said.

The priest looked into his eyes. 'I'm glad you appreciate this simple wonder, my Lord. Now, your eye is of course drawn to the mosaic floor, a fifth century depiction of the nativity story. But it contains unexpected secrets. Master Valiani gave you a key, did he not?'

Cosimo reached into his tunic.

'Ah,' exclaimed Father Enrico, and he walked to a particular spot on the floor. 'The craftsmen of the fifth century were masters of their trade. This mosaic is not only a beautiful decoration, it also acts as a repository for artefacts owned by my Order. We are Arians, an outlawed Christian sect. Master Valiani is a senior member of the order. He has left the thing you seek here.' And he pointed down. 'May I have the key?'

Cosimo handed it to him. Father Enrico placed the golden key into a tiny hole in the eye of a figure standing in a group around the holy crib. Turning the key lines appeared around the edges of the mosaic where not a trace had been visible before. Cosimo crouched down and helped the priest lay the slab carefully to one side.

Inside the hole was a plain square wooden box. Cosimo reached in and lifted it out. It was surprisingly light. Placing it on the floor, he opened the lid. Inside lay a bleached bone.

'What is it?' Luigi asked. 'Let me feel.' He touched the bone gently, running his fingers along its length. 'Francesco Valiani told me of this. It is part of the ulna of St Benedict. He purchased it on his journey home from the East.'

'It is not what I expected.' Cosimo turned the object over in his hands. It was then that he noticed an opening at one end of the bone, and strode over to the nearest alcove where the light was strongest. Poking a finger into the opening, he felt something pressed up against the grainy interior of the bone. With great care, he worked it free.

It was the missing piece of Valiani's map, a disc of parchment a few centimetres in diameter. He could just discern some text and tiny illustrations in faded ink. Cosimo allowed himself a small smile. 'Thank the Lord,' he whispered.

There was a slithering sound from the entrance

and he turned swiftly. But Luigi was there before him. 'Get back, Cosimo!' he shouted.

Two men ran into the room. They were dressed in simple hooded robes tied at the waist with rope. In the half-light, their faces were invisible. Each held a sword.

Luigi had forced Cosimo back against the wall and was shielding him with his own body, drawing a short sword from inside his greasy cloak. Father Enrico stepped carefully to one side. He looked completely calm.

'Take another step and you die,' Luigi hissed.

One of the hooded figures gave an amused sigh.

With amazing agility, Luigi leapt forward sweeping his sword upwards. It caught the arm of one of the attackers and sliced into flesh. The man staggered back, his hood slipping down revealing a young handsome face wreathed in dark curls. Luigi struck a second time, cutting nothing but air.

Cosimo drew his own sword and, as he stepped forward, he noticed the priest creep towards the door and slide into the passageway beyond.

Luigi was swinging his sword in a great arc in front of him and Cosimo made a lunge at the second hooded assailant. As he did so, the injured man thrust his sword deep into Luigi's chest. The old man fell back, his weapon clanging on the stone floor. With calculated ferocity, the hooded man plunged in his blade a second time, and with a choking sigh, Luigi lay still.

Enraged, Cosimo went on the attack. There was a clash of steel on steel. The two men retreated, but only for a moment. Fanning out, they came at Cosimo from front and rear. Out of the corner of his eye he caught a glimpse of a hooded figure in white who had appeared at the door to the chamber. And then he just managed to block a wild slash at his head. One of Cosimo's assailants turned to face the new arrival while the other launched another attack on Cosimo. There came the unmistakable sound of steel slicing through flesh, and the man who had killed Luigi screamed, dropped his sword and grabbed at his stomach, blood pouring through his trembling fingers.

As he fell, he collided with his companion. It gave Cosimo a crucial advantage, and he lunged forward. But even off balance, his adversary was agile and determined. He avoided Cosimo's thrust and counter-attacked.

Cosimo felt a burning pain in his shoulder. Stumbling back, he collided with a stone pillar. His attacker's face was suddenly visible under the hood; a long nose, a beard and bright black eyes. Then Cosimo saw the tip of a sword appear through the man's robe. It kept coming, smeared in red. The man looked down in shock at the metal protruding from his chest. He fell forward. Cosimo had no time to step aside and the hilt of the man's sword crashed down on his head.

Chapter 17

Mid-Atlantic, present day

The Gulfstream G500 broke through the cloud line and soared into the open expanse of blue sky. The view was like a winter scene snow globe just before it is shaken. Luc Fournier placed a glass of chilled Cristal on the armrest of his massive leather chair and began to mull over a recent rare failure. Two days earlier he had been on the verge of securing a large consignment of nuclear reactor parts for some Iranian friends when the operation had been blown wide open by MI5, who had seized the shipment in international waters. The cargo hold had contained more than ten million pounds worth of specialist equipment, equipment he had paid for. Naturally, nothing led back to him or his organisation, but such mishaps were potentially damaging to his reputation, and his reputation was his most valuable asset.

Fournier's mobile beeped to indicate a text had

arrived on his private number, one known to very few individuals. He picked up the phone and read the message: SKY NEWS. SOMETHING U SHOULD C. He clicked a remote and a wide screen lit up. He increased the volume.

'First reports indicate that the cell was a crucial link in a massive operation. Anti-terrorist officers believe the total haul is more than two kilograms of the deadly biochemical agent. It remains unclear tonight exactly how the material was to be used. Theories abound, but it will probably be some time before an accurate assessment can determine how this weapon could have been deployed or indeed who the likely targets might have been. One thing is certain though. Coming as it does just two days after MI5 cracked a similar cell dealing in nuclear technology, the police and the security services are claiming a second important victory in the intelligence war against terror. This is Victoria Manley in London . . .'

Fournier stabbed at the remote with barely suppressed fury then threw it across the aircraft, watching it rebound from the door and bounce along the carpeted floor.

Chapter 18

Venice, present day

Leaving Dino beside the prone form of the gunman, Edie and Jeff raced back to the canal. The launch was there and the new chauffeur was pulling Roberto's body out of the water and into the boat.

'Is he alive?' Edie yelled.

The driver didn't answer. Roberto lay on his back. His shirt was stained red, and Edie could see a gash in his left arm, blood pouring from it. His face was blue, his lips white. There was no sign of life.

Edie pumped his chest and breathed into his mouth. Still nothing. She pumped again, then clamped her mouth to his a second time. Suddenly Roberto's head jerked and water gushed out of his mouth, soaking Edie's dress. His eyes snapped open.

'Quick . . . the hospital,' Edie cried.

Jeff leapt back on to the path. The chauffeur ran to

the wheel, engaged the throttle and spun the launch in the water.

Watching the boat roar away, Jeff dashed towards the alley. He had almost reached it when a black shape loomed up out of the darkness and knocked him into the wall. The cloaked figure disappeared into a narrow covered pathway between two houses.

He could hear a low moaning coming from the alleyway. He sped across the cobblestones to find Dino slumped against a wall. His breath was coming in laboured gasps.

'Dino . . . you're hurt.'

His friend was clutching his abdomen, and his clothes were drenched in blood. 'Jeff,' he muttered.

Jeff scrambled for his mobile and dialled the emergency service. 'You saved our lives,' he said. Dino's eyes flickered open, and he smiled weakly.

'Medics will be here soon . . .'

Dino started to shake.

Jeff pulled off his jacket and laid it over Dino. 'Hang on. Please, just hang on.'

He leaned closer when he saw Dino pulling at a silver chain around his neck. 'Jeff, you must have this. You are my only friend.' The chain snapped. Dino shoved it into Jeff's hand and an oval silver locket fell open. Inside were two small photographs, one of a woman with jet black hair. The other picture was of a young girl with brown eyes. She was perhaps six or seven years old and smiling a gappy smile.

'Jeff, my friend. I don't need it. I'll be seeing my girls very soon, very . . .'

Jeff had no idea how long he sat there next to Dino's body. Then suddenly strong arms were lifting him roughly and someone was yelling in his ear. Two police officers forced his arms behind him and clamped handcuffs on his wrists. Jeff protested, but they ignored him. He was frogmarched to the canal where two police launches and an ambulance bobbed in the water. As he was led to the first of the launches he caught sight of a trolley being wheeled towards the ambulance.

The questions went on for two hours. What was he doing with the dead man? How did he know him? Where was the gun? Had he been working alone? What was his motive? But then, as he was about to be led away to a holding cell, he was released. A witness, a resident from an apartment in the tiny street in which Dino had died, had come forward. They had seen everything from the time Jeff and Edie had been cornered until the arrival of the police. The mysterious gunman had shot Dino at close range and then ran off just as Jeff was returning to the alley.

All through the interrogation Jeff had been worrying about Rose. There was no offer of police protection; the officers who had interviewed him still seemed convinced he was involved in some way, but they had nothing to hold him on. He had been allowed to make one call to Roberto's, but no one picked up. After that he had been forced to switch off his mobile. Leaving the station, he turned it back on and tried again. This time Vincent answered almost immediately and reassured him that Rose was safely asleep. His second call was for a water taxi, and ten minutes later he was speeding into the Grand Canal close to Ferrovia.

The Ospedale Civile, the main hospital serving the islands of the Rialto, looked like many of the other beautiful, well-preserved buildings crammed together with such elegance in the heart of Venice. Eight centuries earlier, in the days of Doge Renier Zeno, it had been built to house one of the six important confraternities in the city and was known as the Scuola Grande di San Marco. Through the central arch of a triptych flanked by *trompe l'œil* panels depicting scenes from the life of St Mark, the elders of the district had passed to and fro performing their civic duties. Close to a millennium later, water ambulances drew up alongside the building. Under the same archway, trolleys were wheeled through Perspex doors to enter Accident and Emergency. Once inside, the place looked much like any other Western hospital, and at one o'clock on a Sunday morning during Carnivale, when Jeff arrived there out of breath and feeling sick to the stomach, it was an utterly depressing place.

He found Edie sitting in an out-of-the-way corner of the waiting area close to a soft drinks machine. A modern metal-framed window covered with an aluminium blind separated her from the ancient campo beyond. They embraced and he could see she had been crying.

'He's still in theatre,' she said, as Jeff collapsed in the chair beside her.

'What did the doctors say?'

'Nothing.'

'Dino's dead.'

'Dino?'

'The man who saved our lives. He was a homeless person, a beggar. I'd known him for ages.'

'I'm sorry,' Edie said softly and grasped Jeff's hand.

A trolley slammed through the doors. Two paramedics in green overalls were trying to calm a man who was thrashing around, attempting to pull tubes from his arms and rip off an oxygen mask.

Jeff ran his fingers through his hair, took a deep breath and stared down at the floor feeling utterly wretched.

There was a quiet cough and he looked up.

'Signor Martin, Signorina Granger.' Aldo Candotti was staring at them, his hands clamped behind his back. 'I need to speak with you.'

He escorted them along the hall to a plain room with a table, a few uncomfortable chairs, bare walls in off-white, a striplight in the high ceiling, a concrete floor. Candotti gestured to Edie and Jeff to take seats.

'You understand I have a job to do and I need answers to some very perplexing questions. Signor Martin, Signora Granger, last time we met, in the room of the unfortunate Mario Sporani, I said I was concerned for you because people kept getting themselves killed when you were around. Now we have another corpse on our hands.'

Edie sighed. 'Deputy Prefect, do you not think we would like to help you? We were at a party at the Gritti Badoer. We had a few drinks and left together at about eleven o'clock. As we walked away, a gunman in carnival disguise chased us. Roberto was shot.'

'Yes, yes, I have spoken with the officers who picked up Signor Martin. Some crazed assassin chased you halfway across Venice. Then you were saved by a gallant beggar who just happens to be a friend of yours?'

'I've given a detailed statement,' said Jeff.

'And you have no clue who this gunman is?'

Jeff held Candotti's gaze. 'I have absolutely no idea.'

Candotti snorted.

'Deputy Prefect,' Edie said. 'Believe me when I say I feel like I've been sucked into some sort of nightmare during the past few days. Until last week I was leading a quiet life in Florence, doing my work. The biggest problem I faced was ensuring my infra-red spectrometer kept working and my titrations were accurate. Since then, my uncle has been murdered and I've had my life threatened, more than once.'

Candotti turned to Jeff. 'And you, Signor Martin. Was your life a model of normality also?'

He shrugged. 'I wasn't being shot at, if that's what you mean.'

Candotti stood up suddenly, his face contorted with anger and frustration. 'God alive!' he exclaimed. 'I've a good mind to sling the pair of you in a cell until you find something more interesting to tell me.'

'I'm sorry,' Jeff said. 'I wish we could help.'

Candotti took a deep breath and got to his feet.

'Very well. I cannot force information out of you, although there are times when I wish I could. But I feel I should remind both of you that you are guests in our country. Your position is, shall we say, delicate? You are withholding information pertinent to this investigation, and I want that information. I may not have offered you a carrot tonight; but believe me, next time, I'll be coming with a very, very big stick.'

After Candotti slammed the door behind him, Jeff and Edie returned to the chaos of the Accident and Emergency ward barely exchanging a word, each lost in thought. An hour ticked slowly past before a young doctor in a spotless lab coat strode over with a clipboard in his hand.

'You're Signor Armatovani's friends, yes?' He took a seat opposite them. 'He has been very fortunate. One bullet shattered his left humerus and lodged in his shoulder. It took some time to remove and there has been quite serious nerve damage. The second bullet passed right through him. By sheer luck it missed his spine and every vital organ. There was some internal tissue damage, but that has been patched up. We expect a complete recovery.'

'Can we see him?' Edie asked.

'He is still unconscious and we'll keep him that

way for at least eight hours to help the healing process. If I were you I'd go home, get some rest. Visiting hours start at midday. I'm sure your friend will be delighted to see you tomorrow afternoon.'

Outside, the campo was eerily quiet. Once more, fog had drifted in from the lagoon, shrouding everything in a gossamer veil. Jeff looked at his watch; it was 2.15 a.m. 'Come on, it's not far to my place.'

There were few street lights in this district. Edie shivered and Jeff put an arm around her shoulder, pulling her close.

They turned off the main thoroughfare into a narrow lane that led to a junction. Jeff kept glancing back around them. Ahead, they could see the faint shimmer of a narrow canal and a footbridge; lines of washing were strung out on each side of the passage-way. A scrambling sound from their left made them both jump. A scrawny tabby emerged from the foggy shadows, gave them a contemptuous glance and ran off.

'Shit!' Jeff exhaled heavily and laughed.

A few minutes later they reached the Ducal Palace. Here a few late-night revellers were wandering about and a small group of well-lubricated locals stood under the Torre dell' Orlogio arguing noisily. Jeff and Edie strode on through the walkway on the north side of San Marco, cutting down a narrow passageway that led to the apartment entrance.

After Jeff had let them in to his apartment, Edie threw herself on to one of the sofas and yawned. Jeff busied himself with coffee cups and the espresso machine.

'You know, I've been thinking . . .' Edie said. 'How could Bruno, who died in 1600, direct us to a clue about Vivaldi who was born over a century later?'

'Precisely, Watson,' Jeff said. Somehow, to focus on the mysterious trail of clues was a welcome distraction from the horrors of the evening. 'The only possibility is that Vivaldi, or someone associated with him, knew of the Bruno clue and changed it. Just as Bruno changed Contessina de' Medici's clue on San Michele.'

'But why?'

'Maybe he was a member of I Seguicamme.'

'It's possible, I guess,' Jeff replied. 'Roberto said the group fizzled out, when was it? The late eighteenth century?'

'And when did Vivaldi die?'

'Not sure exactly, 1740s, 1750s?'

'And he spent most of his life here in Venice, didn't he?' Edie continued.

'So you're suggesting some sort of lineage, that

I Seguicamme was a group protecting this Medici Secret that Mario Sporani referred to? That each generation of members felt they needed to improve the clues or make them more obscure?'

'Maybe. But whether or not Vivaldi was involved with I Seguicamme, someone linked with him must have cracked Bruno's clue.'

Jeff came over with the coffees and placed a cup on a low table beside the sofa. Edie lay stretched out, her head propped up on a cushion, gazing up at the ceiling. 'Thanks,' she muttered.

Cradling a cup in his hand Jeff walked over to the vast windows and gazed out at the near-empty piazza. The ornate fronts of the tearooms and the expensive chocolateries were blacked out. The campanile looked like some improbable rocket turned to stone. Running through the events of the evening, Jeff suddenly felt a spasm of anxiety in the pit of his stomach. They had all come so close, so very close . . . and Dino, poor Dino.

He looked over at Edie. She had fallen asleep on the sofa, her coffee untouched. He smiled to himself. He hadn't seen her like that since college days when she would regularly nod off on a friend's sofa even as the party continued around her. He fetched a quilt from the bedroom, laid it over her and kissed her gently on the forehead.

What was going on? It seemed so hard to get a handle on anything. First it seemed Contessina was the focus, then Bruno, and now Vivaldi. It was like a catalogue of the great and the good, a parade of historical notables. And there seemed to be no connection between any of them except this nebulous reference to a secret society, I Seguicamme, 'The Followers'. Could that be the tenuous link connecting a super-rich first lady, a half-crazed heretic and the composer of *The Four Seasons*?

Vivaldi; he had to focus on Vivaldi. Contessina de' Medici had led them to Giordano Bruno and Bruno had led them to Vivaldi. Vivaldi was the new key, and the clue he, or someone linked with him had left would lead to the next piece of the puzzle. But he knew nothing about Vivaldi.

He took a sip of his coffee, and at that moment a much better idea popped into his mind. 'Of course,' he said aloud. 'Of course.'

Chapter 19

Venice, May 1410

He was floating. Everything was perfect; he felt no pain. All fear had gone. But most of all, he experienced an overwhelming sense of relief. The pressure had lifted, and with it, all the expectations placed upon him. No one could touch him here in this paradise. No one could insist that he fight. Now there was nothing to fight for, because nothing mattered. He could live like this forever, just floating. It was like being a newborn baby again.

And then a face appeared. Was it his mother? She was standing over him. She was calling his name. He felt her soft hand on his cheek, stroking his face, brushing the hair from his eyes. 'Cosimo,' he heard her say. But then her voice grew faint and he was floating again, floating in the warm ocean of happiness he had quickly come to treasure.

*

Tommasini and Niccoli were seated in a small boat at the meeting point, Saint Silvestro on the Grand Canal at the edge of the San Polo district. The night was still and silent. They could see in the distance the lights of the huge houses on the edge of the canal.

Niccolò Niccoli was the first to notice the woman. Wrapped in a long grey shawl that covered her head she was carrying a lantern that threw little light.

'You are Niccolò Niccoli,' she said matter-of-factly.

He nodded.

'I have an urgent message.'

'From whom?'

'That I cannot reveal. The message is this: your friend Cosimo has the thing you seek, but he is hurt. He is in good hands. A ship awaits you.' And she glanced at the other man in the boat.

'Cosimo's hurt?' Niccoli asked.

'Not seriously.'

Niccoli felt relief flood through him. 'Who are you?'

'I am Caterina Galbaoi. You must let me bring you to the one who sent me. There is no time to waste.'

Ambrogio joined them on the pathway. 'This could be a trap Niccolò,' he said, keeping an eye on the woman.

'It is no trap,' she responded, calmly. 'Blood has been spilled tonight. By dawn your friend Cosimo will be wanted for murder. You will all be arrested and tried as accessories. The Doge is a man besieged, and he is cunning. You will have no hope of survival, and all that Master Valiani has done for you will be for nothing.'

'Valiani?'

'Master Valiani is my uncle.'

In a flash, Niccoli drew his sword and had the tip of the blade at the woman's throat. 'Prove it,' he hissed.

The woman took a deep breath and drew her hand from under her shawl. She was wearing a silver band topped with a large rectangular garnet.

Sheathing his sword, Niccoli bowed low. 'Please accept my humble apologies, signora.'

The boat approached the island of Giudecca across the broad canal to the south of the main islands of the Republic. The two men rowed while Caterina guided them through a waterway running south from the Grand Canal into the open waters of the lagoon. The water was glassy still and pitch black, but out here away from the confines of the sick city, the air seemed fresher.

Behind the surrounding wall stood some of the

grandest palaces in Venice, each nestled in lush grounds, home to many of the noblest families in Italy. These people were rarely seen by most Venetians. With the first news of plague they had disappeared completely, believing they would be safe here.

It was very dark, but, as they passed a promontory, lights glimmered ahead and gradually a ship's mast emerged from the gloom. Drawing closer, they began to make out the shape of the hull. It was a caravel of around fifty tons. Two triangular sails were unfurled, limp in the oppressive stillness.

Behind them a large bireme approached, propelled through the water by a score of oarsmen. Two archers stood aft with crossbows raised to eye level. They wore the livery of the Venetian Navy, emblazoned with the lion of St Mark, gold on red.

'Hell!' Niccoli exclaimed, as a bolt slapped the water beside them.

The gap between the two boats was narrowing quickly. A flurry of bolts ripped through the air. One hit the side of the boat, the rest flew low over their heads. Then half a dozen arrows whistled past, falling ten metres from the bireme. Their pursuers were under fire from the caravel.

A second volley rained down across the water and an archer at the bow of the pursuers' boat screamed and fell forward into the cold lagoon. A third, larger shower of arrows was fired, and several more bolts shot back from the bireme. There were more screams as arrows found flesh.

With a final desperate effort, the Florentines drew in alongside the caravel. Niccoli lifted Caterina on to the rope ladder dangling from the side of the ship, and, as a hail of bolts hit the side of the ship and bounced off the hull, she pulled herself aboard. Tommasini climbed up the ladder as fast as he could. A bolt missed him by a hand's width. Before the last of the companions was aboard, the anchor was hauled up and the caravel began to move.

'A lucky escape, my friends.'

Niccoli was the first to reach Cosimo. 'The young woman said you were injured.'

'A mild concussion, nothing more.'

Niccoli noticed a nasty gash on Cosimo's forehead. He had a black eye; the sleeve of his tunic had been cut away and there was a large bandage about his arm.

'A little more than that, by the look of you,' said Niccoli and he pulled Cosimo's head back gently. 'But it appears you've been well tended to.'

Cosimo slapped his hand on his friend's back.

'So what in God's name is going on?' asked

Tommasini. His blond locks were plastered to his face with sea spray and his cheeks were still ruddy with the exertion of their narrow escape.

'I know little more than you,' Cosimo began. He told them the bare bones of what had happened from the time he left the Ducal Palace until he had came to aboard the ship little more than half an hour earlier. 'Before you ask, I have absolutely no idea who my saviour was. But I know I owe him my . . .'

He trailed off as he saw the expressions change on the faces of his friends. They were staring past him. He turned round to see Caterina. Close behind her stood a figure dressed in white, holding a lantern at shoulder height.

'I think you mean you owe *her* your life, Lord Cosimo,' Caterina said.

They watched as the figure in white pulled back the hood. Long black locks tumbled over white cloth.

Cosimo crossed the deck in three strides. 'Contessina!' he cried. 'My darling, Contessina . . .' Then he stopped. 'I don't know whether to pinch myself or to seek a medic. Am I imagining things? The blow to my head, perhaps?'

'My love,' Contessina said. 'I am not imaginary.'

The blood had drained from Cosimo's face. 'Gentlemen, if you will excuse us, I think my lady and I need to talk.'

They sat in the captain's quarters, a narrow hutch of a room containing nothing more than a map table, a slender bunk and an uncomfortable oak bench.

'You killed two men tonight,' Cosimo said.

'Three. I could not let the priest go.'

'The Contessina I left in Florence less than two weeks ago could not have killed a fly.'

'Cosi, I'm sorry I was not honest with you.'

'I don't know who you are anymore.'

'I'm still the same woman, your betrothed, the woman you claim to love.'

'Contessina . . .'

She leaned forward and placed a finger on his lips. 'Let me tell you the whole story, my love. You know that Master Valiani was Niccolò's teacher. Well he also taught my elder brother, Marco. One day, I was in the library when Marco was having a lesson. Valiani had asked my brother a question about mathematics and he did not know the answer. Valiani tried another. Marco could not answer this one either. It was hopeless.

'Eventually, Valiani grew quite agitated. I was worried my brother might be in for a beating. Then suddenly, Valiani snapped his head towards me and said: "You are a fool boy. Even your little sister could answer these questions."

'I don't know what came over me. Perhaps I was

254

scared for my brother, or maybe for myself. I just blurted out . . . six and four. Suddenly Valiani broke into a smile. "Very good," he said. "Let's try another." I must have given the correct response because he smiled again.

'The master was fascinated by me. He sent my brother away with some homework and quizzed me further. You see, Valiani is many things. He is a Humanist, of course, but he is also an elder in the heretical sect known as the Arians. They reject the concept of the Holy Trinity. As a consequence, they are anathema to Rome. Valiani is also a master of many Eastern Arts unknown in Italy, a champion swordsman and a man steeped in arcane knowledge. He became my teacher and my guide. He was always gentle, always kind, but I knew I was little more than a specimen for study. He schooled me in Latin and Greek, in mathematics, philosophy and history. He trained me with the sword and the bow. I was taught to ride and to sail.

'It was our secret, and, as I say, I was little more than an experimental subject for the Master. Then, perhaps five years ago, he told me that he was about to embark on what would almost certainly be his final voyage. He had never married and had no heir. He joked that if only I had been born a boy everything would be so much easier. And he pleaded with me never to let my talents go to waste, because he believed that one day something would happen to change things and I would be important to him, important to the Humanist cause, important to the world of learning.

'Two weeks ago, Valiani appeared in my life again. He told me of his discoveries and the secret of the map. He explained how he intended offering you and your friends the opportunity to seek out the treasures of Golem Korab, but he also wanted me to be what he called "his insurance".

'No Cosi, don't get me wrong,' Contessina said quickly, and touched Cosimo's hand. 'It is not that Master Valiani did not trust you or have faith in your abilities, but he was convinced that two heads are always better than one. He knew he could not tell you about me, and he also knew the time was not right for me to tell you this tale, not then, not in Florence.'

'But . . .?'

'Cosi, I just want you to understand this. I was not sent to interfere in any way. The master knew there would be many dangers for you along the way. He knew that some hint of what you were seeking would find its way to the avaricious and the villainous. He had heard rumours of plague and war; and, thanks to the brave and noble Luigi, he was also suspicious of Father Enrico. But he only learned of all this recently and from Florence he could do nothing about changing the hiding place for the map fragment.'

'And what of your family, Contessina? You could not have simply walked out of the house.'

'Valiani smoothed that over for me. My parents believe I am staying with my brother's family in Padua.'

'You deceived them?'

'We are both capable of that, Cosimo.'

'And how did you get to Venice?'

'I travelled with Valiani to Ravenna. This vessel, *La Bella Gisela*, is owned by a wealthy Genoese trader, another former pupil of Valiani's and a fellow Arian. She is making for Ragusa with a cargo of fine fabrics, alum and salt.'

'How did you know I would be attacked?'

'I had no idea, but Master Valiani knows the Doge to be a devious and calculating man. Your assailants were from Steno's personal guard. The priest was also in the pay of the Doge.'

There was an icy silence between them.

'It seems,' he said at length, 'that I have been played for a fool. By everyone.'

For the next two days Cosimo remained alone in his cabin. This was the way he dealt with problems. He cut himself off and kept his own counsel. His friends knew not to interfere. Ambrogio had other worries; he had spent the whole voyage laid out on the deck with a bucket between his knees. Niccolò was an experienced seafarer whose family had been keen mariners, so, much to Ambrogio's chagrin, he felt entirely at home aboard ship.

Contessina had never seen Cosimo turn in upon himself like this. It upset her, although she could understand how he felt. He had come to believe that somehow she had betrayed him, that she had been wearing a mask more deceitful than any Venetian carnival disguise, that he had been tricked into loving someone different.

La Bella Gisela was hugging the Dalmatian coast. It was a large but fast ship, and with the cooperation of the captain, Cosimo monitored its course as they travelled south. This was a region under Venetian sovereignty, territory held against the Turk. Crossing the Bay of Venice some twenty nautical miles west of Trieste, they approached St Bartolomeo north of the Savudrija peninsula. From the south of Istria, where the peninsula ended suddenly, they skirted the islands of Kvarnerić lying to the west of the mainland. Here, many inlets and sheltered coves offered safe havens for ruthless pirates, rival groups who had long ago staked out the waters from Trieste to Split.

It was during the early morning that Cosimo was awakened from a deep sleep by the vessel pitching and rolling. An hourglass he had left loose on the small work table in the corner flew across the room just missing his head. Scrambling from his bunk, he lost his balance and fell against the table, crashing on to his back.

The deck was awash and the crew were struggling desperately to batten everything down. Cosimo made his way slowly to the bridge where the captain was fighting a losing battle to keep control of the helm. The wind was howling, the sails looked fit to burst. Cosimo could only stand upright by clinging on to ropes strung out along the port quarter.

Another wave hurled the ship upward like so much driftwood. As the wall of ocean rolled on, water poured down on the ship, thudding against the sails and crashing on to the deck.

A scream came from the bow. Cosimo caught a glimpse of one of the crew being swept overboard. A huge wave made the ship yaw wildly, flinging him across the deck. There was nothing to hold on to. His eyes were smarting with salt water and he could barely focus on the world around him. Something crashed into his head and another spasm of pain ripped through him. Blood poured into his eyes.

Clawing desperately at the air, he caught hold of a loose rope.

All he could see was red. Then he heard a dreadful cracking sound. The main mast smashed on to the deck, crushing two sailors beneath it.

He tried to pull himself along the deck but he could not keep a grip on the rope. He gasped for air as he was hit by another cascade of water. The captain had disappeared and the helm had been smashed to pieces. Cosimo could hear a woman screaming above the roar of the elements. Contessina was clinging to the aft bulwark, her arms wrapped around a vertical strut.

He clawed his way towards her. She saw him and screamed his name. With reserves of strength he didn't know he possessed, he hauled himself forward. Moments later, he had reached her side. She was utterly exhausted and could barely speak. Blood ran freely from a cut above her hairline.

A roar came from the front of the ship and *La Bella Gisela* found herself perched at the summit of a mountain of water. The black raging ocean crashed down all around, a great primordial torrent, swallowing everything. Contessina gripped him so tightly it felt like they were merging, becoming one.

'So this is it,' Cosimo thought. 'This is what dying is like.'

He felt so small, so insignificant, so irrelevant, a dot, a pinprick, nothing. And as the ship tumbled back, somersaulting like a toy boat in an infinity of water, he felt a strange sense of relief. It would soon be over.

Chapter 20

Venice, present day

Situated on a narrow alleyway off Via XXII Marzo, Giovanni Tafani's office was only a short walk from Jeff's apartment. Behind the dull concrete façade, Edie and Jeff found themselves transported back three centuries to baroque elegance and classic Venetian grandeur.

Jeff had been very reluctant to let Rose out of his sight, but she was violently opposed to the idea of tagging along to listen to them ramble on, as she put it, to some boring old man about a long-dead composer. And she was more than happy to go along with Maria who had suggested she take Rose with her to visit her family in Mestre where her younger brother had a smallholding.

Tafani met Jeff and Edie at reception and led the way to his large office on the first floor. His eyes, covered the night before by a delicate gold mask, were weary.

'I'm afraid your call this morning caught me by surprise,' he said showing them to a pair of leather armchairs in front of his impressive oak desk. 'You'll have to take me as you find me, a little worse for wear! So how may I help you?'

'We'd like to pick your brains,' Edie said lightly. 'Roberto tells us you're the greatest authority on Vivaldi.'

'Did he now? Well, that is a wonderful compliment. How is the maestro?'

'A little worse for wear too,' Jeff answered and glanced quickly at Edie. 'We were wondering if you could tell us if Vivaldi had any esoteric interests. Was he interested in any way in the occult?'

'He was certainly a rather odd character,' Tafani replied quickly. 'He was known as *Il Prete Rosso*, "the Red Priest", because of his flaming red hair, and he had an on-off relationship with the authorities at the Pio Ospedale della Pietà where he was Master of Violin.'

'Pio Ospedale della Pietà? What's that?' Edie asked.

'The Devout Hospital of the Mercy. There were four of them in Venice in the late seventeenth century. Their purpose was to give shelter and education to abandoned or orphaned children; quite enlightened for the time. Vivaldi was responsible for teaching music and he was commissioned to write concerti for the orphans to perform in public.'

'So tell us more about his uneasy relationship with the authorities.'

'He was a practising priest for only a few months. There were ugly rumours that he seduced teenage girls in the orphanage, that he dabbled in unsavoury sexual and occult practices, but there's absolutely no evidence for it. I'm fed up with so-called revisionist history. It seems none of our heroes is immune, as though modern society needs to bring down the masters to make us feel better about our own lack of morals. I think it says more about our own age than it does about the great men and women who are responsible for our cultural heritage.'

'I take your point,' Edie gave Tafani a reassuring smile.

'Did Vivaldi stay in Venice his entire life?' Jeff asked.

'No, no, he did travel a bit. In fact, when he was young he was sacked from the orphanage. But they had him back after a year.'

'What did he do during that year?'

'He taught the children of a noble family in Padua. The Niccoli family, I believe.'

'The Niccoli family of Florence?' Edie exclaimed.

'Um, yes. I think they did originate from there. But they had been in Padua for at least two centuries by Vivaldi's time. Why?'

'You don't have any information about the year Vivaldi spent there do you?' she asked.

'You might be in luck.' Tafani was beginning to respond to Edie's rising excitement. 'Vivaldi left a very complex will. He died far from home, in Vienna. He'd applied for a job at the Imperial Court, but the Emperor, Charles VI died soon after he arrived and the composer was stranded, penniless and without a patron. A few weeks later, he was dead. Some of his papers remained in Vienna. Others went to relatives in various parts of Italy, and some ended up with his closest friends here in Venice. There is a rather well-known set of documents, the so-called "Confessional", which Vivaldi gave to his closest friend, the painter Gabriel Fabacci.'

'What's "the Confessional"?'

'Come, I'll show you,' Tafani stood up.

'You have it here?' Edie was incredulous.

Tafani smiled. 'Not exactly. But we have a computer archive with almost everything linked to Vivaldi that's ever been written.'

He led them from the room along a galleried passage. A few moments later, they found themselves in a library, with two rows of computers in the middle of the room.

They pulled up chairs and Tafani clicked a mouse as he talked. 'What I am about to share with you is a particularly fascinating document. Vivaldi contracted scarlet fever in Vienna, and was in a delirious state for several days before he finally succumbed. Most scholars believe he wrote this testament on his deathbed, that most of it is fantasy and delusion from a genuine man of God who was fearful for his mortal soul.'

The words: *La Confessione* appeared on the screen. 'It's quite long, but fortunately we have it in several languages. We get a fair number of foreign scholars visiting Venice solely to access our database.'

Tafani found the English version and opened the file. Standing up, he said, 'I'll leave you to peruse this. I hope I've been of some help. Come and see me before you leave.'

Before them on the screen was a document called 'The Taking and the Returning'. They began to read.

I am dying. What I say now is the absolute truth as I see it, a truth I wish to impart before I meet my Lord God, the Almighty Saviour of All Men.

My confession begins with my father,

Giovanni Battista. When I was a boy, he was working for an architect commissioned to remodel an old house on Calle della Morte. An odd feature of the house was a metal column that ran the entire height of the building from the foundations to the roof. To this day no one knows why it was put there. My father was a labourer working in the basement of the house. One day he came across a stout metal box lying just beneath a hemispherical compartment at the base of the metal column. He secreted away the box, and when he was alone later he managed to force open the lock.

I think he was a little disappointed because the box did not contain gold or jewels. Instead, he found the fragment of a letter. It was written on very old parchment and much of it was crumbling. It had been composed in Latin, a language completely alien to him.

My father died a few years later and I inherited both the box and the letter. But it was not until 1709 in my thirty-second year that I took any notice of the heirloom. It had lain forgotten for many years. One day, I was emptying a cupboard to make room for some new manuscripts and scores when I found it.

It was a fragment of a letter written by none

other than Contessina de' Medici, the wife of Cosimo the Elder. It was addressed to a man named Niccolò Niccoli. Tragically, much of the original has been lost but what remains I offer here.

The Thirteenth Day of June, Year of Our Lord 1470.

My Noble Niccolò,

It is now almost six full years since the passing of my beloved Cosimo and you and I are growing very old. It will soon be time for me to fulfil the promises we once made and to complete the task begun so many years ago . . .

. . . Don't misunderstand me my dear friend, I admire your industry and believe the account you wrote over half a century ago is of the highest order of scholarship and literary skill. However, I am fearful. I have no need to remind you of the delicacy of the matter. No one must know the truth of our great discovery – at least not in our own time. I trust your integrity and know you will be cautious, you would never let your

narrative fall into the wrong hands, but I do not have such trust in others, and sadly, we are near the end of our days . . .

. . . I plan to visit the map-makers very soon and through them I shall hide the treasure . . . I have the vial with me here as I write in readiness for hiding from sight what happened in Golem Korab . . .

. . . Would you allow me to place your writings with the treasure? . . . for safe keeping? Here, for you alone is the clue:

. . . With the map-makers . . . the Divine cloth . . .

The iron cross . . . at the dead centre . . .

Your friend,
. . . Contes . . .

I was immediately captivated and mystified. It was particularly frustrating that the last section had been damaged and that parts of the clue had been lost. Needless to say, I felt compelled to learn more.

It so happened that a few weeks later I was summarily removed from my position as Master of the Violin at the Pio Ospedale della Pietà. It appears I was not liked by some of the older administrators. Fortunately, I had a small inheritance from my father and I had managed to save a little money of my own. I spent some time tracing the Niccoli family, who, it turned out, were of the most noble and ancient blood. Niccolò Niccoli's direct male descendant now lived in Palazzo Moritti, a large estate close to Padua. Persuading the head of the Pio Ospedale della Pietà to write a letter of introduction for me, within a week of losing my position in Venice, I found employment as a music teacher to the youngest generation of the Niccolis.

At the Palazzo Moritti I had plenty of leisure time. I taught for just two hours a day. The rest of the time I spent in contemplation and musical composition. But I was there for one particular purpose: to learn as much as I could about the connection between the Medici and Niccoli families and to fill in the spaces in the narrative written by Contessina. What was the nature of her journey? And what was the reason for their obsessive secrecy?

I found answers in the grand library, a

monument to the recently deceased head of the family, Michelangelo Niccoli who had been an avid collector of arcane literature and the family archivist.

The crucial text was contained in three volumes of journals written by Niccolò Niccoli. I cannot divulge their contents, for they speak of the most terrible things. I read every word the man wrote. I was so captivated by his story that I was almost caught in the library, which was a strictly private place for the family. Indeed, I was so fascinated, I stole the three volumes, handed in my notice as soon as I could, and returned to Venice.

For the next six months, all my spare time was taken up in copying the journals of Niccolò Niccoli. I did have every intention of returning the originals to the family. When I was finished with the transcription, I sent the books anonymously to the Palazzo Moritti via a discreet intermediary.

I was slowed in this quest to unlock the secrets of the Medici because much of the later part of the journal was written using some form of encryption which took me years to unravel.

Now I can at least feel some sense of pride that I had the strength of will to stop. I have come to the end of my life, and I entrust the letter and the copies of the journals to my closest friend, Gabriel Fabacci. I would take them and destroy them myself but I feel unable to even look upon these documents again. I shall advise my friend to destroy the collection, or to perhaps send them to those who have the most right to them, the Niccoli family.

May the Lord have mercy upon me.
Antonio Vivaldi.
26 July 1741, Vienna.

Jeff pushed his chair back. 'So, this fragment of Contessina's is the "venerable document" Bruno referred to. In his own account he said he had a clue, but had found nothing. His servant, Albertus, must have placed the letter fragment in the Gritti Badoer where it was found almost a century later by Vivaldi's father.'

'So now we obviously have to get our hands on the journals of Niccolò Niccoli.'

Jeff was about to reply when his mobile rang.

'Dad, it's Rose.'

'Hi honey.'

'Just got a call from the hospital, Roberto's awake and wants to see you.'

'So you've actually read the transcription? That's incredible.' Tubes emerged from each of Roberto's arms, a pulse oxymeter was placed on a stand beside the bed next to a bleeping heart monitor. His face was bruised, a line of steri-strips held together a gash on his forehead, and his upper lip was split. He was clearly in a great deal of pain, but trying not to let it show. 'Any news of the gunman?'

'Candotti seems to have as little to go on as he had after Sporani's death.'

'No doubt he'll be around here to question me as soon as the doctors give him the all-clear.'

'Get the gorilla at the door to stop him.' Jeff and Edie had almost not made it into Roberto's private room thanks to the vigilance of his personal guard, a three-hundred-pounder in a black suit.

Roberto grimaced as he laughed. 'Oh Lou's a pussycat when you get to know him.'

'Not sure I want to,' Jeff replied rubbing his arm where it had been grabbed as he had made to enter the room a few minutes earlier.

'Tafani was helpful though,' Edie said. 'But we've drawn a complete blank with the Gritti Badoer clue.'

'Don't worry about that; it's my job. Do you have it, by the way?'

Jeff handed Roberto the notepaper from the hotel.

'Thanks. You need to follow the Vivaldi lead. Get to Padua as soon as you can.'

'Easier said than done.'

'Nonsense. Just call the Niccoli family.'

'Oh, of course . . . easy,' Jeff began sarcastically, and stopped. 'Hang on! Don't tell me: you know them.'

'Well, as a matter of fact . . .'

Edie laughed and leaned forward to caress Roberto's cheek with the palm of her hand. 'You're priceless.'

'Why, thank you . . .'

There was a gentle rap on the door and Aldo Candotti entered.

Roberto did his best to smile. 'We were just talking about you, Deputy Prefect.'

Jeff walked towards the door and Edie gave Roberto a kiss on the cheek.

'And Jeff,' Roberto called, his face grave. 'Take Rose with you.'

The Palazzo Moritti was once part of a vast country estate situated some three miles from the centre of Padua. Over the centuries, tracts of land had been sold off and now it was a mere shadow of its former glory, a grand house in an exclusive outer suburb.

Edie, Jeff and Rose had left Venice early in a rented car. Rose had not been overjoyed by the idea of having to tag along, but Jeff would not take no for an answer. For most of the journey she had sulked in the back, listening to her iPod.

Arranging an interview had indeed proved to be every bit as simple as Roberto had claimed, and Giovanni Ricardo Marco Niccoli, the twenty-third Barone, had been more than happy to meet friends of Roberto's.

The palazzo was situated off the main road along a quiet, tree-lined lane running west out of Padua. A broad gravel driveway took them from a pair of grand wrought-iron gates, through a copse of cypress trees to the beautiful fifteenth century Palazzo Moritti reputedly designed by a disciple of Brunelleschi. An elegantly dressed butler met them at the huge front door and escorted them through an echoing hall to a drawing-room.

Barone Niccoli was expecting them. He was a tall man, dressed in an expensive dark blue suit. He had white wavy hair and his hazel eyes were warm and friendly.

'Welcome,' he said, his English only faintly accented. He shook Jeff's hand and kissed the back of Edie's. 'And you must be Rose. A real English rose, I see.'

275

Rose beamed and all her pent-up anger evaporated instantly. 'I imagine,' Barone Niccoli went on, 'that you are less than pleased to be dragged out here on your papa's business. Am I right?'

'Ignored us the whole way here,' Jeff declared.

'Dad . . .!'

Niccoli laughed. 'Well, I have the perfect antidote for boredom.' And with those words, two young men strode into the room. They wore ripped jeans and T-shirts, but their features were classically aristocratic. Even more striking was the fact that they were, to the eye of a stranger at least, absolutely identical.

'Rose, my sons, Filippo and Francesco.'

They each shook Rose's hand. 'You like scramble biking?'

'Well . . .' Jeff interrupted.

Rose glared at him.

'I've never tried it, but I'd like to.' She shot a challenging look at both adults.

'It's quite safe, Jeff, they get padded up and wear helmets,' Niccoli explained.

A few moments later, Edie and Jeff were sitting with the Barone, cups of coffee on a table between them.

'So, tell me more about what has brought you here. Is Roberto all right by the way? I was a little surprised he didn't call personally.'

'He had an accident. Nothing too serious, but he'll be in bed for a few days.'

'I'm really sorry to hear that. It would be nice to see him again. I was very fond of his father.'

'We're researching a TV documentary,' Edie said. 'The president of the Vivaldi Society in Venice put us on to you. Apparently, the composer stayed here for a few months around 1709 and 1710.'

'Yes, that's correct.'

'And he became fascinated with the journals of one of your ancestors, Niccolò Niccoli, the condottieri who was also a close friend of Cosimo the Elder.'

The Barone reached for his espresso and took a sip. 'Yes, I can see the attraction for television. The story has many connections between some really fascinating historical characters. My illustrious ancestor was the first to elevate our family into the aristocracy. We owe him a great deal.'

'The journals are of particular interest,' Jeff went on. 'The episode involving Vivaldi coming here to teach members of the family was such an anomaly. We're interested in the report that he stole the journals but returned them later in a fit of guilt.'

Niccoli chuckled. 'That's true, although I think the story has been rather exaggerated.' He sighed. 'Well, I'll help you as much as I can. Until fairly recently, we had several copies of the journals. During the 1920s, the well-known British historian, J.P. Wheatley spent a year here translating the originals and working through the version Vivaldi had transcribed and returned to my ancestors after what you call his "fit of guilt". But then there was the fire.'

Jeff and Edie exchanged concerned looks.

'You haven't heard about that? It was over thirty years ago, sometime in 1977. I was at Oxford. My father was ailing, my mother, the Baronessa had died, which in a way was a relief. She loved the library and would have been devastated by what happened.'

'Arson?' Edie asked.

'Yes, turned out to be some horrible little thugs from the city. The police caught them, but nothing could bring back what had been lost. Half the library was destroyed: several priceless Bibles, a first edition of Galileo's *Starry Messenger* – again almost priceless. We lost over two thousand books, including Vivaldi's edition of my ancestor's journals and almost everything translated by Professor Wheatley. A few pages from the first volume were all that could be saved.'

'But the originals survived?'

'Possibly.'

'What do you mean?'

'The arsonists were also thieves. Some volumes were taken from the shelves before the fire was started. However, they were pretty inept. During the following year, several extremely valuable tomes were located. It was, after all, practically impossible for them to sell the books. We found a Petrarch, an Aristo, two Boiardos, and a set of original Leonardo anatomical drawings.'

'But the journals never showed up?'

'Sadly, no.'

Jeff looked at Edie, her disappointment was clear to see and mirrored his own.

'I'm sorry I can't be of greater assistance.'

'You mentioned a part of one volume that was saved from the flames. You have that still?'

'Yes, but it's little more than a fragment of the original.'

'May we see it?'

The Barone drained his cup and placed it back in its saucer. 'Follow me.'

They passed along a broad corridor, emerging into a wide room. To one side, glass windows offered a view of lush gardens, a lake, a pale blue summer house on stilts at one end of the water. The opposite wall was panelled, a row of portraits, the family nose repeated almost like a xeroxed image: Renaissance Warhols.

They passed through a set of double doors and down a plainly decorated passage. Stopping by an archway, the Barone ushered them into the library, a vast, windowless room. There was nothing to indicate it had been rebuilt in the late '70s. Two ancient-looking sofas stood back-to-back in the centre. Every square inch of three of the walls was shelved and crammed with thousands of books.

'I'm envious,' said Jeff.

'Our greatest treasures are kept here in these glass cabinets,' Niccoli said. 'After the events of 1977 it was clear we had to be a little more careful.'

He unlocked one of the cabinets by punching a number sequence into a key pad. Below three shelves of leather spines lay two wide drawers. As he pulled on the handle of the lower one, Edie caught a glimpse of tissue paper and laminated sheets. The Barone slowly removed a leather folder, and took it over to a small table.

Inside, four sheets of paper had been professionally preserved under plastic. Each of the pages was ripped, and burn marks were clearly visible along the edges of two of the sheets. One of the pages was fragmented into three and had been fitted together to allow the text to be read.

'This is all that remains of the English translation?' Jeff asked incredulously.

'Tragically, it is all that survives of the three volumes. According to the forensics report we received some six months after the fire, there is some evidence Vivaldi's copy was destroyed in the fire. Some ninety-five per cent of Professor Wheatley's three-volume translation was also burned. Some tiny fragments of charred paper with the same watermark as these pages were discovered. But, the true originals, in my ancestor's hand . . . well, I hope they haven't been dumped in a river or used to clad pipes. I prefer to imagine someone, somewhere, is treasuring the journals, even if they have no right to them.'

'May I?' Edie said.

'Of course. Please take your time. Read these sad remains. I have a few boring chores to perform.'

. . . rescue was truly a miracle, but Cosimo did not appreciate it at the time. He learned a great deal about his betrothed, but what he learned was perhaps too brutal to accept readily. The finer details of his adventure in Venice was only related to me much later – the story of the extraordinary Luigi, the treacherous priest and the fight in the chapel . . .

. . . the captain and all but six of his crew

perished in that dreadful storm. I do not know how I reached dry land. All I remember is cold, cold water and screams. I found the body of Caterina, drowned and bloated. To my incomparable relief and joy, Cosimo and Contessina had survived but were in shock, as was Ambrogio, who came through the ordeal with only minor cuts and bruises.

We had been washed up on a beach close to a fishing village. Some old men found us and took us in. Everyone was very kind. A few supplies from our ship were eventually washed ashore. We took what we needed for the rest of our journey and left the remainder to be shared amongst our rescuers. It was the least we could do for those who had given us food and shelter.

The surviving crew members remained in Ragusa to await a ship headed for Italy. We tarried in that fine and noble city just long enough to find our bearings and to prepare for the journey south-east into Macedonia. Some of the valuables we had salvaged from the *Gisela* we exchanged for horses, supplies, maps and the services of local guides . . .

. . . a wild land. Only a dozen years earlier this place had been overrun by the Turk. The people, almost all of them poor farmers, lived little better than slaves. The Sultan controlled, with an iron grip, everyday life in this sorry province, while the people were spiritually yoked to the Constantinople Patriarchate . . .

. . . We were in great danger of course. On the one hand, we deemed it wise to avoid the many soldiers who kept the peasants in line, and on the other, we were vulnerable to attack by *ajduks*, the members of the local resistance movement. By the third day, having made a safe crossing into Macedonia, we had reached the more remote regions, the foothills of the Dinaric mountains, and the highest peak, Korab itself . . .

. . . such harsh and inhospitable country. Ambrogio was complaining all the time, of course. Contessina and Cosimo were inseparable and operated almost as a single person, not only strengthened by what they had been through but driven by a burning ambition. I was weary, I admit that. But, as the most experienced traveller, my companions relied upon me . . .

. . . we saw light in the distance high in the sky close to where Korab stood in the darkness . . . mountain road took us directly east. Along the way we passed by a few deserted houses. Further on we found a hamlet of stone huts; they had been razed. Inside one lay two black husks, a mother and child incinerated in the blaze as they clutched each other.

In all my travels, this was the single saddest sight, one that will stay with me for ever. The smell of burned flesh and charred straw still hung heavily in the air. Some terror had passed this way a short time before, perhaps the previous night.

By early the next evening, we reached the summit of the mountain and there, as the sun hung low in a ruddy haze, we caught our first sight of the monastery of Golem Korab . . .

. . . The abbot, Father Kostov was a tall, muscular man. Even in his shapeless roughly woven habit he possessed an indefinable dignity. He had been educated at Genoa and Paris and spoke four languages. We were questioned long and hard before being allowed into the monastery, but once the abbot accepted us as guests we were treated with all courtesy . . .

. . . first night we dined with the abbot in his

spartan chambers close to the dormitories of the monks and told him of our mission. He explained the danger they were in. A local warlord named Stasanor had devastated the nearby villages, and was turning his avaricious eyes upon them . . .

. . . was three days after our arrival before we were shown the library . . . many wonders that made all our travails worthwhile. From then on Cosimo and Ambrogio Tommasini were seen only rarely; the good abbot had given them the freedom of the place and permission to copy anything they wished . . .

. . . but an atmosphere of dread pervaded the monastery . . . fear of Stasanor was ever present. The monks felt it, and so too did we.

. . . by the purest coincidence . . . the night of the attack . . .

. . . the good abbot came to us after evening prayer and said he wanted us to know something about his monastery, something no outsiders had ever been privy to. And so it was we learned of the Miracle of Saint Jacob and saw his work . . .

Chapter 21

Toronto Airport, present day

Luc Fournier's phone rang as he descended from the Gulfstream G500.

'This is the second failure.' The heavily accented voice was immediately recognisable. 'You will understand my colleagues are upset.'

Fournier said nothing.

'You have twenty-four hours. If you do not meet your obligations our relationship will be terminated. Is that clear?'

'Perfectly,' Fournier responded coldly. 'But please don't ever threaten me again. In forty-five years I have never once failed to deliver. I will not fail you . . . unless, that is, I choose to.'

The laboratory was a single storey concrete edifice hidden from the main road by a copse of trees. Behind it stretched snow-covered fields. The nearest houses stood over half a mile from the building, and even these were owned by Canadian Grain Supplies, one of Luc Fournier's many anonymous companies that acted as a front to his real business.

The limo pulled up outside the main building and the driver ran around to open the rear door and to hold an umbrella aloft, shielding Fournier from the few flakes of snow that descended from the grey sky. It was minus 5 degrees centigrade and the men's breath billowed into the crisp cold air.

Fournier was met at the door by the head of the lab team, Dr Jerome Fritus. With barely a nod in greeting he led his employer along a corridor to the central rooms of the laboratory complex. Fritus was not one for small talk and he knew Fournier did not like unnecessary conversation.

The main room in the complex was white-walled and sterile, an environment that perfectly reflected the barren isolation of the frozen fields and the snow-laden sky outside. Fritus led the way to a wide counter upon which stood a cubic glass container. Inside this lay the tablet stolen from the Medici Chapel.

In that moment, all Fournier's concerns and frustrations evaporated. Nothing else mattered, Afghan terrorists included. He was in the presence of a timeless wonder, something bigger than all of them.

'I have your initial report on the inscription,' Fournier said, 'but what else have you discovered?'

Fritus stood with his hands clasped behind his back and stared at Fournier. Unlike any other of Fournier's many employees he seemed to have no fear of his employer. Fournier found this refreshing, but as soon as Fritus's usefulness had passed he would be quietly eliminated.

'It is a perfectly proportioned rectangle 3.9 by 1.9 centimetres,' Fritus replied. 'The inscription must have appeared on the surface only after the stone had been hydrated by water vapour in the air. The green writing is made from a sulphurous compound that changes colour when water molecules are incorporated into its crystalline structure.'

'And you've managed to date it?'

'Carbon dating is of course impossible as the tablet is made from inorganic materials. However, I have been able to come up with a pretty accurate age using a new comparative analysis technique. The tablet is made from Amanorthosite, a form of what's called intrusive igneous rock, characterised by the presence of small amounts of the mineral, letomenite. Letomenite changes its chemical structure when it comes into contact with air. This means we can compare the amount of change in this compound on the edges of the Medici tablet with material inside the tablet. This will tell us when the piece of stone was first cut into its present shape.'

Fournier was suitably impressed. 'But surely, all the time it was inside the body in the chapel the stone was sealed from the air.'

'Correct,' Fritus replied as though he were talking to a keen student. 'But there was air in the body when it was buried and molecules of oxygen would have been able to seep into the corpse. The lettering on the tablet only appeared after the tablet was exposed to the air because it needed water vapour which could not have been able to find its way past the embalming fluid around the object.'

'So are the dates right? Is the tablet genuine?'

'By my calculations the stone of the tablet was first cut and exposed to the air between 500 and 600 years ago. I can't be any more accurate than that.'

'You don't need to be,' Fournier replied. 'It's enough to confirm the tablet is not modern. What else have you discovered?'

'How do you know there is more, Monsieur Fournier?'

Fournier raised an eyebrow.

Fritus didn't need any more encouragement 'I found something very strange. Trace amounts of a chemical called Ropractin.'

'Which is?'

'Metapropyl dimethylphosphonochloridite, if that helps. It's a close relative of Sarin, but much deadlier. At room temperature it is a liquid, intensely green in colour, semi-fluorescent. It's about a thousand times more poisonous than Sarin, deadly in concentrations of a tiny fraction of a milligram per kilogram of body weight.'

Fournier had stopped listening. After all these years, finally he understood the central mystery of Niccoli's written account of his journey to Macedonia. He knew now what the Medici Secret was.

Chapter 22

Padua, present day

The black-haired man watched them enter the grounds in the hired car and drove on to park a hundred metres along the lane. His head throbbed still from the blow he had sustained the previous night. And deep inside him seethed a vengeful anger.

By the time he reached a copse of trees opposite the entrance, the three of them had disappeared inside. He circled the house, watching as two teenage boys entered through one of the back doors. A few minutes later, the boys re-emerged with the girl.

The pounding in his head was clouding his judgement. He closed his eyes and went through some of the mental exercises he had been taught in Special Forces. Clearing his mind he took deep breaths. When he opened his eyes again, everything seemed clearer.

Moving silently through the trees, he reached another vantage point, some way from the house, in an area of rough grass and shrubbery. The three youngsters were chatting animatedly beside a pair of scramble bikes.

Having put on their helmets, the two boys showed the girl how it was done. They shot off on a circular route over mounds and skidded around tight bends. Part of the course followed a muddy path just a few feet from where he stood, but he knew they would not see him.

He had absolutely no qualms. Killing was what he did for a living. He did not need to hate his targets. Indeed, he felt nothing for any of them. His instructions were to acquire every scrap of information possible. Whatever the cost. His client was paying generously. So, he planned to dispatch the boys, take the girl and swap her – dead or alive – for that most precious commodity: information.

One of the brothers came tearing round the nearest bend spraying a plume of mud around him. Revving the bike, he roared over a mound, flew through the air and landed elegantly. Raising his pistol, the assassin steadied his arm with his free hand. The boy rushed towards him, skidded and sprayed more mud high into the air. The bike twisted and spun out of control. The boy picked himself up and rode back to the others. The moment had passed.

The second boy started his ride with an impressive

wheelie before roaring away; but as he approached the first mound, the back wheel lost its grip. He flew over the handlebars and landed hard in the mud.

Standing, legs parted, knees slightly bent, the assassin swung the gun, aiming it at the head of the kid clambering back on to the bike. He started to squeeze the trigger.

'Guys?'

Quickly, he lowered the gun and took a step back into the trees as a short, plump woman with pink spiky hair came into view.

Filippo straightened up in the saddle, killed the engine and climbed off, letting the bike fall to the wet ground.

'Sorry to spoil your fun,' the man heard the woman say. 'Cook's made tea and cake.'

Francesco rolled his eyes. 'What now? We've just got started.'

'Take it or leave it guys, but the chocolate cake's something else.'

'This is our tutor, Matilda,' Francesco explained to Rose. 'Matilda is from America and she takes food *very* seriously.'

'As you can tell,' Filippo added behind his hand, making Rose and his brother laugh.

The gunman watched from the shadows as the four of them turned to walk back to the house.

Chapter 23

Venice, present day

It was dark by the time they reached Piazzale Roma and returned the hire car. The canalside cafés and bars were beginning to come alive as the water taxi glided along the Grand Canal. It took no more than ten minutes to reach the Ospedale Civile.

Roberto's room was quiet, the lights dimmed. A TV was on in the corner, the sound off. Roberto was awake and sitting up in bed. His face looked sore, the bruising more lurid than it had been the day before. 'Ah, my intrepid researchers,' he said, 'and the lovely Rose. I *am* honoured.'

Rose could not disguise her shock, but stepped up to the bed and kissed him gently on the cheek. 'How are you feeling?'

'Oh, pretty good young lady. And you?'

'I had the best time.'

Roberto gave Edie and Jeff a quizzical look.

'Barone Niccoli has two boys, Francesco and Filippo. Identical twins. And they really are identical,' said Rose excitedly.

'Ah.' Roberto obviously found it painful to smile.

'So, how are you bearing up?' Edie asked, taking his hand.

'Can't complain. Pretty nurses, good food, plenty of time to relax.'

Edie frowned.

'Oh, and the most entertaining chats with Candotti. I sent him packing yesterday. Told him I wasn't up to talking. He came back this morning, rather contrite.'

'Doesn't sound like the Candotti we know and love.'

'I took the precaution of having a word with the Chief of Police, Prefect Vincenzo Piatti. I told him you two were being harassed.'

'Is there anyone you don't know?'

'I don't know him, actually. But it appears he knows me.'

'Won't that wind up Candotti even more?'

'Maybe . . . but frankly I don't care. I don't think any of us should trust anyone with what we know. Candotti is just doing his job, but the police can't protect us right now and I believe the best way to keep information from people like him is simply to avoid them. Anyway, enough of that. What did you discover?'

Edie told him about Barone Niccoli's library and the fate of the journals. 'It made for a fascinating read,' she concluded. 'But frustrating. It doesn't get us any further.'

Roberto was silent for a moment, lost in thought.

'And you?'

'Well luckily, I at least have made some headway. The clue from the Gritti Badoer; I've had little else to think about.'

'What about the nurses?' Edie said, smiling sweetly.

Roberto raised an eyebrow, then continued. 'That line of music is fascinating. On the surface it seems pretty obvious. Each note must refer to a letter which I thought would spell out a sentence.'

'It didn't?'

'No. The letters spelled out nonsense. Then I began to think about the Roman numerals, IV and V. It struck me I might need to transpose the notes into a different key and these numerals marked the way.'

'What do you mean?'

'Well, you can play a piece of music in any key. It's the intervals between the notes that creates the melody. The etching on the hemisphere was of a stave with a succession of notes. This series of notes can be transposed; all the notes can be moved up or down to change the key. The Roman numerals were telling us something. There were two bars of music in the clue and under the first bar was the number IV, under the second was V. It became clear that I had to transpose the notes in the first bar to the perfect fourth and the notes in the second bar to the major fifth.'

'And that gave you a series of notes that spelled out a readable message?'

'Er, no.'

'No?' Jeff was starting to feel irritated but realised that they had to humour Roberto because he was clearly enjoying teasing out the information bit by tantalising bit.

'I was surprised too. I thought I had it. But then it clicked. In the copy you made of the etching there was no clef in the notation.'

'And a clef is . . .?'

Rose giggled. 'Oh Dad!'

'Sorry.'

Roberto waved to Rose inviting her to explain.

'The clef is the symbol at the beginning of the musical stave. Most common is the G clef.'

'Thank you, Rose, a textbook description. I assumed the notation was written using this. Then I started to wonder. The next most common form is what's called the bass clef, or F clef. And hey presto, when I used this, it worked.' He paused for a moment. 'Could you possibly pass me some water?'

Edie handed him a glass. He took a sip and then rested his head back on the pillow.

'Where was I? Yes, the bass clef. The first bar of notes spelled out: G, A, B, followed by two rests, then an E, a rest and an F.

'G A B - - E - , and F?'

'Exactly. The second bar read: A rest, an A, two more rests, an E, a rest and another A. In other words: - A - - E - A.'

'A bit like hangman,' Rose said.

'That's right,' Edie responded. 'Fill in the gaps. Tafani mentioned that Vivaldi had entrusted the fragment of the letter from Contessina de' Medici to a friend, the painter Gabriel Fabacci. G A B - - E - F? Gabriel. F, Gabriel Fabacci. Perfect!'

'OK, what about the - A - - E - A?' Edie asked.

'That took a little longer. But a smattering of local history goes a long way. In 1741, the year Vivaldi died, Gabriel Fabacci was commissioned to paint a fresco in a church called Chiesa di Santa Maria della Pietà. Vivaldi performed there almost every Sunday, and he was choirmaster for more than thirty years. Its popular name is

La Pietà. Put in the missing L, P, I and T and you have it.'

'So, let me get this straight,' Jeff said, trying to keep pace. 'The clue at the Gritti Badoer must have been left by Vivaldi's friend, Fabacci, after Vivaldi's death and it leads us to his fresco in La Pietà? Why didn't he just take the information Vivaldi gave him, track down the journals of Niccoli and claim the so-called Medici Secret for himself?'

'You might well ask the same of Vivaldi,' Roberto replied.

'In his "confessional",' said Edie, 'he tells us that what he learned scared him so much he couldn't even contemplate taking things any further.'

'I thought initially that this might also have been the way Fabacci thought. Perhaps he too was a God-fearing man. But there were more prosaic reasons for his tardiness. Shortly after finishing his fresco, only a few weeks after he inherited his friend's documents, Fabacci was killed, drowned in the lagoon. All he managed to do was plant the clue in the Gritti Badoer. The knowledge of the Medici Secret died with him.'

'But why bother to leave any clue at all?' Edie asked.

Roberto sighed and shook his head. 'Who knows? Maybe he couldn't let go completely. Maybe he believed that in some better, brighter future someone would learn the secret and make good use of it.'

'So what do we do now?'

'Well, it's all there, isn't it? We have Fabacci's clue linked with his fresco in La Pietà. He even tells us when any intrepid investigator should look for it: sunset.'

Jeff was nodding, but he looked pained.

'Jeff?' Edie said. 'What is it?'

'This is all fine, but shouldn't we also be wondering who else is on the trail? Was that gunman after it, or is he just a hired assassin? If it's the latter, who's employing him, and why?'

The room was silent for a moment, lights from the TV flickered unfocused on the darkened walls and ceiling.

'I don't think any of us can answer those questions, Jeff. At least, not for the moment. But if it puts your mind at rest, at least a little, I have some people looking into who shot me.' And for a fleeting moment they could all see in Roberto's expression an aspect of him none of them had witnessed before, an aristocratic steeliness that verged on menace. 'Let's all concentrate on solving the central mystery,' he added softly.

Jeff was just about to reply when Rose suddenly

pointed at the TV. 'Look, isn't that the Medici Chapel?'

They all turned to see Jack Cartwright talking to camera with the cold stone of the crypt behind his head. Edie grabbed the remote and found the volume control.

'You are quite convinced of this?' A reporter was holding a mike close to Cartwright, who looked a little overwhelmed by the lights and cameras.

'Totally. We have confirmed our suspicions using DNA analysis,' Cartwright replied. 'The body assumed to be that of Cosimo the Elder, the first Medici leader of Florence is an impostor.'

'So who is it?'

'At the moment, we have no idea. We don't know when, why or how the body was switched, if indeed it ever was. Perhaps this unknown person was buried as Cosimo de' Medici; which of course begs the question: where is the real Cosimo? And why was he buried elsewhere?'

'I don't fucking believe this,' Edie said quietly. 'The bastard. I've got to get back to Florence . . . right away.'

'That's ridiculous,' Jeff said.

'Do you really expect me to just sit here while that conniving bugger steals my thunder? It was always my theory the body in Florence was not Cosimo's

301

and, as soon as my back is turned, Cartwright gets in there.'

'So phone him. Yell at him, but don't go, not now.'

A few minutes later they were exiting the lift from the private ward and walking towards the doors leading to Campo SS Giovanni e Paolo. Edie plucked her phone from her shoulder bag and dialled. Rose looked worried and her father placed a reassuring arm around her shoulder.

'Look, before you start . . .' Jack Cartwright was clearly startled by Edie's call. 'It's not what it seems.'

'What is it then, Jack?'

'Did you see the whole broadcast?'

'Well, no . . .'

'I made it clear at the very start that the idea was yours.'

'But why did you have to say anything at all?'

'I didn't mean to,' Cartwright replied. 'You don't know what it's been like here since you left. The police have been here with forensics twice. They've brought back files, taken others. I've had no privacy. They've even installed bloody CCTV cameras.'

'What's that got to do with . . .?'

'I didn't tell the press anything. Some damn reporter came snooping around and told *me* the results of our research. Said he would like me to talk on air. When I said I didn't want to, he made it clear they would just broadcast an item about it anyway. On balance, I thought . . .'

'You thought you'd go on national television and announce an unproven hypothesis, one that wasn't even yours.'

'Yes.'

'OK, Jack. What's happened has happened. I have some business to finish off here, but I'll be back no later than the day after tomorrow. And Jack, please don't say another word on TV, or anywhere else.'

After dropping Rose off at the apartment, Jeff and Edie arrived at La Pietà around 5.15 p.m., with the western sky a magical patchwork of orange, red and purple. Sunset was a little over a quarter of an hour away.

The church stood on Riva degli Schiavoni and looked out across the lagoon to San Giorgio Maggiore. Little remained of the fifteenth-century building Vivaldi had worked in; most of it had been rebuilt during the mid-eighteenth century, a structure designed by the architect Giorgio Massari.

'It's funny,' Jeff said gazing at the late-Baroque interior. 'In all the time I've lived in this city I haven't set foot in this building.'

'It's pretty incredible, if a little OTT.'

They walked along the aisle, admiring the elaborate cream and gold pillars and the spectacular ceiling fresco by Tiepolo. Windows ran along each wall to left and right, and between these were small frescos by a variety of artists.

The fresco they were seeking was the first on the right-hand wall. It was of a Madonna and child. Angels hovered above them, the colours still vibrant. The Madonna, taking up much of the left side of the fresco, was holding the Christ child in one arm. With the other she was pointing towards three men on mules. The mules were laden down with caskets. At the very top of the fresco, in the centre, was a large star, its rays a semi-circle of golden daggers. The lower half of the picture lay in shadow, and although the movement was barely perceptible, the shadow was slowly creeping up the fresco as light from the sinking sun was refracted by the rear windows of the church.

The seconds ticked by.

'It's five thirty-one,' Edie said. 'Sunset. So what now?'

'I don't know. What are we . . .?'

'There,' Edie said so loudly an elderly couple turned and glared at her. 'There, look. The Madonna's hand.'

The sharp division between the umbra and the sunlight now ran directly along the Madonna's arm and through her pointing finger. It traversed the picture and crossed the wall to another fresco immediately to the right. They ran over to the neighbouring image on the wall. The picture was cut in two about one third lit-up, two-thirds in shadow. The dividing line sliced through blue sky, cut the tops off a mountain range, decapitated an angel and scythed through a building.

'Christ!' Edie exclaimed.

Jeff peered at the fresco. 'Is that what I . . .?'

The line dissected a tiny image of a building that could only be the Medici Chapel in Florence. Beneath it was a line of writing: SOTTO 400, 1000.

The sky was darkening as they emerged from La Pietà and headed west towards San Marco. Lights had come on along Riva degli Schiavoni. The evening crowds had begun to swell, and as the vaporetti arrived from the Lido, tourists bustled their way on to the thoroughfare. A brisk wind churned the lagoon, making the moored gondolas dance and clatter.

Crossing San Marco, they entered the hallway to the apartment. The whole place was deserted, but, as they walked towards the stairs, they heard a faint gurgling sound. The concierge behind the desk was spasming violently, a bullet wound an inch wide in his throat. His face and the entire inside of his desk was drenched in blood.

Jeff tried to suppress his rising panic. 'Edie!' He shook her shoulders and she snapped to attention. 'Call the police.'

Jeff took the stairs to his apartment two at a time. Emerging on to the landing, he could see his door was ajar. A tall, pale man dressed in a dark suit was standing by one of the sofas. He had Maria pulled close to him. The silencer of a gun was pressed hard up against her right temple. She was whimpering, her eyes wild with terror.

Jeff retreated quickly into the hall.

'I'll blow her brains out, Jeff.' The voice was raspy, strongly accented. 'You know that, don't you? Then I'll kill the girl. I know Rose is here, somewhere. And I'll find her.'

Jeff walked slowly into the room, heart thumping. 'What do you want?'

'What a silly question. The clue, of course.'

'What clue?'

Jeff glanced down as liquid suddenly splashed to the floor between Maria's legs. The gunman saw it too. He pulled the trigger and half of Maria's head flew across the room.

Jeff threw himself back into the hall and collided with Edie, nearly knocking her over.

Edie grabbed his arm. 'What the hell's going on?'

'Rose,' he croaked, rushing back into the room.

It looked like an abattoir. Blood splattered the walls and ceiling. The gunman was nowhere to be seen.

'Oh my God!' Edie raised both hands to her face in horror.

'We've got to find her,' Jeff muttered.

They ran down the corridor.

The first room was empty. Two more rooms lay ahead, one to the left, one to the right. They were about to enter the second bedroom when the gunman reappeared, his pistol raised.

'Good evening, Signorina Granger. What do you think of the new colour scheme? *Très chic*, no?' Two paces brought him nose to nose with Jeff. 'Give me the clue,' he whispered. 'Whether I kill you or the lovely signorina, I will find your little daughter and finish giving the apartment a makeover. So, last chance guys . . .'

He put the pistol to Edie's forehead.

A voice came from the end of the corridor. 'Drop your weapon.'

For a second, the gunman hesitated. But then he lowered his gun.

'*Drop it.*'

The place was suddenly full of uniformed men in Kevlar vests. One grabbed the gunman and cuffed him. Another ran forward to pick up the gun and bag it.

'Thanks,' Jeff said and strode past Aldo Candotti, who made no effort to stop him.

At the far end of the corridor was a small bedroom. Just inside could be seen the faint outline of a door and a tiny handle sunk into the wall. Rose's secret hidey-hole. Jeff gripped the handle and pulled, praying his daughter was safe. He flicked on the light switch. The bulb had broken. But there was just enough light for him to see inside. It was a long, narrow room kitted out with a miniature sofa, a low table and a squat cupboard containing a few books.

'Rose?'

No reply.

'Rose? It's Dad. Everything's OK. You can come out.'

Edie and two police officers approached.

'Jeff, what . . . .?'

'I thought she'd . . .' Edie hugged him and he buried his face in her hair.

There was a scream from the living room. Dashing back along the corridor, they saw Rose, her face alabaster white.

Chapter 24

Macedonia, June 1410

Abbot Kostov led Cosimo and the others through the refectory, along a gloomy grey corridor and down a staircase into the crypt. They walked in silence, the abbot lighting the way with a single flickering torch until they reached a circular room with a low, domed roof. In the centre stood a stone pillar on which was perched a glass container about the size of a man's hand. Inside was a slender cylindrical vial a few centimetres long, closed at each end with a brass cap. A strange, sickly green liquid filled three-quarters of the vial.

Cosimo moved forward, but the abbot's arm darted out to stop him. 'My friend, do not take a step closer,' he said firmly.

Cosimo obeyed.

'This is our most sacred place,' the abbot said. 'We have been custodians of this object for more than one hundred years. It originated in the village of Adapolin in the Sunun region far from here. The local villages were struck by a terrible plague that killed indiscriminately, but Adapolin itself was spared. Not a single person fell ill there.

'A man named Jacob, a simple farmer, possessed the object you see before you, this sacred vial. As their neighbours perished, Jacob instructed the elders of Adapolin to erect a pillar in the town square and to mount a barrier around it. He then placed the vial on the pedestal and all the villagers, the women and the children, the elders and the young men filed past the low wall. Each was made to kneel in brief prayer and then to cross themselves.

'By autumn of that year, Adapolin had become famous as the miracle village. The sick and the lame flocked there for healing. Many returned home with tales of the miraculous cures and the protective qualities of Jacob's vial. But Jacob himself was very ill. It was almost as though he had absorbed the dark vapours and allowed himself to become the Devil's vassal. His skin became covered in sores, his eyes almost sealed with blisters, and he lost all his hair.

'One day the villagers awoke to find the vial and Jacob had disappeared. It was Abbot Andanov, five generations before my time, who took in the sick stranger. Jacob died two days after arriving here, and was buried in the grounds of this monastery. My predecessors have kept the vial safe all this time.'

There was a sudden great booming sound from overhead, and the whole room shook. Screams followed, and the sound of running feet.

The abbot gripped Cosimo's arm. 'It has begun,' he croaked. 'We are under attack.'

A young monk stumbled into the room. His face was streaked with blood. 'Father,' he gasped. 'Stasanor . . .' He sank to the cold stone floor and lay still.

'Quick, come with me.' Abbot Kostov slammed the door behind them and locked it, then beckoned them to follow him up the stairs. The refectory was deserted, but they could hear the clang of steel, screams and roars of men close by. And they could smell burning.

'You cannot help us now.'

Cosimo took the Abbot's hands. 'Father . . .'

'Go my friends. God will guide us. I must leave you.'

'Cosimo, our weapons are in the rooms,' Niccoli snapped. 'That's too far away. We'll have to split up.'

Three men appeared at the end of the corridor. Two of them carried broad swords, the third, a mace.

Niccoli grabbed a torch from a bracket and

advanced towards them. Emerging into an open space, a cloister at the heart of the monastery, they could hear screams, the crackling of ignited wood and straw. The air was heavy with the stench of burned flesh and spilled blood.

'We must scatter,' Tommasini cried above the noise.

'Agreed. We have to get out. Make for the lake. There's a copse of trees on the far shore.'

Cosimo turned and felt Contessina grab his arm. 'I'm not letting you out of my sight,' she said.

Panting, Tommasini made it back to his room. Slinging a bag over his shoulder, he unsheathed his sword and dashed back into the corridor. It was filling with smoke. He began to choke and realised he had not the slightest idea how to make his escape. Someone rushed towards him and he shrank back against the wall. The man ran straight past into the darkness. Then he felt a hand grip his shoulder. He screamed and a voice hissed in his ear. 'Master Ambrogio.'

He could just make out the features of one of the monks, Father Daron, the librarian. 'We must rescue the sacred vial,' he hissed. 'Follow me.'

The stairs to the crypt lay on the far side of a courtyard. An arrow whistled past Tommasini's ear.

He had no idea from where it had come and just kept going across the uneven flagstones. The monk was only a couple of paces ahead of him, bent almost double. As they reached the stairs a tall figure emerged from a doorway to the left. He charged at them, sword raised.

The monk fell back using Tommasini as a shield. But the Florentine was prepared, all senses heightened. Before the raider could land a blow, Tommasini thrust his sword forward. Side-stepping the crumbling body, Tommasini lost his sword, but had the presence of mind to grab the dead man's weapon.

Downstairs, Father Daron fumbled for the key and finally managed to unlock the door. He slammed it shut behind them and the pair found themselves in a chill blackness.

Feeling their way along the passageway they made for a faint light, and in moments they were back in the circular chamber.

Tommasini watched as the monk's fingers darted across the surface of the crystal box. A panel slid open. Father Daron reached in and gingerly grabbed hold of the vial. Behind them, they could hear the door being beaten down.

'Quick! You must take this.' Father Daron pressed the glass cylinder into Tommasini's hands. For a second, Ambrogio allowed himself the luxury of studying the object in the fading light, marvelling once more at the intensity of its colour, the heaviness of the liquid in the tube. Images from the past flashed through his mind. The hands of the saintly Jacob holding this very object, this miraculous thing.

There was the sound of boots on stone.

'I shall place myself in the hands of the Lord,' Father Daron said. 'You must escape.' The monk handed Tommasini one of the wall torches and pushed him roughly towards the far side of the room, where he pulled aside a rug that lay on the floor. There was a faint outline of a door in the stone. The monk plucked a key from his pocket and inserted it into a tiny aperture. Tommasini helped him lift the lid. A ladder disappeared into darkness. Tommasini climbed on to the top rung as three men charged into the chamber. The monk pushed his head down and the Florentine almost lost his grip. The door crashed down over him.

Tommasini found himself in a tunnel barely head height and no more than a few inches wider than his shoulders. Stumbling towards a fork in the tunnel, he took the left branch out of pure instinct. His breathing was laboured in the fetid air and sweat ran down his body. Trying to still his pounding heart, he listened for sounds of pursuit. It was impossible to detect anything above the roar of fire, explosions and crashing masonry. He pushed on down another tunnel. He had only intuition to guide him. After thirty paces, he turned a corner and saw a solid wall of rock ahead of him. He had reached a dead-end.

Another explosion directly overhead shook the walls and part of the ceiling started to collapse. Pieces of stone and tile cascaded down and a large chunk of rock almost knocked Tommasini over. He kept his balance, but his torch was snuffed out. With his left hand, he felt inside his tunic to make sure the vial was intact, then, clutching his sword, he shuffled slowly towards a tiny chink of light.

'I must save as much of the library as I can,' Cosimo whispered. 'It is what we came here for. We cannot leave everything to be totally destroyed by this Stasanor.'

Contessina gripped his hand.

'Across the courtyard,' Cosimo insisted and pointed to a door in the far wall.

To their right stood a chicken coop and next to that a well-stocked vegetable garden dissected by a narrow path. To their left, an open door led into an empty laundry. Contessina almost tripped over the body of a man in a black leather tunic. She snatched up his sword, whirling round as Niccolò Niccoli, armed now with a broadsword, came stumbling backwards towards them trying to fight off two men.

Contessina sprang forward to help. The bandit swung at her with his mace. It missed her head by an inch. The man was inexperienced with the weapon and slow to regain his balance. With lightning speed, Contessina slashed her assailant from neck to groin. Plucking the mace from the dirt, she tossed it towards Cosimo. Niccoli's assailant was distracted momentarily and Niccoli lunged forward driving hard steel into his mouth. The blade emerged through the back of the bandit's neck just below the base of his cranium. Niccoli left it there and they ran towards the door on the far side of the courtyard.

Niccoli gripped the handle and cautiously eased the door open. Another short, narrow passageway led to a flight of stairs. The door to the library stood on the right. It was locked and bolted.

Cosimo took a violent swing with his mace, and the lock splintered with the force of the blow. A torch was hanging just inside. From his pocket, Niccoli withdrew a small flint and ignition iron in an ebony box. Flicking the iron over the flint, he produced a spark that lit a knuckle of kindling. He dipped the oil-soaked torch on to the tiny flame and it caught immediately.

Many of the shelves in the library were already

bare. Cosimo rushed forward into the adjoining room. The floor space was covered with crates, some piled three high. The abbot had only that evening begun making safe some of the monastery's most precious items to be stored in a maze of catacombs beneath the building. Almost all of the crates were strapped with narrow ropes, some were sealed with wire and a heavy waxy material. Two baskets stood beside the boxes. One was filled with goblets, plate and assorted silverware; the other contained a pile of religious icons, paintings on wooden boards, gold and silver crucifixes, chalices and incense holders on chains still exuding pungent odours.

Cosimo removed the lid from the nearest crate, carefully lifting the papers closest to hand. He opened a dusty cover, blew across the front page and read the Greek lettering. It was a manual for aqueduct designers written by one Umenicles. He picked up a frayed parchment with amber burn marks running across it.

'This is in the hand of Herodotus himself,' he said, barely able to believe his eyes. The next volume contained pages of geometric diagrams and mathematical formulae. It was a work by a Greek disciple of Euclid.

'My heart bleeds looking at these wonders,' Contessina sighed. 'What can we do?'

'I suggest we make haste,' Niccoli muttered.

But Cosimo was in another world. He felt both sick inside and elated. It was almost too much to comprehend. 'What can we do?' he said at last.

'Not much, I fear.'

'Niccolò, we cannot leave these books; how can we possibly choose?'

Contessina crouched down and placed a gentle hand on Cosimo's shoulder, but it was too late. The marauders were already on their way. Their shouts echoed down the passageway.

'Quick!' Contessina hissed and grabbed Cosimo.

'We must save what we can!' Cosimo pressed a handful of precious texts into Contessina's arms, then began to stuff what he could into his pockets and under his belt. Niccoli scooped up a couple of scrolls, then yanked Cosimo behind the tallest pile of crates. A moment later, two of Stasanor's bandits rushed into the room.

Before they could get too close, Niccoli and Contessina sprang from their hiding place. Niccoli had the torch in one hand and his sword in the other. His torch made a fiery arc in the air. It seared one of the men across the face and he screamed. Then thrusting forward, Niccoli found the bandit's throat with his sword and slit it open with a single movement. Blood sprayed in a great plume and the man sank to his knees clawing at his neck. Contessina was quick to reach the other guard. Surprise gave her a distinct advantage. Her startled opponent barely had time to parry her first blow before she had slipped under his guard. He was dead before he hit the ground.

Out in the passageway they could hear more voices approaching. Niccoli extinguished his torch. Falling back into the shadows, they held their breath. Two more intruders ran past them into the storeroom, emerging a few seconds later. They did not spot the three Florentines pressed into a dark recess.

'What now?' said Contessina.

'Follow me.' Niccoli checked the corridor and slid away.

Past the storeroom and an almonry, through another door they found themselves in the chapel. Skirting the edge, dodging between stone columns they quickly reached the altar. A young monk, a boy no more than thirteen or fourteen years old jumped up from behind the altar holding a crucifix. His face was bleached with terror. Seeing Niccoli, blood smeared across his face, sword glinting in the half-light, he screamed, dropped the crucifix and bolted. Niccoli leapt up the stone steps to the corner of the room where a narrow doorway led to a broad corridor. They could see a group of bandits running towards the chapel.

'The tower must be to the right,' Niccoli whispered. 'I believe there's another way out from there.'

They were not spotted as they made their way inside. A solitary figure stood in the centre of the room. He looked like a rabbit startled in the light of a firebrand, his helmet askew. He could barely have reached puberty, a twin of the young monk, but a boy who had lived a very different life. He eyed his sword lying on a wooden bench close by. Niccoli tilted his head to one side and raised his eyebrows.

It took just a few seconds to bind the boy's hands and to gag him. As Niccoli did this, Contessina and Cosimo scanned the room. In a wooden truck pushed up against the curved outer wall of the tower room they found rope and a pair of grappling hooks, leftovers from a few years earlier when the monastery had undergone repairs.

A half-opened door led to a ramp that ascended to a mezzanine level. They had no choice but to clutch their swords and what they had managed to salvage from the library and make a run for it up the ramp. At the top stood a parapet and beyond that the black of night. To their left, a passage led back into the monastery. Contessina peered over the wall and could see the ground some ten metres below. Grass stretched away into the gloom.

Niccoli snatched up a grappling hook as Cosimo swung the other down on to the parapet. They tossed the ropes to the ground below. Niccoli went over first. Cosimo steadied Contessina as she swung her body over the stonework and slithered expertly down. Cosimo reached the ground a few moments later. As he landed, a pair of books fell out of his tunic. He bent to grab them, but Contessina was too quick for him. '*No*,' she snapped, as two arrows thudded into the turf beside them.

They zig-zagged down an uneven slope. Glancing back, Cosimo saw a group of riders spurring their horses towards a wooden bridge close to the walls in an effort to head them off. He was exhausted and slowing almost to a halt, gasping for breath.

'Come on, Cosimo,' Contessina screamed at him and ran back again. She put her arm around him. 'Not far now, if we can . . .'

At that moment, the lead horseman emerged from the shadows of the monastery, shocking them with the speed with which he had crossed the distance from the walls. He raised a spear and let it fly. Contessina sprang forward and pushed Cosimo out of the way. He was sent sprawling, and the rider peeled off, the hooves of his mount almost crushing Cosimo's head.

Niccoli grabbed one of Cosimo's arms while Contessina caught the other, they stumbled across the last few metres of open ground and into the trees. 'Don't stop now,' Niccoli cried, speeding up and yanking on Cosimo's arm.

'Let go,' Cosimo snapped and pulled both arms free. 'I'm not a child.' With a final burst of energy he didn't know he had left in him, he sheathed his sword and drove forward through the undergrowth. They could still hear voices, but they were receding now. For the sake of the few precious works they had rescued, he could not stop, not while there was an ounce of breath left in him.

The rain started to sluice down as Ambrogio reached the meeting point. He ached all over and his hands and face were cut and bleeding. Pausing for a moment, he took out the vial and held it up to the light. The green glow seemed more intense now. In its glass container the mysterious liquid seemed almost alive, and Ambrogio could sense its latent power. He couldn't help smiling to himself. His master knew far more than he did about this miraculous thing. But he was the one holding it at this very moment. Returning the vial to his tunic, he heard a twig snap. He unsheathed his sword and crept cautiously into the sparse trees.

The man was almost on top of him before he saw him. He stifled a yelp, and sprang back.

'Ambrogio, it is I.'

'Niccolò! Thank the Lord.'

The two men embraced. Ambrogio stiffened as two more figures emerged from the gloom. Then he broke into a broad smile as he saw Cosimo and Contessina striding towards him.

Chapter 25

Venice, present day

Vincent had closed the heavy drapes and dimmed the lights leaving the fire to cast its comforting glow across the room. Edie and Jeff were on the sofa, each cradling a large brandy while Rose slept fitfully on a leather chesterfield under the window on the other side of the library. Jeff's apartment had been sealed off, still the subject of forensic investigation. Candotti had told them they had been tailed by a police unit, a move that had clearly saved their lives. Roberto had insisted they stay at his place and had only stopped demanding he be moved there himself when Edie threatened to pack up and leave, alone, on the night train to Florence if he did.

Even though the police had followed their movements since they had left Roberto's hospital room, Jeff and Edie had been quizzed at length by two senior police officers and had recounted the events leading up to the shooting several times over: how they had visited La Pietà simply as tourists, to look at the famous frescoes; how they had then left there just after 5.30 p.m. and returned to the apartment. They each gave detailed descriptions of the gunman and clarified that it was he who had chased them the night before, injured Roberto and killed Dino. They also confirmed this killer was the man who had hijacked Roberto's launch and murdered the driver, Antonio.

A female counsellor had talked to Rose alone, and later, with Edie and Jeff. But Rose really only calmed down once she was inside Palazzo Baglioni. She seemed to have a natural affinity for the place and had bonded closely with Roberto. She felt safe inside the ancient walls of the canal-side residence. She had swallowed a special nightcap created by Vincent from what he claimed was a secret recipe that had been in his family for generations and had drifted off to sleep to the mellifluous sound of Brahms' Intermezzo in A. As Jeff had kissed her goodnight, the last thing she said was, 'I can't believe it, Dad. I only popped out of the apartment for a few minutes.'

Jeff gazed over at his sleeping daughter.

'The young have remarkable powers of recuperation,' Edie said quietly.

'I guess this must bring back some horrible memories for you.'

She smiled. 'Years of therapy have plastered over the cracks. I was just eight, a lot younger than Rose when my parents were killed. That's not to say I don't remember it. I do. Every detail, as though it were yesterday.' She seemed to want to talk and Jeff was happy to let her. 'I've relived the experience so many times. It never loses its potency, but I've come to terms with the fact that it really *did* happen. I really *did* walk into that makeshift lab in the desert and find my mum and dad practically floating in their own blood. It was simply an opportunist killing; the murderer got away with a few dollars. That was three decades ago, and the clocks don't stop, the world doesn't halt on its axis, even if you think it should.'

'And now you work with the dead.'

'Oh yes.'

'In a strange way, it must help.'

'Not sure about that, but it keeps things in perspective.

Jeff gave her a quizzical look.

'Look at Cosimo de' Medici. He was one of the wealthiest men who ever lived. Within the limits of his time, he could do almost anything. He kick-started the Renaissance for God's sake. And what is he now? Wherever his real body lies it will be, at best, a pile of crumbling bones inside a beautiful jacket with solid gold buttons.'

Jeff thought of poor Maria. Her life so violently and needlessly extinguished. And Dino too, who had paid the ultimate price for saving them. That was only two nights ago, but already it felt like a lifetime away. Where was Dino now? Had some element of his being really found his wife and daughter? Had the agonies of their lives finally been washed away? Or was everything Dino had once been now nothing more than a slab of meat decaying in a mortuary nearby?

Jeff shrugged his shoulders and looked up at the ceiling. 'Questions with no answers,' he mused. 'I guess it's only at times like this we stop to consider what life really means. And what do we conclude?'

'We each conclude something completely different,' Edie said.

'But there are some basic truths, aren't there?'

'Probably not,' Edie replied.

'It's all smoke and mirrors, all meaningless, don't you think? Whether or not you believe in an afterlife, the only thing that really matters is what you leave for others, be it great works of art, wonderful music people will listen to for centuries after you're dead, or something as simple as being remembered as a good person, someone who gave more than they took.'

'Maybe,' Edie drained her glass, and poured herself another. 'But whatever you do, whatever you leave behind gradually decays and eventually vanishes. I see it every working day. Eventually nothing remains, nothing at all. Bones crumble to dust, and the dust is blown away in the wind.' She took a large gulp of her brandy. 'And what we *do* vanishes too, doesn't it?' She didn't wait for Jeff to reply. 'One day Mozart's music will be forgotten, the words of Jesus will mean nothing. Whatever they contributed will have faded beyond memory. As the great George Harrison put it: all things must pass.'

'Quite so,' Jeff said and raised his glass in a mock salutation. And they both laughed.

'So, what now?' Edie said, wiping her eyes.

'Obviously, we leave for Florence first thing. All of us.' Jeff glanced over at Rose, feeling a stab of guilt for landing his daughter in all this mayhem. Then came anger, anger for being so powerless to shield her from the horrors she had witnessed.

Chapter 26

Toronto, present day

The call to a Venetian number was made by one of Luc Fournier's junior assistants and patched through to the speeding limo en route to the airport.

'Good evening,' Fournier said. He heard an intake of breath as the man at the other end of the line was about to speak.

'There's no need for you to say anything,' Fournier was clipped and precise. 'Let's make this as simple as possible. I want you to intervene personally. Do you understand? . . . Good. That's all. Don't fail me.'

Chapter 27

Venice, present day

The two men wore identical grey suits. One had a pair of aviators perched on the bridge of his nose even though it was 10.30 at night and black as a coalface outside the police station. The other, taller man had spiky bleached blond hair, with black roots. He was chewing gum. They approached the main desk and the officer in charge, Gabrielli Risso eyed them, a faint tingle of fear edging along his spine.

'Yes?'

The man wearing the sunglasses silently surveyed the room. The other took a wallet from his pocket and held it up close to the desk officer's face. ROS: *Raggruppamento Operativo Speciale*, an elite division of the Carabinieri, an anti-terrorism unit.

'How may I help you?' Risso asked.

Still chewing on his gum, the blond man said, 'We're here to collect the prisoner.'

'If you mean the murder suspect brought in from San Marco this evening, he's still being processed.'

'Get your commanding officer here . . . now.'

Risso stared into the man's slate-grey eyes and decided not to argue. He lifted the receiver and punched in three numbers.

A few moments later, a middle-aged man dressed in the uniform of a Vice Provincial Commander appeared. 'Commander Mantessi.' He had a strong Neapolitan accent. 'My duty officer tells me you're interested in the San Marco murder.'

'Is there somewhere we can be more private?'

The Commander indicated a room off the main hall. It was empty apart from a steel table. There were metal bars at the single square window in the wall opposite the door. The man wearing shades stood silently at the end of the table. The blond man sat down.

'We have been sent to transfer the prisoner.'

The Commander lowered himself into a seat opposite, placed his arms on the table and inter-locked his fingers. 'I've heard nothing about this.'

'Our Commander emailed you this evening.'

'I have not received an email.'

The ROS officer kept his eyes fixed on Mantessi and withdrew a sheaf of papers from an inside pocket of his jacket. 'Here.'

Mantessi glanced at them and stood up without a word. 'Wait here.'

In less than a minute he was back in the room. 'There's no record of this request other than the document you showed me. There's no email,' he said simply.

'I anticipated that eventuality,' the ROS officer said. 'You cannot rely on the new technology. So I took the liberty of contacting your superior, Deputy Prefect Aldo Candotti.' He handed Mantessi his mobile. The commander took it as though he had been offered a stale halibut. Placing it to his ear, he said. 'Yes, Deputy Prefect. Yes, that is correct. But sir, we have no formal . . .' He glanced at the ROS officer who was gazing at his shoes and rocking on his heels. The other officer appeared to be staring straight at him, but it was hard to tell for sure. 'That's correct sir. Yes, naturally. I see . . . Very well . . . Goodnight.' He made a show of finishing the conversation even though Candotti had already hung up.

The ROS van pulled up at the back entrance to the police station. The prisoner had been cuffed, his hands behind his back. Four officers escorted him to the doors of the van. He smirked at Mantessi who watched the process from the doorway. Two uniforms pushed the prisoner's head down to clear the frame before they closed the doors and banged on them to tell the driver all was secure. The van sped away. A black Alfa Romeo 159 carrying the ROS officers swept out behind it.

The two vehicles crossed Ponte della Liberta and took a turning off to Mestre, the lights of Venice dipping behind them. The main road twisted north and plunged past fields skirted by olive groves before it narrowed to a two-lane street with modest stone houses on either side. The van and the car pulled off into a lane and stopped. The two men jumped from the Alfa Romeo and met the driver of the van midway between the vehicles. The lane was slushy underfoot. Sleet had only stopped falling an hour before. Their breath hit the cold air and swirled around their faces. They swapped keys. The car reversed, swung around in the lane and skidded off while the two ROS officers jumped into the cabin of the van, fired the engine and continued on along the muddy track. A mile further on, they could see headlights in the night. They slowed and pulled over under the branches of a tree close to a black car. Running round the back of the van, they opened the doors.

'God, am I glad to see you,' the prisoner exclaimed and scrambled out into the chill air.

One of the ROS men patted him on the back. 'Good to see you too, Giulio.'

The other officer quickly unlocked the cuffs. Giulio rubbed his wrists. One of the men offered him a cigarette. He took it gratefully and lit up, following them around the side of the van.

The headlights switched off and a burly figure emerged from the black car. Aldo Candotti had his hands in the pockets of a shin-length black coat that flapped around his legs. He shook hands with the three men. 'Excellent work,' he said, his voice flat. 'Now gentlemen.' He turned to the two ROS officers. 'If you could wait here for a moment. I would like a private word with Giulio.'

Candotti put one meaty arm about the prisoner's shoulder and led him down the leafy lane under the trees.

'I am really grateful,' Giulio gave Candotti a big smile. 'I will soon have the information you need.'

'The problem is,' the Chief of Police replied, 'you seem to have generated . . . how shall I put it? Rather a lot of bad PR, Giulio. Your idea of grabbing the girl at the apartment was so crude, I had to intervene personally.'

Giulio's fingers pinched the cigarette between his lips. Pulling it away, he tossed it to the ground and crushed it under the toe of his shoe. When he looked up, Candotti was holding a pistol an inch from his forehead. Giulio tensed and took a step back.

'Inefficiency is excusable in many people, Giulio,' Candotti said wearily. 'People can accept it if a pop star turns up late for a show or a painter needs just that little bit longer to finish his masterpiece. But assassins? Well, it doesn't work, does it? Surely you can see that.'

Giulio's mind was racing. No situation was ever irretrievable. He stole a glance towards the vehicles, seeing the two men looking directly at them.

'I would say I'm sorry I have to do this,' the Chief of Police said. 'But I do so hate clichés, don't you? Now, shall I get you on your knees and shoot you through the head or would it be more sporting to let you run and shoot you in the back?'

The gun went off and a large hole was blasted in the middle of Giulio's forehead. 'Or how about I make it a surprise?' Candotti enquired. Pocketing the gun, he picked his way back to the car, trying to avoid splashing mud on his shoes. He was already firing up the engine as the two policemen approached. Candotti let the window down. 'Bury him in the woods,' he said, staring into the cold eyes of the blond ROS officer. Without another word, he sped off down the track, out on to the main road and back to the Most Serene Republic.

Chapter 28

Florence, present day

By the time they reached the Medici Chapel it was late evening. All the trains from Venice had been booked out until the afternoon and so they had hired a car. What with a visit to Roberto, another trip to pick up some things from Jeff's apartment and another appointment at the police station to obtain clearance to travel to Florence, it was 4 p.m. before they had left Piazzale Roma.

Jack Cartwright met them at the foot of the stairs leading down into the burial chamber. He shook Jeff's hand and gave Edie a contrite look. She rolled her eyes and walked straight into her uncle's old office.

The police had returned everything they had taken away for analysis, but only one of the lab staff, Sonia Stefani, had come back from leave. The computers had been reinstalled, the files checked; everything was as it should be. In fact, it was eerily similar to the way it had been a week earlier, almost as though nothing had happened.

Jack pointed to the ceiling. 'CCTV,' he said. 'The police recommended it and the insurers insisted upon it. Bloody intrusion if you ask me.'

Edie shrugged. 'It's good of you to come back so early,' she said to Sonia. 'It's much appreciated by Jack and me.'

'To be honest, I was bored out of my mind. You've been in Venice?'

'Yes, I needed a little break,' Edie lied. 'This is my friend Jeff, and his daughter, Rose.'

They all shook hands.

'So what's been happening?' Edie asked. 'I heard about the TV report of course.' She glanced towards Jack Cartwright who was sitting in a swivel chair at Carlin Mackenzie's old desk.

'You see these here,' Jack said, pointing at an image on his computer screen; bands of colour that looked like a soldier's ribbon bars. 'Only two days ago I obtained some brand new software that allows us to sequence a workable amount of DNA from the tiniest source. This meant I could get a much more accurate lock on the nature of the DNA we extracted from the body thought to be Cosimo. As a comparison, here are samples from four other members

337

of the Medici family.' He punched some keys and several sets of coloured strips appeared beneath the first one.

'You would expect matches in this region.' He moved the cursor along a stretch of coloured blocks. 'But there's nothing.' He looked up at Edie. 'The body we've been studying cannot possibly be a Medici.'

'So who the hell is it?' Jeff asked.

'That I can't tell you. But I've discovered some interesting facts. I compared the sample with the International HapMap.'

'The what?' Jeff asked.

'Sorry. Since the human genome was mapped a few years back, we now have something called the International HapMap Project, a catalogue of SNPs.'

'Which are?'

'Single nucleotide polymorphisms,' Edie interrupted. 'Tiny amounts of human DNA that vary most commonly from one individual to another; the bits of the genome that contribute to a person having, I don't know, blue eyes, say. Or a hairy back.'

'Or a nose like my mum's,' Rose interjected.

Jeff put an arm around her shoulder.

'Whatever,' Cartwright said. 'The point is, I was able to compare the DNA from this body with over three million SNPs in the catalogue and I found that the corpse is that of a man who was born in Scandinavia. As far as we know, Cosimo de' Medici never went within a thousand miles of Scandinavia, ergo the body is definitely not Cosimo's. I suggest it is probably the body of a court servant or a slave.'

'And what about the woman?' Jeff said.

Jack stood up suddenly. 'Are you two ever going to tell me what the hell's going on?'

Edie swallowed. 'What makes you . . .?'

'Edie, why have you rushed back here? How come Jeff is so curious about everything all of a sudden?' He took a deep breath. 'I do read the papers, you know. Four deaths in fewer days. A famous visconte shot, a man who happens to be a friend of yours, Jeff.'

'I'm sorry, Jack,' Edie said. 'It wasn't my plan to keep you in the dark.' She noticed Rose's eyes getting bigger by the minute.

'Nor you,' Jeff said to his daughter.

Edie gave Cartwright the bare bones of the story, leaving out the critical information they had gleaned from the clues.

'And obviously you found something at La Pietà that brought you back here?' Jack said when she had finished.

Edie nodded.

'And, clearly, you haven't heard the latest.'

'What do you mean?'

Cartwright paused for a moment, savouring the dramatic reaction his remark had produced. 'The suspected killer has escaped from police custody.'

'What!' Jeff and Edie snapped in unison.

'Only made public this evening, just before you arrived in fact. No trace of him.'

'Dad?' Rose asked querulously.

'Wait a moment, darling,' Jeff said. 'It's all right.'

'What exactly did you find at La Pietà?' Jack Cartwright enquired, grim-faced.

'There was a fresco.'

'I know. The place is full of bloody frescos!'

'There was an image of this chapel. And some writing: SOTTO 400, 1000.'

'What's that supposed to mean?'

' "Under" in Latin,' Edie said.

'I know that,' Jack muttered.

'That's it. I've no idea what the rest means.'

Cartwright turned to Jeff. 'And you?'

'I thought it might be a combination or a number code, but . . .'

'You've obviously been tangled up with this for too long,' Jack said. 'You can't see the wood for the trees. Why mix Latin with modern numbers? 400, 1000? Must be telling you something. Change the

400 and the 1000 to the Roman system and what do you have? CD, M.'

'CD, M . . .'

'C-o-s-i-m-o D-e M-e-d-i-c-i?'

Jeff and Edie looked at Cartwright as if he had just revealed to them the meaning of life.

'Brilliant, Jack.' Edie broke into a slow smile.

'Under Cosimo de' Medici,' Jeff said. 'Hate to spoil the party, but haven't we just come full circle? The artefact you found the night Professor Mackenzie was killed. That was "under" Cosimo de' Medici.'

'Except it wasn't Cosimo.' Jack retorted.

'Oh for Christ's sake!' Edie exclaimed. 'This is ridiculous!'

'No, no – hold on, hold on.' Jeff perched himself on the edge of a desk and stared at the floor. 'The other body, the woman. You've been assuming that was Contessina de' Medici, right? But the artefact was under the body posing as Cosimo. Maybe whatever the clue from La Pietà is leading us to is under the other body.'

'What makes you think that?'

'Well,' Jeff replied. 'CD, M might stand for Cosimo de' Medici, but it could just as well mean Contessina de' Medici, couldn't it?'

It took them half an hour to remove the body

from the alcove, a nerve-racking procedure requiring patience and a great deal of experience to avoid ending up with a pile of powdered bone and rags on the laboratory floor. Edie and Jack transferred the body of the woman from its resting place on to a trolley which Rose had helped prepare with Sonia. She didn't want to be left out of anything any more. And Jeff calculated that ultimately, this was better than packing her off at every opportunity. She had faced the most terrible adversity and had shown herself to be a courageous and resilient young woman. He found himself watching her, admiring her as she worked. He was feeling distinctly proud.

The two palaeopathologists had donned gowns and latex gloves and prepared to begin their investigations. Edie positioned a powerful light close to the trolley while Jack adjusted a loupe in his left eye. Neither spoke. Jeff noticed for the first time the blinking red light of the CCTV camera in the lab and thought what odd footage it would be recording.

'The body is in pretty much the same sort of condition as the male,' Edie noted as she inspected the clothing and a few strands of grey hair around the corpse's temples. 'Quite possibly buried at the same time.' She clipped some of the hair and placed it in a test tube which she stoppered and labelled. Cartwright dusted some fibres from the woman's dress and put these into a similar tube.

Much of the woman's clothing had disintegrated, especially on her underside, leaving a layer of cloth like a sheet lain over the body. Between them they carefully removed this, placing the various pieces on a table nearby that had been covered in plastic. They then laid another sheet of clear plastic over the garments.

The skin of the body was brown, the colour of old teak in patches under the arms and around the pelvis. In places, it had disintegrated to nothing, revealing tawny bone. 'OK,' Edie said. 'Let's take a look "under" the body.'

Repeating almost precisely what the team had done little over a week earlier, Jack pivoted the body on to its side. They could see the shape of the spine and the ancient bone where many of the vertebrae had become exposed as the flesh and skin had disintegrated. Then Edie saw it, between the sixth and seventh rib in the space where intercostal muscles and tissue had once been. A silvery object.

'Turn her back over,' Edie instructed and helped Jack turn the featherweight body.

'Anything?' Jeff asked, leaning in to get a closer look.

'I think so. Jeff, could you . . .?'

'Sorry.' He took a step back.

Repeating the procedure Carlin Mackenzie had followed, Edie sliced open the remains of the woman's chest. She could just see, nestled in the dried-out tissue, the edge of what looked like a small metal container. Several of the woman's ribs had turned to powder. Edie carefully eased away a bone fragment and with a soft brush she dusted the cavity, before sliding her latexed fingers into the opening.

The room was silent – the four of them stared at the object Edie had retrieved. It was a metal box no more than two inches square with a tiny clasp along one side. She walked over to a small table and placed the object carefully on to a plastic sheet.

It was plain. The metal appeared to be silver, or a silver alloy. It looked as new as the day it was made. Jack leaned over and adjusted his loupe, then he removed it altogether and pulled over a magnifying glass on a stand.

'There's not a mark on it,' he said.

'Can we open it?' Jeff asked.

Edie lifted the clasp with a pair of tweezers and eased open the lid. It rolled back smoothly. Inside lay a small silver key on a bed of faded purple velvet. Along the shaft of the key were the words: GOLEM KORAB. Edie plucked it from the box and held it

344

between latexed finger and thumb. She had just turned it over to see if anything was written on the other side, when she heard a strange voice.

'Bravo.'

A tall man with blond spiky hair was standing halfway down the stairs into the burial chamber. They had been so engrossed none of them had heard him arrive. He was clapping slowly, the sound muffled by black leather gloves. He stopped, put his hand into the pocket of his jacket and withdrew a revolver. 'It appears I've arrived at just the right moment. Now . . .' He stared directly at Edie. 'Please replace the key and step back from the table.'

Edie didn't move.

'Very well.' He raised the gun.

'Edie!' Jeff yelled.

The man smiled, but kept the gun fixed on them. 'Very sensible.' He was at the table in three paces, lifting the key from the box. 'Pretty, isn't it?' He slipped it into his pocket. 'Now, I'm very sorry but I am going to have to kill you anyway. My employer would not like my visit made public, and well, neither would I. Get on your knees.'

None of them moved. He slammed the gun against the side of Jeff's face and sent him sprawling across the floor.

'Dad!' Rose cried and rushed over to his side.

'On your knees,' the gunman repeated.

Jack and Edie obeyed.

'Face the wall. And you.'

Trembling, Sonia followed suit.

'Now, who'd like to go first? I think the youngest, don't you?'

Jeff acted instinctively, and made a lunge for the gunman's hand. With a strength he didn't know he possessed he head-butted the blond man and heard his nose crunch. The gun skittered across the floor. The blond man stumbled back, just managing to grasp the edge of a table, breaking his fall. But Jeff still had the momentum of rage and desperation. He punched the gunman hard in the solar plexus. With a grunt, his opponent bent double.

Jack and Edie were both on their feet now too, and Sonia reached down to pick up the gun. He might have been outnumbered, but the blond man was no ordinary bar brawler. Blood pouring from his broken nose, he caught hold of the trolley with the body and shoved it hard towards them. It shot across the floor, collided with a computer rack on a mobile stand and slammed into a corner of the lab where two work-benches met. The mummified corpse slid diagonally off the trolley and on to the stainless steel top of the workbench, scattering beakers and racks of test tubes, and landing head-first but miraculously intact in a tangled nest of wires and paper. Knocking Rose to one side, the gunman took the stairs three at a time.

Jeff dashed over to Rose and pulled her to him. 'You OK, sweetheart?'

'I'm fine, Dad. You're the one who's bleeding.'

Jeff's hand went up to his head where he had been struck by the barrel of the gun.

Sonia brought over a cold, wet cloth and dabbed gently at the wound. It was not deep but already the skin around it was starting to bruise. 'Shouldn't we call the police?' she said.

'Shouldn't we first check that bastard isn't still here?' Edie said.

Jeff took the gun from her and ran upstairs. But there was no sign of the gunman anywhere. After all, he had what he had come for.

'Well, that looks like the end of our adventure,' Jack said.

'That could be just as well,' Jeff replied ruefully.

'I saw what was written on the key,' Edie said. 'GOLEM KORAB.'

'Sounds like an Indian pudding,' Sonia said.

Rose was the only one to laugh. But then her expression became more serious. 'Hang on, Edie,' she said suddenly. 'You saw what was on one side of the key. What about the other?'

'Unfortunately I didn't get to see that. Our friend with the peroxided hair interrupted us just as I turned it over.'

They were silent for a moment, but then the spell was broken by Sonia. 'The CCTV cameras,' she said, her eyes wide with excitement.

The others stared at her blankly.

'You might not have had time to see the other side of the key, but they would.'

'Sonia, you're a genius,' Edie exclaimed.

Removing the memory stick from the camera in the lab, Sonia slotted it into a multi-media reader connected to one of the Macs.

'You know how to work this?' Edie asked as Sonia took over the keyboard and began tapping at some keys.

'I've picked up a few tips from my brother. He works for a security firm in Milan. These cameras are pretty standard. They record on to these sticks and then they're wiped automatically every twenty-four hours after the original images have been stored on a hard drive. So all we need to do is fast-forward to about twenty minutes ago,' Sonia said.

Most of it showed an empty lab. Then they saw Sonia enter and leave. A little later, Jack Cartwright came in from the corridor and stayed for an hour or so working at one of the computers. Fast-forwarding, Sonia found footage of Edie and Jack working on the body on the trolley. They watched Edie remove an object from the corpse, place it on a table, open it and take out the key.

'That's it,' Edie said. 'Go back.'

Sonia tapped at the keyboard and the film went into reverse. She slowed it until it was tumbling back in time frame by frame.

'There,' she said.

On the screen they could see Edie's latexed finger and thumb holding the key.

'It's impossible,' Jeff said despondently. 'You can't make anything out.'

'Hang on,' Sonia said, her fingers dancing over the keys. The image on the screen grew larger and shifted to the right, stopped and began to grow again. The key filled the screen, but it was blurred.

'Just need to enhance this . . .'

A few seconds later, Sonia sat back. 'Voilà!'

They could just make out a faint etching at the top of the key. It was the impression of a single-storey building and a word: ANGJA. In the centre of the building were two tiny characters, M and D.

★

At 7 a.m., Pisa airport was almost empty, more reminiscent of a large bus station than an international airport. Rose, wrapped up in her thick winter coat, was sipping at a polystyrene cup of weak tea Jeff had just handed her.

'You really don't have to pack me off home, you know, Dad,' she said and ran a gloved hand along his arm, clasping his palm.

'I'm afraid I do, Rose. Believe me, I regret it, but we've had one too many frights.' He felt furious with himself for having put his daughter's life in danger, for ruining her trip to Italy, for exposing her to such horrors. 'I'm . . .' he began.

'Dad, there's no need. It's not your fault. Look at it this way, how many girls my age get to see such action?' She laughed. 'Think of the stories I can tell . . . I'm joking,' she added quickly, seeing her father's face drop. He managed a tired laugh and gave her a hug.

'So, promise,' he said holding her at arm's length, 'promise, not a word to anyone, not even to your mother . . . especially not to your mother.'

'Cross my heart.'

They turned as Edie approached.

'All set?'

'Yep. Passport, tickets, money,' she said with a grin at Jeff. 'At least I had all three last time I was told to check two minutes ago?'

Edie laughed and kissed Rose on the forehead. 'We'll see you soon.'

Rose went up on tiptoes and gave her father a kiss on the cheek.

'Ow!'

'Oh God! Sorry, Dad!'

'No problem.' He fingered his bruised face gingerly.

At the security check he said, 'Phone me when you get home, yes?'

'I will, and please Dad, take care. I don't really understand what's been going on with you guys; but maybe it's time you went to the police?'

'Yeah, maybe Rose. Maybe. But don't worry. We'll sort it all out. And you'll be back in a few months, OK?'

'Try and stop me.'

With that she was gone. On the other side, she collected her bag and turned one last time to wave to Jeff and Edie before entering the wide corridor that led to the departure gates.

Rose was sitting reading a magazine when a voice announced in Italian, and then in English, that Business Class passengers could board the BA flight to Gatwick at their convenience. She folded her magazine, slipped it into the side pocket of her bag and stood up.

'Rose,' said a voice behind her.

She turned, startled, then smiled. 'What are you doing here?'

Chapter 29

Ragusa, June 1410

By the time sunlight had begun to leach across the eastern sky, Cosimo's party had left the monastery many miles behind. Three days later, they had reached the coastal city of Ragusa.

It had felt good returning to civilisation, and they did not dwell on the hardships they had faced. By the time they reached a tavern situated in the midst of Ragusa's thriving harbour, the sun was setting, casting a warm, golden glow across the shimmering water of the bay. Sailors were cleaning the decks of their boats and stallholders scrambled to sell off cheap their remaining stock of fish and vegetables. Laughing children played around the ropes holding fast the boats to the quay and chased each other round the nets and crates as the adults talked and drank.

Cosimo was in buoyant mood. The adventure had been extremely risky, but worthwhile. The haul from the monastery was truly astonishing, including as it did a collection of essays by Martial, a commentary on Homer and a wondrous text that appeared to be a very early copy of a Platonic discourse. He had also managed to save a chunk of an original Aristotle text, and, most prized of all, an almost complete original work called *Histories* by the great Herodotus. They all slept like logs that night, their first in a good bed since the night before the raid on the monastery.

Cosimo knocked on the door. He banged again, harder this time. Still no reply. 'Ambrogio . . . Ambrogio,' he called.

Contessina and Niccoli waited in the corridor behind him. They turned as the innkeeper approached swinging a large set of keys.

'You are concerned for your friend? Perhaps he drank a little too much last night.' The man chuckled and rubbed the bristle on his chin.

He unlocked the door and pushed it open.

Ambrogio lay sprawled on the bed.

'Hah! I'll leave you to help him with his headache,' the innkeeper said merrily.

Contessina held Tommasini's hand. 'Ambrogio,' she whispered. He twitched when she called him again, and his eyes flicked open.

'You look terrible,' Cosimo said. 'Thought you

could hold your drink a bit better than that!'

He stopped suddenly at the corner of Tommasini's bed. The floor was smeared with blood and a foul-looking yellow liquid. Lying on its back, fangs drawn back, was a large brown rat. A huge tumour, almost the size of its cranium had sprouted on its head. Its eyes were still open, and tracks of dried blood ran down its fur.

'Ambrogio, are you sick?' Contessina cried.

Tommasini tried to sit up. Wincing, he grabbed his forehead. His eyes were ringed in black, lips dried and cracked, skin deathly pale.

'I, I couldn't sleep.' His voice sounded brittle.

'What on earth's this?' Cosimo said, pointing to the floor.

Tommasini looked down at the floor and turned away quickly. 'My God! Poison?' he croaked.

'I hope it's just that . . . I really do.'

Silver stars punctured the ebony of night as Cosimo leaned on the rail of the ship and looked out at the inky calm of the ocean. The *Zadar*, the trade ship they had boarded at Ragusa was fast, but no vessel could be fast enough for him. All he wanted was to be home, to walk the streets of Florence and to have time to study the great treasures they had saved from the barbaric Stasanor.

A voyage of seven days hugging the coast north then bearing west and south would bring them to Ancona, which meant giving Venice a wide berth. It would be a two-day ride before they reached home. Feeling suddenly cold, Cosimo pulled tight a rough woollen blanket he had draped across his shoulders.

Cosimo was awoken by a shrill scream. Pulling on his breeches in the dark, he nearly lost his footing. Emerging on to the deck, he saw Niccoli and Contessina appear from the stern. They looked bleary-eyed in the cold grey of early morning. A young crewman came rushing towards them, his eyes black with shock. Cosimo was about to grab him when he heard the captain's voice.

Captain Davonik was a big man with a long, pepper and salt beard, dark brown eyes and weather-beaten cheeks. He had followed this route to Ancona a thousand times and people claimed he had brine for blood. 'What is it, Kulin? You look like you've seen a ghost.'

The young boy was shaking and could barely form words. The captain gripped Kulin's upper arms. 'Calm yourself.'

The boy pointed mutely to the railings on the port side.

All around the ship, as far as the eye could see, the

surface of the water was a mass of dead fish. They were of all shapes and sizes and species. They bobbed in the water, a thousand eyes staring blankly at the leaden sky.

It was nearly sunset and Cosimo was alone in the hold sitting at an upturned crate that served as a table. Thoughts jostled for his attention, each one madder than the last. It was dark here save for a flickering circle of yellow produced by a single candle perched on the upturned box. He was surrounded by boxes of spices and exotic foods from Turkey, Persia and beyond. There were baskets filled with fabrics of many textures and a rainbow of colours. Soon these would be transformed into the latest fashions and sold to the wealthy of Naples and Genoa, Venice and Florence. There could even be in this very shipment, he mused, the silk for his beloved's wedding gown.

In front of him lay an opened book, a volume which would have been considered the greatest prize in any library in any city in the world. It was a tract by a Greek historian named Thucydides, who, almost a thousand years earlier, had composed a funeral oration for the famed Athenian politician, Pericles. Cosimo read the words aloud to himself: ' "And we shall assuredly not be without witnesses. There are mighty monuments of our power which will

357

make us the wonder of this and of succeeding ages.'"

Contessina appeared in the doorway. She was carrying a flagon of wine and a large bowl of bread and fruit. 'Sit, Cosi,' she said and smiled gently. 'I swear I've not seen you eat since we came aboard.'

'You think I need fattening up?'

'Definitely.'

Contessina placed the wine and food on the makeshift table and sat down next to Cosimo.

'I'm not at all hungry,' he said.

'Nor me. But we should eat.'

Cosimo poured some wine. The ruby liquid, rough and potent, came from vineyards close to Ragusa. 'Has Captain Davonik offered any kind of explanation for what happened this morning?' he asked wearily.

Contessina shook her head. 'None whatsoever. He told me he has been working the Adriatic for over thirty years. He was younger than the boy Kulin on his first voyage, and he has never experienced anything like this. He's completely mystified.'

'If I allowed my sense of reason to falter for a moment, I'd say this was the Devil's work.'

Niccoli entered the room. 'I need to talk to you about Ambrogio,' he said.

Contessina offered him some wine. He refused, but sat down at the table.

'It must have been two hours before dawn. I could not sleep. I kept thinking about that rat in Ambrogio's room. Eventually I got up, and went on deck.

'The night was unusually calm. I could see the island of Lastova a long way off to starboard. And then I noticed a basket had been lowered over the side of the ship. And there, lying flat on his belly, was Ambrogio, with his hands in the water. I saw a flash of green. It came and went so quickly, I couldn't be sure.'

'The vial,' Contessina said.

'Why didn't he tell us?'

From the deck came loud shouts.

Cosimo was first to the ladder. He held out a restraining hand to Contessina when he reached the top.

Ambrogio Tommasini was almost naked. A filthy vest and ragged undergarments clung to his wet body. He was crouching like a wild animal, face and arms covered in huge sores and swellings that seeped a yellowy liquid. His eyes were wild. Blood dripped from his nose and mouth. His hair, once a beautiful mop of blond curls, had fallen out, except for a few stringy wet patches plastered to his bloodied scalp.

The captain and the ship's mate were standing a few feet in front of him, staring, petrified.

'Get back!' Tommasini screamed. 'Get back. Don't touch me. I am cursed.' Then he spotted Cosimo and the others. 'Cosi . . . Cosi.' Tears tumbled down his cheeks merging with the blood.

It began to rain.

'Ambrogio, what have you done?'

Tommasini looked puzzled.

'Why did you keep this thing a secret? Why didn't you . . .?'

Tommasini took two stumbling steps towards them. A crazed expression broke through the grotesque distortions of his face.

'Cosimo, oh noble, virtuous Cosimo. You should hear yourself. Perhaps then you would realise why you make so many people want to puke.'

The rain was now coming down in earnest. 'What did you hope to do, Ambrogio?'

'I had my instructions, Cosimo.'

'What do you mean?'

'Surely you don't imagine you and the Humanist League are the only ones interested in the findings of men like Valiani, do you?' He coughed and retched. Blood splattered the deck. When he lifted his head again, he looked like a ghoul from Hell. 'And Valiani,' he gasped. 'Well, he hasn't exactly been secretive about his travels, has he? The Holy Father knew of Golem Korab before any of us.'

'The Holy Father? What are you talking about?'

'You have a short memory, Cosimo. You forget. My father was chief theologian to Cardinal Baldassare Cossa, as His Holiness was once known. I grew up in the household of the future pope.' Tommasini tried to smile, but the result was a horrible gargoyle's grin.

'You're telling me Pope John knew of this vial?'

'He, he knew the old monastery held secrets. An emissary from Macedonia mentioned the place, years ago and then . . .' Tommasini looked to the sky, his face contorted in agony. 'The Holy Father learned that Valiani and others were on the trail. I was called to Rome to speak with His Holiness. He knew of my links with you. I was well placed to pass on any information I might stumble upon.' He grimaced again and clutched his side. 'Then, when Valiani turned up out of the blue, I felt as though I had been handed it all on a plate. I admit I did not relish the prospect of a journey into the Macedonian mountains but, well, it was for the most noble of causes.'

'Oh?'

'Yes, Cosimo, believe it or not, other people do have different ideals. My master, Pope John has enemies bearing down on him from all sides. He is a military man as well as a spiritual leader . . . He, he . . .' Tommasini's legs began to buckle under him.

He fell to his knees. 'The Pope . . . hoped there would be some . . . something of great value in the library of Golem Korab . . .'

Tommasini's eyes burned with profound self-loathing. 'Oh God, Cosimo, my friend, my loyal friend . . . I'm so sorry . . . I, I . . . opened the vial . . .'

His lips continued moving, but now nothing was coming out. With a low groan, he lurched forward like a half-empty sack of flour.

They had all gathered on the deck of the *Zadar*, the captain and crew, Cosimo, Contessina and Niccolò Niccoli. Ambrogio Tommasini's body lay in a make-shift shroud perched on the edge of the ship's railing. Spots of rain hit the deck creating dark brown smudges the size of ducats.

Cosimo could not stop himself thinking of those who had died, lost in exchange for what? Ideas, a few scraps of paper, words, words left by long-dead men. The pain was almost too much to bear. He looked up to the sky and let the droplets of rain spatter on his face, let them run down his cheeks, impostors for the tears he still could not shed.

Had the Pope known of the vial all along? Cosimo could only think the worst and must act accordingly. The vial must be hidden away and never be allowed to fall into the wrong hands. Lifting his head he said,

'Dear Lord, take my friend Ambrogio who was cut down so cruelly and so young. Ambrogio fell into temptation, a temptation that destroyed him. He has suffered terribly for his sins. I pray his soul may rest in eternal peace, for he was a good man, a true and loyal friend, a man, weak like us all. I forgive him and I pray that in your infinite wisdom you, Lord, may forgive him too.'

He nodded to the captain and the shrouded body of Ambrogio Tommasini slid into the sea.

Chapter 30

Macedonia, present day

As the heli-jet came in low over Skopje airport, Jeff could see the city below, a low-rise mass of white buildings skirted by green mottled mountains. An hour later, they were through customs and being driven across the city in a black Toyota Landcruiser Sahara. Their driver and guide took them out on to the freeway heading west. The road climbed slowly as the landscape grew more mountainous. It was late afternoon by the time they reached the foothills of Golem Korab, the tallest mountain in Macedonia and the site of an ancient, now-ruined monastery. This stood beside a wide stretch of water, Lake Angja. Using a software package called Google Earth that enabled them to zoom in to within a few metres of any spot on the surface of the planet, they had checked over the site and were able to pinpoint a large stone cube, a featureless building on a small

364

island close to the centre of the lake. There was no information available about the building but, from the slightly blurred images on Google Earth, it looked like some sort of marble mausoleum. Crucially, it was the same shape as the outline of the building etched into the key.

The main road soon petered out and the four-wheel drive Toyota turned off on to a steep dirt track. After about thirty minutes, they reached a hikers' base, called Refuge Karadjek. From here, the guide had told them, a leisurely climb would bring them to the ruins.

Jeff and Edie pressed on up the mountain alone. They each had a rucksack, torches, food, and walkie-talkies because there was no signal here for their phones. They had also packed a lighter, emergency flares and a change of clothing. Jeff was also carrying an inflatable kayak made from ultra-light carbon fibre.

It was freezing cold, but stunningly beautiful, a hard and brittle beauty, like a cubist-era Picasso or a woman past her prime but radiant still with cheekbones chiselled from ice. It reminded Edie of childhood holidays in Scotland, walking through the Grampians. She hadn't then appreciated the spectacular skyscrapers of rock and the long spindly lakes squeezed almost into oblivion by the pincer movement of ancient stone; but now she could see the wonder of it all.

The monastery reared up like the remains of a fossilised wood, great columns of stone soaring into the sky, jagged and irregular. Looking at it now, Jeff could visualise how once, long ago, it had been a magnificent sight, a monument both to the ingenuity of man and to his piety, for this had been a place of worship as much as a sanctuary where hardy souls had vowed to dedicate their lives to their God. And there, immediately behind it, perhaps a hundred feet down the other side of the hill, Lake Angja. It lay in the shadow of the mountains. Shafts of evening sun broke through the clouds and cast pools of brilliance on the hills close to the water. But the lake had the appearance of black glass, utterly still and forbidding, almost alien.

'Can I see the printout?' Jeff asked. The wind had come up and they had both pulled on their fur-lined hoods. Jeff compared the Google Earth image with the copy they had made of the schematic etched into the key. 'The island must be just around that promontory,' he said, pointing vaguely north-east.

Passing close to the remains of the towers, they found a rough path between the rocks that took them down to the edge of the lake. A small island was visible about a hundred metres across the still black water. Trees obscured much of the shoreline but they could just make out the sides of a squat building, its walls straight and unadorned.

They dumped their rucksacks and Jeff slipped the protective cover from the kayak and let it unfurl on the shingle. He pushed a small lever on the side and a canister of gas opened, inflating the kayak. Together they pushed the boat into the water and clambered in.

There was no current, so the crossing was easy. As they stepped on to a rocky outcrop of the island, they were struck by the stillness, and the almost complete silence all around them. The building dominated the island, a giant marble slab, featureless and foreboding. The walls were smooth, immaculately crafted to the point of complete blandness, leaving only the grain of the stone to offer texture or to break its uniformity. It reminded them of something Albert Speer would have dreamed up for Adolf Hitler's fantasy of the Third Reich.

They circumvented the building twice before finding the door. It was a narrow marble rectangle made from the same piece of stone as the wall. The grain flowed from the door across the seam to the wall. The door would have been almost invisible when closed, but now it was slightly ajar. The lock had been tampered with recently, and there was still the residue of some lubricating oil. Jeff felt a tingle of excitement shoot down his spine.

'You don't have to go any further, Edie,' he said, pulling a torch from his bag.

'Don't be bloody ridiculous.'

'Perhaps one of us should stay here anyway, just in case.'

'Oh sod off, Jeff. In case of what? Don't you think it's a bit late for that sort of thinking?'

'OK,' he said, ducking under the lintel and flicking on his torch.

Their feet echoed on the marble floor of a narrow corridor. Their torch beams cut spectral tubes of illumination through the darkness and they could just make out the far wall, another featureless stone barrier. But as their eyes adjusted to the void they could see a faint patch of light and the blankness of empty space gave way to an outline, a rectangular opening and a corridor beyond.

The distant light was just enough to see by and they flicked off their torches. The stone walls were as smooth and plain as the rest of the mausoleum: cold, soulless marble that glistened very faintly. Instinctively, they moved to the edge of the corridor, clinging to the wall and slowing their pace. As they approached the end of the passageway they could see another rectangular opening cut into the stone. A vast metal door opened into another corridor, and through the opening on to a high-ceilinged chamber. The walls were splashed with orange light that danced and shimmered over the stone. Edie slid around the stone and leaned into the room as far as she dared.

It was vast, a circular chamber with a domed roof, almost a hemisphere, but pinched at the centre like the domes of St Basil's Cathedral in Red Square. The walls and the floor were constructed from the purest white stone. In the centre stood a massive block of black marble.

At first, Edie couldn't understand how the room was lit. There were no torches on the walls. But a channel, perhaps two feet wide cut into the floor, ran around the perimeter of the room and flames licked the air with their roots in a viscous black liquid. Someone had obviously been here very recently.

This does not bode well, thought Jeff. But it was too late to turn back now.

They left their rucksacks by the entrance, and walked over to the black object, which lay directly beneath the apex of the ceiling. Along one edge were three deep steps. They took them slowly. Reaching the top, Edie gasped and almost lost her footing. 'My God!' she exclaimed.

Beneath a glass canopy, two large caskets lay side

by side. One casket contained the body of a woman who was wearing what looked like a wedding dress, except it was cream and laced in pale blue. A gossamer veil covered her face. The man in the other casket wore a long gown of royal blue velvet with gold brocade. Their faces had crumbled, the skin frayed along the chin and across the cheeks. Their hands lay on cream silk, the flesh all gone, which made their identical rings of white gold and amethyst look many sizes too big. Beside the nearest casket stood two marble columns. Upon the left pedestal sat a plain rectangular wooden box, about a foot long. On the column to the right was a gold plaque with words in Latin etched into it. All they could understand immediately were the words: COSIMO ET CONTESSINA DE' MEDICI.

'Quite spectacular, is it not?' The voice came from the entrance.

They spun round.

'You're wondering where we've been? Believe me, this place is a rabbit warren.'

A tall, lean man in a black suit, his dyed black hair swept back over his ears, emerged into the light. Beside him walked Aldo Candotti carrying a gun nonchalantly at his side. And behind them, Jack Cartwright came forward. He had a young woman with him: Rose. Cartwright kept her right arm yanked up behind her back, and her mouth was gagged with a length of black cloth.

Jeff dashed down the steps, an inhuman growl coming from deep inside his chest. Candotti grabbed Rose from Cartwright and shoved the gun hard to her forehead.

'Now, let's all try to remain calm, shall we?' The tall man in black declared with a faint smile.

'Who the hell are you?' Jeff snapped. 'And what are you doing with my daughter?' He took a step towards Candotti who pushed the barrel harder into Rose's head, making her groan.

'My name is Luc Fournier.' He signalled to Candotti to ease off.

'And you,' Edie spat. 'What the hell are you doing here?'

Cartwright did not reply.

'Signor Cartwright has been in my employ for some time,' Fournier said. 'You look surprised, Signorina.'

Edie rounded on Cartwright, eyes blazing. 'It was you! You killed your own stepfather.'

Cartwright's expression of denial looked like it was painted on.

'Poor Jack,' Fournier interjected. 'Poor Jack was always playing second fiddle, always overshadowed by the great Carlin Mackenzie. It was easy for me to find an ally. He jumped at the chance to tell me everything that was going on. It was I who obtained the Medici journal in 1966. It seemed quite possible there would be other treasures buried in the crypt. I didn't want anyone else stumbling upon them, now did I?'

'So you knew about the artefact immediately after it was discovered and you killed my uncle to steal it?'

'That was regrettable.'

Edie glared at Cartwright. 'You piece of shit,' she snarled.

'We are not here to settle family disagreements.' Fournier was clearly enjoying the role of master of ceremonies. 'There are far more pressing matters. This chamber was designed by Contessina de' Medici and built a few years before her death, a mausoleum in which she and her beloved husband could lie together for all eternity. All very touching. But my only interest lies with the contents of that rather unassuming little box over there.' He pointed to the pedestal standing beside the tombs.

'As you have doubtless learned already, Cosimo de' Medici and his future wife Contessina travelled to this place almost exactly six hundred years ago. On that voyage they were accompanied by two men, Niccolò Niccoli, and Ambrogio Tommasini. They had left Florence under the auspices of a travelling mystic and philosopher named Francesco Valiani who guided them to a library in the monastery where it was believed important ancient documents were hidden. But they, or rather Ambrogio, found much more. He discovered a strange substance that could protect people from disease, but which could also kill, a biochemical agent.'

'What does any of this have to do with us?' Jeff snapped. 'For God's sake, let my daughter go.'

Candotti ignored him.

'The contents of that box have a great deal to do with you, Signor Martin,' Fournier said, 'and Rose is my little insurance policy. You and Signorina Granger are a remarkable couple. I knew you would find a way to get here, after all you've been through. In fact I was relying upon it. Because you have a vital piece of information I need.'

'We do?'

'I need four numbers,' Fournier said. 'Four Roman numerals to be precise. And I have only two, those etched into the key retrieved from the Medici Chapel, the numbers D and M. That presents me with a problem.'

Jeff shrugged his shoulders.

'But it also presents you with one, Signor Martin.' Fournier smiled his sinister smile. 'On your travels you came across two more Roman numerals, which were overlooked by my people. We could have all been saved a great deal of trouble this afternoon if someone had used their initiative. Now you will please give me those two numbers.'

'Why should I?'

'Because, Signor Martin, if you do not, the lovely Rose here will very quickly end up as dead as Cosimo and Contessina.'

'IV and V,' Jeff said.

'Thank you so much. You see how easy it is.' Fournier walked up the marble steps to the pedestal and the locked box. A barrel of four individual metal cylinders comprised the lock. He stared at them for a moment then rolled them into position. 'Other than the monks of Golem Korab,' he said. 'Ambrogio Tommasini was one of the few people ever to see what was contained in this box. He tampered with things he did not, could not, understand and paid the penalty. After his death, the Medici secreted away this box. But our good friend, Niccolò Niccoli, wrote a journal about their adventure in which he left a series of cryptic clues. Apparently, the secret could be revealed using four numbers and the words: to be a god. Placed in the correct sequence, the numbers IV, V, M and D spell DIVVM or DIVUM . . . God.'

The latch clicked open, and Fournier raised the lid.

Reaching down, he carefully lifted the vial level with his eyes. 'Amazing!' he murmured.

'Will you please let Rose go now?' Jeff said. 'You've got what you came for.'

Fournier nodded to Candotti, who reluctantly loosened the gag and shoved Rose away. She stumbled, but Jeff moved forward quickly to catch her.

There was a discreet cough from the doorway. Candotti swivelled round and aimed his gun.

'There's really no need for that, Deputy Prefect,' Roberto said, taking several paces into the room. He was limping slightly, his left arm was in plaster from shoulder to hand and it lay in a sling. His face was still badly discoloured.

'Visconte Armatovani.' Fournier gave the briefest of bows. 'To what do we owe the pleasure?'

'How could I resist, Monsieur Fournier? I was worried about my friends here. I also had some enforced leisure time in the hospital to do some thinking. And, even if I say so myself, I do have a rather fine library. By great good fortune, copies of some parts of Niccoli's journal had fallen into the hands of my ancestors. I have learned some remark-able things about that . . .' and he nodded towards the glowing tube in Fournier's hand.

Fournier raised an eyebrow, 'Oh, really?'

'This is the great secret which the Medici realised had to be hidden from the sight of men. To them it was a miraculous substance. To be sure, it had sent one of their friends to a most hideous death, but the contents of that vial could protect people from the plague. But Cosimo and Contessina had seen at first hand how such a thing could corrupt. Men would be willing to sacrifice their very souls for something like this. I'm sure you would love to tell us all about it, Monsieur Fournier.'

Fournier's eyes gleamed with triumph. 'The vial contains a very rare biochemical agent called Ropractin. You've all heard of Ricin and Sarin, both very nasty chemicals that in tiny quantities can kill thousands. Ropractin comes from a mould called Tyrinilym Posterinicum, found in damp climates. Refined and purified, it produces a liquid that has a fluorescent green hue. In trace amounts Ropractin kills bacteria like a super penicillin. But, above a certain concentration, it causes the rapid onset of some very unpleasant diseases for which there are no known cures.

'The Medici discovered this the hard way. They had no idea where this vial came from originally, and probably none of us will ever know. Perhaps some anonymous alchemist discovered it. Who knows?'

'But the point is,' Roberto interrupted. 'You have not come all this way to help combat disease, or for medical science . . .'

'Do we have to listen to all this, Luc?' Candotti blurted out. 'You can't trust this man . . .'

Fournier turned slowly towards the Venetian Police Chief. 'You amuse me, Aldo.'

Candotti looked puzzled.

'A man such as yourself talking about trust. You have sold your career and the trust placed in you by the good people of Italy. And for what? The few pieces of silver I have passed your way.' He shook his head, tutting. 'And you, Signor Cartwright,' Fournier went on. 'Do you have any pearls of wisdom to add? Any words of warning about who we may or may not trust?'

Cartwright remained silent.

From his jacket pocket Fournier removed a snub-nosed pistol. He raised his gun and shot Cartwright and Candotti between the eyes.

Jeff crouched down shielding Rose with his body. Fournier had turned his gun on Edie, but he didn't fire. Roberto had a Beretta M9 in his good hand aimed directly at Fournier's head.

'Edie, Jeff, Rose, get out of the way.'

They took cover behind the tomb.

'You and I have no quarrel,' Fournier said quietly.

He began to back away towards the door. 'And you dare not shoot. If I were to drop this vial . . .'

Roberto held the Beretta steady for a second, then lowered it. Fournier dived to one side. Crouching low to the ground, he fired once, wide of his target, sped towards the exit and disappeared.

Edie, Jeff and Rose emerged from behind the Medici sarcophagi, averting their eyes from the carnage just a few feet away.

'We can't just let that maniac go,' Edie said.

'What do you suggest?' Roberto responded. 'We're not the police. Anyway,' his eyes flickered towards Candotti's body, 'they weren't a great help.'

'Roberto's right, Edie,' Jeff said. 'Remember why we got into this in the first place? To find out who killed your uncle. We know the answer now.'

'Oh great,' she growled. Marching up the marble steps, she stared down at the empty box, hands on her hips. Then suddenly, she yelled and kicked the base of the pedestal.

There was a loud cracking sound from the floor beneath her feet, followed by a high pitched whine and the sound of stone grinding on stone. The pedestal toppled to one side, sending the empty box clattering down the steps. From a point above the entrance to the chamber, a massive stone block slid down from the lintel. It slammed into the floor, making the whole room shudder.

No one moved. All they could hear was the steely sound of small stones and debris falling from the ceiling on to the marble floor.

Tears welled up in Rose's eyes. 'We're trapped aren't we?'

'There's always a way, sweetheart,' Jeff said and put his arm around her shoulders.

In place of the column was a perfectly square hole. Inside lay rows of wooden tubes. Jeff reached in, lifted one out and put it on the floor carefully before picking up another, almost identical tube.

'Scrolls, like the one Sporani found in the Medici Chapel,' Roberto said.

Jeff removed a few more, then spotted something lying underneath. 'There's another box.'

'Can you lift it out?'

'No, it's fixed in place. There's a lock, identical to the other one.' Jeff rolled the cylinders to form the right combination. There was a satisfying click and he lifted the lid.

An identical vial lay nestled in the velvet padding. On the inside of the lid, inscribed in gold was a line of Latin. Roberto translated it: ALL MEN ARE TREACHEROUS.

Jeff lifted out the vial and held it up. It weighed

almost nothing and shimmered luminous green in the light from the oil burners.

'I know this sounds crazy. But it seems almost alive.'

'For fuck's sake Jeff, be careful,' Edie muttered.

'It looks pretty robust,' Jeff replied. 'Thick glass or crystal. If Tommasini killed himself he must have opened it. Look, this has been expertly resealed.' He pointed to the end of the tube where a stout brass cap joined the glass, a waxy substance had been moulded into the join.

'OK, but even so . . .'

'So,' Jeff said, passing the vial to Roberto. 'Two vials. One real, one fake?'

Edie laughed suddenly, an edge of hysteria to it. 'Bloody marvellous. We have the vial, but we're shut in with no way out.'

'Damn it!' Jeff walked over to the door. A thin line around the edge was the only indication that there had ever been an opening at all. 'This is ridiculous. How can this happen? How could fifteenth-century engineers construct such a thing?'

'They weren't the first,' Roberto replied. 'Four and half thousand years ago the Great Pyramid was sealed up immediately after the pharaoh was buried. It was all done automatically using an ingenious system of ropes and pulleys. Don't forget who we're dealing with. The Medici were not your average citizens. They had amazing resources at their disposal, and Cosimo and his pals were steeped in ancient knowledge.'

'And the Humanist ideal,' Edie sneered. 'Not much good to us now.'

'What did you say?' Roberto snapped.

'The Humanist ideal . . .'

'Of course!'

Roberto raised the vial to eye level. 'The Humanist ideal.

'What are you going on about, Roberto?' Edie glared at him.

'Cosimo and his friends were driven by the power of knowledge, but they were also very high-minded. They believed personal integrity was paramount. Note the inscription.' He pointed to the lid of the box. 'They realised the power of the vial. They knew it could destroy their world. That's why they hid it here.'

'So what are you trying to tell us?' Rose asked shakily.

Crouching down, Roberto placed the vial back in its box and shut the lid.

For several moments nothing happened. Roberto stepped back, keeping his eyes glued to the opening in the floor.

'It's not . . .' Jeff began and stopped. A low rumbling came from the floor and the box sank down into the stone stairs. They watched it descend three feet, four, five. It stopped and a stone block slid across the space sealing the box deep inside the tomb. Then came a new sound, from across the room, the grating of stone on stone. It grew louder. They ran down the steps, reaching the floor as the block of stone in the doorway began to lift. They dashed towards it and ducked under the rock, almost falling over each other into the dark corridor on the other side.

They were picking themselves up in the darkness when, without warning, the block stopped moving. There was a moment of silence. Then came a noise like the growling of some monstrous beast. It grew louder and louder. A tremendous crash came from inside the chamber and they could see through the opening great boulders tumbling through the air and smashing to the floor.

'Quick! The ceiling is coming down,' yelled Roberto. Jeff grabbed Rose and they made their way as fast as they could towards the exit, Roberto limping a few feet behind the others. The walls were shaking and the floor began to crack and splinter. Towards the end of the corridor, they felt a massive jolt like a seismic tremor. Rose screamed. In the grey light they saw a chasm a metre wide shudder across the floor and up the wall. Edie helped Roberto cross the fissure. He slipped, landed heavily and convulsed in pain. 'Come on . . . the exit is just ahead,' Edie screamed above the noise.

Catching up with Jeff and Rose, they all kept running as fast as they could, not looking back.

Lathered with sweat, they emerged into the air. The cold hit them like a sledgehammer, but it was a relief. Night had fallen, and it was not easy finding their way back on to the shingle. But then, the darkness was ripped away as an intense beam of light broke over the mausoleum and a helicopter roared into view, before it banked away to the north.

They could hear voices coming from the direction of the monastery. And out of the night another bright beam cut a swath through the darkness. A small motor launch roared up on to the beach. A Macedonian police officer jumped out and splashed his way to the shore. Roberto led the way and Jeff held Rose close as they crossed the rough ground to follow the policeman.

The chopper was back and was swooping low over the water as they covered the short distance to the edge of the lake. As they made dry land, another officer saw them, broke into a run and called into his radio for assistance.

Outside the old monastery it looked like the aftermath of a military operation. Close to the towers they could see figures in bulky white biohazard suits erecting a large inflatable decontamination tent. The chopper returned to hover over the towers and another was perched on a narrow plateau of rock a dozen metres from the entrance to the ruins. A policeman instructed them to follow him. Inside the helicopter, three men in biohazard suits sat with rifles across their laps. On the floor behind the pilot, his hands cuffed behind him, was Luc Fournier. His face was badly bruised and his suit ripped.

'Is this the man?' the policeman asked Jeff.

Fournier did not even look up.

The policeman gave the pilot the thumbs up.

As they ducked away from the whirling blades, Roberto said, 'OK, so I arranged a little back-up.'

Jeff could not resist laughing, and with a grin, Roberto leaned forward to ruffle Rose's hair. 'You two go and get warmed up,' he said. 'I think we're all going to be put through decontamination.'

Two paramedics ran up and escorted Jeff and Rose to the ambulance chopper.

'You certainly know how to put on a show, don't you Roberto?' Edie said, her eyes gleaming.

'You complaining?'

'No!' She laughed and looked away.

'I want to show you something before we get checked out.'

She slipped her hand through his good arm. 'You are the most extraordinary man I have ever met. How on earth did you find your way here?'

'I called the Medici Chapel, hoping to reach you, but instead talked to Sonia. She told me about the key and Candotti. Google and my library did the rest.'

'Ah yes, your library. I can just picture Vincent heaving all those books to the hospital.'

'Made a change from grapes.'

They passed the remains of the western tower and skirted the outer wall of the monastery. A path led directly to a circular stone platform, which then afforded them a vista of breathtaking beauty. Lake Angja lay stretched out before them, glistening in the moonlight like a black and white photograph taken with a starburst filter. They could see the mausoleum, a flattened cube of dark stone on the island off to the west. It appeared fathomless, and now they knew that it did indeed harbour many secrets inside its walls.

Roberto put his arm around Edie as they stared out at the water. 'It's not hard to imagine Cosimo and

Contessina standing on this very spot six centuries ago, is it?' he said.

'Puts things into perspective.'

'They must have been very much in love.'

She turned to look at him, surprised.

'Contessina didn't just create this whole thing to hide the vial,' Roberto said, his eyes fixed on the incredible view. 'This place obviously meant a great deal to them. It was their special place and she wanted them to be here together for eternity.'

'I didn't realise that the Visconte was such a terrible romantic.'

'Maybe,' he replied with a sly smile. 'But I was also thinking what a sacrifice they made.'

'How do you mean?'

'In the fifteenth century people believed that the body was sacrosanct. Just think of their obsession with Holy relics. Yet they allowed their beautiful tomb to be destroyed just to stop anyone unworthy taking the vial.'

'Did they though?'

'Of course they did. I think the Medici Secret is safe, at least for a while. I don't intend telling anyone about it. And I get the feeling our friend Luc Fournier is going to be locked away for a very long time. Naturally, there will always be people like Fournier. But there will also be people like Cosimo and Contessina . . .'

'It was understanding what made them tick that got us out of there.'

'A lucky break.'

Edie gave him a doubting look and they were silent for a moment, savouring the peerless atmosphere of the place.

'And at the very least they certainly looked peaceful before the roof came down, did they not?' Roberto said finally.

'They weren't really there though were they, Roberto?'

'Perhaps not, but we were, so their legacy lives on. Perhaps in another six hundred years someone else will learn of the Medici Secret. And, who knows? They may even live in more enlightened times. It would be nice to think that one day there might be no place for people like Fournier and nothing to be gained from trying to sell death to the highest bidder.'

'What? You mean the Humanist ideal?'

'Something like that,' he whispered, pulling her close and lowering his lips to hers. 'Something like that.'

The Facts Behind the Fiction

The Medici Secret is of course a work of fiction but, as with my first novel *Equinox*, many elements of this story are also based in fact. What follows is a summary of those elements and the truth behind them.

Ancient Manuscripts

The Greeks and Romans were great chroniclers. Unfortunately for human civilisation much of what was written in ancient times has been lost. The magnificent store of knowledge destroyed when the library at Alexandria was razed was one of the worst losses. But many texts disappeared in other, less dramatic ways.

Some of the vast literature of Greek and Roman civilisation was preserved in the monasteries and royal libraries of Europe and Asia Minor, and many documents survived the Dark Ages. It was largely thanks to the Florentines that this knowledge was retrieved by Europeans and used as the basis for the tremendous blossoming of civilisation we call the Renaissance.

The great fourteenth-century Italian philosopher, Petrarch, gathered about him a collection of like-minded adepts who shared a fascination with the Classical tradition. They believed there were perhaps thousands of manuscripts and documents in the original Latin and Greek secreted away in private collections and in isolated monasteries. Many of these men made it their life's work to seek out such treasures.

A generation after Petrarch, some of the most significant finds in the area of ancient 'scientific' studies were made. One of the most important figures in this quest was Niccolò Niccoli. During the second decade of the fifteenth century, Niccoli discovered *Astronomica* by the Roman writer Manilius, along with Lucretius' *De Rerum Natura* and several books about mining and agriculture including *Silvae* by Statius and *De Re Rustica* by Columella. A few years later, Bracciolini found Cassio Frontinus' *On Aqueducts*, which had provided the cornerstone of Roman architectural technique, and Cicero's *Brutus*, a book that soon became politically controversial because of its portrayal of the virtues of a monarchical form of government.

What was significant about these finds was that they were written in the original Latin and were mostly unadulterated. This meant that for the first time the Florentine elite of the late fourteenth and early fifteenth centuries could read the words of the great thinkers of the Classical era exactly as they had been written.

This was a tremendous advance. But perhaps even more important is the fact that, when these works were translated and interpreted, it was soon realised just how much the scientific thinking of Roman scholars was actually based upon an older source: the ideas of the Greeks, and in particular, such figures as Archimedes, Aristotle, Pythagoras and Plato from the golden era of Greek learning between 500 and 250 BC.

The inevitable result of this was a new and intensified search for the original Greek sources of scientific knowledge. Inspired by what had already been found, many of the richest people in Florence began to send emissaries abroad to locate and to purchase on their behalf anything they could find in the original Greek.

Until this time, the only original Greek manuscripts in Western European hands consisted of a few fragments of Aristotle and scraps of Plato along with some tracts of Euclid, all jealously guarded by monks or in the hands of a few devotees. Petrarch himself was reputed to have owned an original manuscript of Homer, but could not read a word of it. On the authority of the Roman writers to whom he referred, he accepted that Homer was a great poet and would kiss the book every night before retiring.

During the first three decades of the fifteenth century, several hundred original manuscripts found their way to Florence, largely from the East; where once Crusaders fought for Christendom, Western emissaries now bartered and purchased intellectual capital from the Turk. A single Florentine agent, Giovanni Aurispa returned after one particularly fruitful voyage in 1423 with 238 complete manuscripts.

In this way, the intellectual community of Florence acquired complete versions of Aristotle's *Politics*, the histories of Herodotus, the dialogues of Plato, the *Iliad*, the *Odyssey* and the plays of Sophocles, along with the medical writings of Hippocrates and Galen.

With accurate translations of a growing collection of Greek texts came the startling realisation that everything the Florentines had achieved culturally so far had been surpassed almost two millennia earlier by the Greeks. But this discovery did not act as a destructive force. It inspired them not only to emulate but to dare consider improving upon what the ancients had achieved.

In 1428, a committee was organised to instigate a series of changes to the education system of Florence. One of the trustees of the Studium, which lay at the cultural heart of the city, was Cosimo de' Medici, then a young banker living in Rome. He persuaded the clerical institutions of Florence to provide an annual 1,500 florins to add two new chairs to the rostrum of subjects. The existing curricula consisted of medicine, astrology, logic, grammar and law, and to these were added moral philosophy and a professorship of rhetoric and poetry. This provided a new syllabus for every student in Florence, and formed the foundation of the system adopted throughout Europe that remained in place within the universities of England, France and Italy until the eighteenth century.

Biochemical Weapons

The biochemical at the centre of the novel – the Medici Secret itself – is Ropractin. This is a fictional chemical but its structure and properties are very close to a real biochemical agent called Sarin. This biochemical is also known by its NATO designation of 'GB'. Sarin is an extremely toxic substance and its sole application is as a nerve agent. It has been classified a weapon of mass destruction by the United Nations, and its production and stockpiling was outlawed by the Chemical Weapons Convention of 1993.

Sarin became famous in 1994 when it was used by the Japanese religious sect Aum Shinrikyo whose fanatical members released an impure form of the biochemical during several connected incidents, which together resulted in the deaths of more than a score of people and injured hundreds of others.

Biochemical and biological weapons have been known for centuries. The earliest example of a biological weapon comes from a time predating the story of Cosimo and his associates in *The Medici Secret*. In 1346, the bodies of Tartar soldiers who had died of the plague were thrown over the walls of the besieged city of Kaffa (now Fedossia in the Crimea) to infect those within. Four centuries later, during the French and Indian War in North America in the 1760s, the English gave blankets contaminated with smallpox virus to the natives.

Chemical weapons were used on several occasions during the First World War, and, in more recent times, the late leader of Iraq, Saddam Hussein, is known to have gassed thousands of Kurds and used biochemical weapons during the decade-long war with Iran that began in 1980.

Today, the use of biochemical and biological agents by terrorist groups is a very real fear for Western governments. Huge resources are deployed in an ongoing effort to stop such substances falling into the wrong hands, but many believe that it is only a matter of time before some nihilistic individual or organisation somewhere obtains sufficient quantities of a deadly agent to cause mass murder in a Western city. It is sobering to realise that there may well be a Luc Fournier out there now formulating such a nefarious plan.

Further Reading: *Biochemical Weapons: Limiting the Threat*, Joshua Lederberg, MIT Press, Boston, 1999.

Giordano Bruno

Giordano Bruno was a mystic and a philosopher who rejected both the priesthood and orthodox religion to become a man abhorred by the Inquisition. Born in Nola near Naples in 1548, he joined the Dominican order. But, after discovering a wider philosophical outlook through the work of Copernicus and other unorthodox thinkers, he turned his back on religious dogma. He wrote many books of radical philosophy, the most famous of which was *The Ash Wednesday Supper*.

Bruno lived in London for a short time and is believed to have worked as a spy for Queen Elizabeth I. He associated with many of the mystics of the day, including John Dee, and he may have met William Shakespeare who is known to have become interested in many of Bruno's ideas.

Early in 1592 Bruno moved back to Italy at the invitation of a nobleman named Giovanni Mocenigo. Ostensibly, this was so he would become a tutor to this wealthy patron. While in Venice, he taught in Padua and made the acquaintance of Galileo and other thinkers of the time. However, the invitation from Mocenigo was a trap, and in May 1592 Bruno was arrested in Venice and put on trial before the Venetian Inquisition. He was then transferred to Rome. There he remained in a filthy cell for seven years. He endured terrible torture at the hands of the Pope's right-hand man, Robert Bellarmine and was burned at the stake in Campo de' Fiori in Rome on 17 February 1600.

Although Giordano was murdered by the Inquisition, today he is considered to be the first martyr of science and philosophy, a man who refused to back down from his opinions about the nature of the universe. Galileo was well aware of Bruno's treatment at the hands of the Roman Curia and did not want to share the same fate. Bruno's legacy has grown as the Catholic Church has diminished, but he remains anathema to orthodoxy and even now, over four centuries after his death, he has not been pardoned for his so-called heretical views.

Further Reading: *The Pope and the Heretic*, Michael White, Abacus, London, 2002.

Cosimo and the Medici

My drawing of the character and early biography of Cosimo de' Medici in *The Medici Secret* are as accurate as I could make them. He was born in Florence in 1389. His family did live in a house on Piazza del Duomo, his father was named Giovanni di Bicci de' Medici who did found what was by 1410 already a great bank.

In reality, Cosimo had two younger siblings, Lorenzo and Pierfrancesco. Lorenzo was sixteen in 1410 and Cosimo's half-brother Pierfrancesco was not born until 1431, twenty-one years after the events described in the novel. However, the essential fact that differentiates the fictional and the actual Cosimo is that, in reality, he never did make a voyage of discovery to Macedonia, or anywhere else. However, intriguingly, he did come very close to it. His intimate friend Niccolò Niccoli tried to persuade him to join him on a journey to the East, but Cosimo's father refused to allow it, and Cosimo acceded to his father's wishes.

Cosimo was a Humanist. He was extremely interested in culture and learning and he did a great deal to spark the Renaissance. Although he did not actually travel far himself, he paid others to retrieve anything they could from far-flung places, including Macedonia.

Cosimo was, like his father, a great businessman and he did much to further expand the horizons of the family bank. Most importantly, he handled papal finances. This was crucial in the evolution of the Medici dynasty and it made him the wealthiest man of his time.

But of course, the Medici had enemies – not the Tommasini family – and there were constant rivalries between them and other great Italian families. One, the Albizzi tried to have him assassinated, and when this failed they succeeded in having him imprisoned in 1433. But within a year, Cosimo was back in Florence and had acquired greater power and influence. For the next thirty years he was, in all but name, leader of Florence.

Cosimo was married to Contessina de' Bardi in 1416 and they had two children, Piero and Giovanni. Upon his death in 1464, Cosimo was indeed named *Pater Patriae*, Father of his Country. His eldest son, Piero then became the Florentine leader. Known as Piero the Gouty, he was plagued with bad health and died in 1469, just five years after his illustrious father. His son Lorenzo became, after Cosimo, the most highly regarded and successful Medici of them all. Known as Lorenzo the Magnificent, he was, like his grandfather and father, the first citizen of Florence, and for twenty-three years he was effectively the political leader of the city state, guiding Florence through a period of unprecedented stability and growth.

The character of Contessina as portrayed in the novel bears almost no relationship to the real-life wife of Cosimo de' Medici. According to official histories, she had no special physical powers and was not educated by a magus such as Valiani, but she was certainly a very intelligent and loyal woman, who was devoted to Cosimo and supportive of his endeavours.

Further Reading: *The Rise and Fall of the House of the Medici*, Christopher Hibbert, Allen Lane, London, 1974.

Da Ponte

Antonio da Ponte was the designer of the Rialto Bridge in Venice which was completed in 1591. The story about the Devil and da Ponte's wife and child has been adapted from an old Venetian fable in which the site supervisor at the bridge, Sebastiano Bortoloni, was the person visited by Lucifer.

Florence Flood

On the night of 3 November 1966 Florence suffered the worst natural disaster in its long history. At about 4 a.m. a huge volume of water from the Valdarno Dam caused the Arno to burst its banks. The water swept away cars and trees, crashed into churches and ancient palaces and burst into steel-lined vaults. Gas, electricity and water supplies were cut off and the city's electric clocks stopped at 7.26 a.m. At its highest, the water reached over six and a half metres in areas around Santa Croce.

At least thirty people died, and 50,000 families were made homeless by the flood. In addition, 15,000 wrecked cars were strewn about the streets and 6,000 shops were put out of business. According to the best estimates, in the space of a few hours, some 14,000 works of art were damaged along with three to four million books and manuscripts.

Golem Korab

This is not an Indian pudding but the tallest mountain in Macedonia, rising to almost 10,000 feet above sea level. The area is dotted with lakes but there is no Lake Angja and no monastery on the mountain. If there was ever a castle close by, it has completely vanished.

Humanism

As Europe was dragged from the bleakness of the Dark Ages, an awareness of what could be achieved and a conviction that humanity could do better than it had done already was a tremendous spur to adventurism, both in word and in deed. It led to the age of discovery, and to the beginnings of modern scientific thinking as well as providing a fertile ground for the artistic endeavours we see as emblematic of the Renaissance.

The importance of this shift in perception cannot be overestimated. With a few notable exceptions, such as Roger Bacon, people since the fall of Rome had been paralysed by a deep-rooted sense of unworthiness. Central to their thinking and encouraged by Christian dogma, was the notion that humans were mere creatures of God, pawns in a world where the forces of nature and the will of the Lord were everything, a world in which the individual was totally without significance. Such thinking could only lead to a stagnant society, and although the belief that God controlled the universe and was directly involved in all aspects of human existence dominated mainstream thinking until the Darwinian revolution, some Renaissance figures thought differently.

Some of the greatest intellects of the Renaissance believed whole-heartedly in the idea that human intellect should be treasured and nourished. In this paradigm shift, we may see the impact of Platonic philosophy evolving into what has been called human virtue, a central tenet of Active Humanism. At the heart of Platonic philosophy is the concept that humanity can find God through unravelling the secrets of Nature. For Plato this was the foundation of 'inspiration', and it became a crucial element in the thinking of many of the best minds of the Renaissance. A number of great and influential figures such as Leonardo da Vinci, Giordano Bruno, Machiavelli and Cosimo de' Medici understood this Platonic ideal.

Many Humanists subscribed to the view that virtue stood apart from conventional religion and saw it as an entirely human quality that could bring the individual closer to the essence of Nature. Indeed, the early Humanist scholar Leon Battista Alberti once wrote that those who possessed virtue were 'capable of scaling and possessing every sublime and excellent peak'.

This thinking represented a revolutionary way of perceiving the world, prompted by the great rediscovery of human worth and a positive realigning of the role of humanity in God's universe. It was a truly essential element of the Renaissance.

I Seguicamme (The Followers)

This is an imaginary secret society, but Venetian history is littered with strange sects and secret communities. Giordano Bruno was involved in various splinter groups of the pan-European Rosicrucians in the Republic, and for centuries Venice was a nexus for magi and itinerant mystics and occultists.

The Venetian authorities were famously lenient towards those the Catholic Church considered heretics and it was a haven for those with radical views. Many alternative philosophies were allowed to flourish in Venice and Venetian publishers pushed the boundaries of what was allowed in a Europe dominated by Catholic dogma.

Mauro's Mappamundi

Father Mauro was a cartographer who lived and worked in a monastery on San Michele in Isola which is the cemetery of Venice. In *The Medici Secret* the details of his story have been elaborated, but the basis of this part of the novel is true. Between 1457 and 1459, Father Mauro did, with the help of his assistant Andrea Bianco, a sailor-cartographer, create as a commission from King Alfonso V of Portugal a very beautiful map of the world (or mappamundi). The map was completed in April 1459, just months before Mauro's death. It was sent to Portugal, but has not survived to the present day. A copy of the map is on display in the Biblioteca Nazionale Marciana in Venice.

Niccolò Niccoli

The description of Niccolò Niccoli in *The Medici Secret* is quite close to what we know of the real man.

He was forty-four in 1410 when the story is set, and he was a Florentine nobleman, who had, in his younger days, been an admired condotierre. He was tough, good in a fight and he understood military matters. He also had a thing about wearing an ancient red toga. But there was much more to Niccoli. He became famous in Italy as a man of high culture who did much to further the course of learning and discovery. He was a great traveller and owned the largest and best library in Florence. His greatest contribution came from his services to Classical literature, both as a copyist and collator of ancient manuscripts. These included works by such luminaries as Lucretius and Plautus. He is also famous as the inventor of italic script. I did, however, change a few details. Niccolò died in 1437, so in reality, he could not have corresponded with Contessina in the 1460s.

Palaeopathology

Palaeopathology is the study of ancient diseases, and the branch of this discipline known as Human Palaeopathology is becoming increasingly well recognised as an important tool in criminal investigation.

The most obvious evidence from a body is some sort of traumatic injury such as a smashed skull or severed limbs, but more subtle deformities may point to such afflictions as oesteoarthritis and gout. Using relatively simple chemical analysis certain diseases (including tuberculosis and syphilis) may also be discovered from surviving bones.

In order to learn more about how a subject lived and died, the palaeopathologist uses genetics. DNA can be obtained from dramatically decayed bodies and modern analytical techniques mean that amazing results can be achieved using very small samples. Also, as genetic science progresses, the palaeopathologist gains more sophisticated tools to study the bodies of those who died hundreds, even thousands of years ago.

There really is a Medici Project involving a team of palaeopathologists who are currently studying the bodies of the family buried in the Medici chapel in the centre of Florence. Indeed, the original inspiration for *The Medici Secret* came from an article on the BBC News website describing the work of this research team.

Venetian buildings

Many of the places mentioned in *The Medici Secret*, such as Harry's Bar, the Gritti Badoer and the

Ospedale Civile are of course real and in the locations described. The historical details about them are also as accurate as I could make them. However, sometimes I've taken the liberty of changing the internal topography of some buildings, and in the case of La Pietà, the art contained therein. As far as I know, there was no real life Gabriel Fabacci, but there is a fresco by Giovanni Battista Tiepolo.

The original La Pietà was built during the fifteenth century. And the present church was designed in 1755 by Giorgio Massari, but the façade was only completed in the last century. Vivaldi did in reality perform many of his most famous pieces of music in La Pietà and he was choirmaster there for many years.

Further reading: The most wonderful book about Venice ever written (and indeed one of the best and most enjoyable books I have ever read) is John Julius Norwich's *A History of Venice*, Penguin, London, 1982.

Venice and the Plague

Like most ancient cities in Europe, Venice was ravaged by plague on many occasions. Indeed, the city may be considered as a nexus for many diseases because it lies at a crossroads between east and west and from its earliest days it acted as a trading hub.

The worst plague occurred in 1347–8. This horror became known as The Black Death, an epidemic that is believed to have wiped out more than one third of the population of Europe. This plague is referred to in passing by Doge Steno when he first meets Cosimo and his fellow travellers in Venice.

Plague doctors did exist, most of them were forced under threats of execution to stay in the city during times of plague and their costume was as I described it. The characteristic beak mask worn by the doctors in the belief that it protected them from infection has become a popular theme for modern-day masks.

People of the fourteenth and fifteenth centuries did also attempt to ward off the plague with what we would consider irrational means, including firing cannons, ringing church bells, dousing themselves with perfumes and herbal solutions, and burning braziers filled with scented plants.

Vivaldi

Born in Venice in 1678, Antonio Lucio Vivaldi is today one of the most popular composers of the baroque era. He is also the most prolific of any classical composer, credited with over 450 works. The most famous of these is, of course, *The Four Seasons*. Written in Venice, it's a piece which describes in musical form the changing moods of the city through the year.

Although there is no evidence that he or any one close to him planted clues in the Gritti Badoer, Vivaldi was born close by. His family were of modest means and he did train for the priesthood, becoming known as The Red Priest because of his bright red hair. He did teach orphans at the Ospedale della Pietà, and many of his compositions were written for performances by the young amateur musicians he taught. The composer was sacked by the governors of the orphanage for some unknown impropriety, and he was reinstated within a year.

Vivaldi lived most of his life in Venice, but in his later years he travelled across Europe; and as described, he died soon after arriving in Vienna where he was due to take up a court appointment. But he did not stay with the Niccoli family and he did not write an elaborate God-fearing will such as that discovered by Jeff and Edie.

ALSO AVAILABLE IN ARROW

Knights of the Cross

Tom Harper

1098. The armies of the First Crusade race across Asia minor, routing the Turks and reclaiming the land for Christendom. But on the Syrian border, their advance is halted before the impregnable walls of Antioch.

As winter draws on, they are forced to suffer a fruitless, interminable siege, gnawed by famine and tormented by the Turkish defenders. The entire crusade is on the verge of collapse. His lord, the ruthlessly ambitious Bohemond charges Demetrios Askiates to find the killer. But as Demetrios investigates, the trail seems to lead ever deeper into the vipers' nest of jealousy, betrayal and fanaticism which lies at the heart of the crusade.

Praise for Tom Harper:

'Tom Harper writes with strident clarity in this epic tale of murder and betrayal, bloodshed and romance. Gripping from the first page, the reader is swept up in this colourful and convincing portrayal of an Emperor and his realm, under siege. Well-researched, and cinematic in its imagery, this is a fast-paced and exciting debut.' *Ink*

'Harper effortlessly draws the reader into the court intrigues and conspiracies of 11th-century Byzantium in his outstanding debut.' *Publishers' Weekly*

'Scholarly but speedy narrative, steeped in medieval horrors ranging from flogging to famine, all anchored in what feels like a passion for history and spelling out the way things were.' *Literary Review*

arrow books